THE PRINCESS PACT

THE FOUR KINGDOMS AND BEYOND

THE FOUR KINGDOMS

The Princess Companion: A Retelling of The Princess and the Pea (Book One)

The Princess Fugitive: A Reimagining of Little Red Riding Hood (Book Two)

The Coronation Ball: A Four Kingdoms Cinderella Novelette

Happily Every Afters: A Reimagining of Snow White and Rose Red (Novella)

The Princess Pact: A Twist on Rumpelstiltskin (Book Three)

A Midwinter's Wedding: A Retelling of The Frog Prince (Novella)

The Princess Game: A Reimagining of Sleeping Beauty (Book Four)

The Princess Search: A Retelling of The Ugly Duckling (Book Five)

BEYOND THE FOUR KINGDOMS

A Dance of Silver and Shadow: A Retelling of The Twelve Dancing Princesses (Book One)

A Tale of Beauty and Beast: A Retelling of Beauty and the Beast (Book Two)

A Crown of Snow and Ice: A Retelling of The Snow Queen (Book Three)

A Dream of Ebony and White: A Retelling of Snow White (Book Four)

A Captive of Wing and Feather: A Retelling of Swan Lake (Book Five)

A Princess of Wind and Wave: A Retelling of The Little Mermaid (Book Six)

RETURN TO THE FOUR KINGDOMS

THE PRINCESS PACT

A TWIST ON RUMPELSTILTSKIN

MELANIE CELLIER

LUMINANT PUBLICATIONS

THE PRINCESS PACT: A TWIST ON RUMPELSTILTSKIN

First edition published in 2017
Second edition published in 2018 (v2.2)
by Luminant Publications

ISBN 978-0-6480801-7-6

Luminant Publications
PO Box 201
Burnside, South Australia 5066

melaniecellier@internode.on.net
http://www.melaniecellier.com

Cover Design by Karri Klawiter

For Faith
this book will always be connected with you in my mind
and while I didn't get to know you on this earth
you will remain in my heart until we meet again in eternity

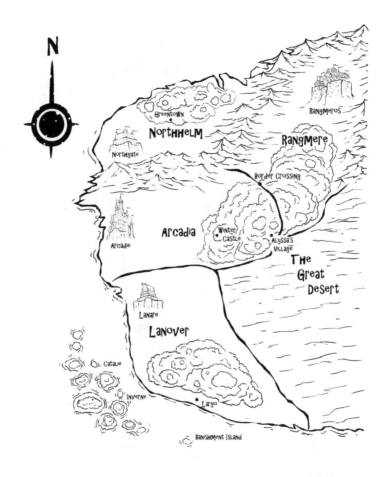

FEAR

$\mathcal{T}$he dark forest was rushing by so fast she couldn't make out details of the individual trees. She tried to pump her legs faster, but the bundle in her arms hampered her movements. She clutched it more tightly and risked a glance over her shoulder.

She wasn't looking for help. She had already made that mistake once before. She had thought then that a godmother might come to her aid, but a monster had come instead. The very same nightmare that now pursued her.

Pain was shooting up and down her legs, and her mouth ached from the cold air she gasped into her exhausted lungs. Fear could only push her body so far, and she had nearly reached her limit.

Just when she thought she would collapse, a dark figure loomed in front of her. She screamed, swerving and falling to the ground. She twisted as she fell in order to protect her burden and landed hard against an outstretched root.

She instantly recognized the silhouette in front of her, and her thoughts rushed back to the small attic room three years ago.

She could feel the rough straw in her fingers and see the dawn threatening through the windows.

And then the glint from the gold that was nothing compared to the avaricious gleam in the eyes of the man who kept her company. She had distrusted him even then, but she had been desperate for help from wherever she could get it. And she had been sure, with the bold certainty of youth, that she would find a way around his bargain.

And so the pact had been made.

"Why do you flee from me?" he asked. His voice had lost none of its arrogant assurance. "There really is no point, you know. You can't possibly escape me. A bargain is a bargain."

She looked down at the precious baby in her arms who was somehow still asleep.

"I'll be coming for her," he said, "when the time is right. So keep a careful eye out for me."

She woke, her eyes springing open and her heart racing, his incongruous high-pitched giggle echoing through her mind.

It was just a dream. It was just a dream, she told herself, but the terror lingered.

She knew that it wasn't just a dream. It was a warning. One day he would come, and he would claim what was his.

A pact is a pact, after all.

PART I
THE TRUTH

CHAPTER 1

*P*rincess Marie Christina Adrienne Camille of Northhelm was bored. She did her best to keep an expression of dutiful interest on her face, but inside she was sighing. The council meeting had already been going for two hours, and the current discussion on trade regulations couldn't have been more dull.

She knew that Northhelmians were famous for their careful attention to detail, and she even knew it was a strength—one that kept her kingdom in peace and prosperity. But ever since she had returned from her visit to the neighboring kingdom of Arcadia, she couldn't quite suppress her restlessness.

Several times she had been forced to restrain herself from asking some particularly serious courtier if they had ever just had fun. She could imagine the shocked look she would receive, and the stories that would immediately circulate about the flighty princess. So far, she had managed to keep the words from tumbling out, but she was sure that one of these days she was going to slip up.

For the past hour, her attention had been focused on the empty chair across the table. Her brother usually filled it, but he had complained to her earlier in the day that the agenda looked unusually tedious. And now his chair sat suspiciously empty.

She had spent the last sixty minutes trying to guess what excuse he had used for his absence. As the minutes ticked by, her ideas became more and more outrageous, so she was confident her brother had used none of them. The heir to the throne of Northhelm took his position with the seriousness and diligence it demanded.

Which meant he must have come up with something truly inspired.

Marie gave up trying to guess the excuse and allowed herself to focus on the most important aspect of the situation: his betrayal of his own sister. William should have known that the sibling code required her inclusion in his brilliance. Surely his excuse could have been stretched to cover them both.

She gave another internal sigh because she knew perfectly well that her brother would charm himself back into her good graces within minutes. She had always had a soft spot for him, and he was well aware of it.

Just as she was trying to harden herself toward him in preparation, the double doors to the council room flew open with such force that they hit the walls with a loud bang.

Marie jumped, but most of the councilors merely flinched, turning disapproving faces toward the intruder.

William strode into the room, and Marie noted with interest that his riding boots were splattered with mud. As tradition dictated, the crown prince was an active member of one of Northhelm's cavalry regiments, and since he was wearing his uniform, Marie guessed that he had somehow orchestrated a change in his shifts.

As far as excuses went, it was beautiful in its simplicity. And she could hardly fault him for leaving her out of it. Not for the first time, Marie wished that there was some similar tradition that required a Northhelmian princess to join a regiment. Marie was certain that she would make an excellent officer.

"William." Her father's voice was, as always, calm and measured.

"I'm very sorry to have missed the start of the meeting." William gave a respectful bow to the assembled councilors. "I have just returned from patrol with news and felt that the council needed to hear my report without delay."

The head councilor nodded and gestured William to take his usual seat. A footman appeared from the hallway and closed the doors behind the prince.

Marie struggled to repress her frustration. Was all of this formality really necessary? If William had arrived to tell them that the palace was on fire, she felt certain that he would still have been expected to calmly take his seat before delivering the news. She allowed a tiny sigh to escape her lips, carefully timing it to be hidden by the scraping of William's chair.

"Your report, Your Highness?" asked the head councilor once William was settled in his seat and the doors were firmly closed.

"This morning, a small group of foresters arrived in Northgate. They claim to be refugees from Greenwood."

Marie raised her eyebrows. They must have been intercepted quickly if the story wasn't all over the palace by now. She felt a little miffed that no one had bothered to inform her of the unusual event, but the feeling was overwhelmed by curiosity. There hadn't been any refugees arriving in the capital of Northgate since one of the larger southern towns had caught fire and burned to the ground. But that was a good ten years ago, and Marie had been only a child.

Greenwood was a much smaller settlement, located just north of the capital. The whole northern part of the kingdom was covered in a large forest and was much less densely populated than the wide plains and farms south of Northgate.

Even among the smaller towns of the forest, Greenwood was

a particularly tiny village. She knew it only because it was located so close to the capital. Many of the youth who were raised there chose to relocate to Northgate; those who remained chose the harder life of the village because they loved the woods and the solitude. Marie couldn't imagine what calamity would have inspired them to seek shelter at the palace.

"My squad rode out immediately to investigate and found the town exactly as the refugees described," said William. "It was completely deserted and appeared to have been ransacked and stripped of everything of value. It would take considerable work to make any of the homes habitable enough to last a winter."

There was a low murmur of surprise around the vast table, and several whispered conversations broke out. It was the only time Marie had ever seen the council close to chaos, so she wasn't surprised when the head councilor cleared his throat loudly and glared around the table. When the other councilors had been shamed into silence, he directed his concerned gaze at the king.

"Did the refugees offer any explanation of this strange situation?" King Richard asked his son.

"Yes, sir," said William. His face remained impassive, but Marie knew him well enough to read the slight inflection in his voice. He was about to say something dramatic, and he was enjoying the anticipation.

"The refugees claimed that a strange man with an unusual accent visited the town several days in a row last week. He spoke openly against the capital and against the crown, attempting to rile up the people. Many of the villagers simply ignored him, but some were swayed by his words. Those individuals began going into the forest to meet with him. They came back with reports of a large band of rebels."

"Rebels." There was neither surprise nor fear in the king's voice.

William nodded. "They have apparently found shelter in a system of caves hidden in the forest, and he is seeking to increase their numbers. Those who arrived in Northgate claim that there was nothing particularly persuasive about his words, but that his manner was strangely beguiling. One of the older men claims that those who followed him into the forest acted bewitched."

"I assume that this strange new rebel is being blamed for the destruction of the village?" asked the king.

"Yes. Last night, those who chose to side with the stranger apparently became angry at the rest of the village for refusing to support him. They gave an ultimatum. Support the rebel cause or be driven from their homes. As you know, foresters are hardy folk, and they ignored the threats. That night a large band of armed men arrived in the town. They ordered the remaining villagers out of their beds and forced them onto the road to the capital. They didn't let them take anything with them, and one of the refugees, who circled back to check on the village a few hours later, found it ransacked and deserted."

There was a long silence after his words.

Marie felt a surge of interest and excitement, followed almost immediately by an equal surge of guilt. She remembered the southern refugees from her childhood. Black soot had lurked behind the children's ears and in their hair while the adults' faces had been marked with a haunting desperation.

Marie's family had greeted them personally in a show of royal support, and one small girl had cried the entire time, clutching a ragged and dirty doll. Marie had been overwhelmed by the people and the noise and felt exasperated by the younger child's wails. Her mother had taken her aside and explained that the girl had lost not only her home but also her entire family in the fires. The doll was all she had left of her old life.

Marie wondered if these new refugees were all right and if any of them had lost family members to the stranger's beguiling words. What kind of princess valued excitement over the well-being of her subjects?

A bad one, she concluded, but she couldn't quite shake the feeling of relief that something had come along to break the monotony.

"This is troubling news, indeed," said the head councilor. "Clearly the matter must be investigated further."

There was a round of agreement from the other councilors, and several seemed about to launch into long speeches on the subject. Before they could get started, however, the king spoke.

"I will take responsibility for determining the truth behind these strange events. And I will report back to this council in one week's time."

A second murmur of assent swept around the table, and several of the councilors looked relieved.

Marie couldn't understand their attitude. She was sure she would go crazy if she had to wait a week to find out more and instantly resolved to insert herself into the investigation. When the councilors began to file out of the room, she hung back.

"I know that look," said a wry voice behind her.

She turned to face her brother. "What look?" She filled her voice with all the innocence she could muster.

"You're in the middle of plotting how to convince father to let you in on the investigation, aren't you?"

"Me? I wouldn't dream of pushing in where I'm not wanted."

William laughed.

"No," he agreed. "You're just an expert at convincing people that they want you around."

"Thanks...I think. I just wish I was as much an expert at getting out of council meetings as you are."

"I would never attempt to 'get out' of a council meeting!" William attempted a haughty expression but couldn't resist grinning at her.

Marie elbowed him in the side, and he was about to poke her in retaliation when they were interrupted by a familiar voice.

"Children." His tone was mild, but these days, their father

only ever called them children as a chastisement, so they quickly resumed serious attitudes.

Only the three of them remained in the council room, and now that the councilors were gone, the king looked worried.

"This is a very concerning development," he said. "We've been receiving word about a new group of bandits in the forest for some time, but this is the first time I've heard them called rebels."

"That's definitely the word the Greenwood refugees used."

"I think you and I need to ask them some more questions," said the king.

"Me too," said Marie quickly.

Her father turned to look at her. After a moment's consideration, he nodded his head.

"Certainly, if you wish it."

CHAPTER 2

$\mathcal{T}$he castle steward had found a place for the Greenwood refugees in an old guardhouse within the palace grounds. It had been empty for some time, and multiple plans to repurpose the building had been lost in the administrative approvals process.

Normally the sight of the building served as a frustrating reminder of Northhelmian bureaucracy, so Marie was glad to see it put to such excellent use. The refugees turned out to be a small band, made up mostly of women, children, and older men. Two of the women had organized the children to play some sort of quiet game in the corner of the common room. The children were subdued but intent on the activity and paid no attention to the new arrivals.

The rest of the group, however, broke off from their various activities when the king strode into the room. The rather harassed looking steward appeared relieved by the arrival of the royals and ushered them to seats at a long table. Marie was surprised at the informality of the whole encounter, but her father and brother seemed unfazed.

Further proof that they get to do much more exciting things than I do. She gave an internal sigh and then felt repentant. Her mother would never dream of complaining or feeling so unsatisfied.

Several of the villagers took seats across the table from the royals. Marie had already observed the refugees deferring to an older, grizzled man who she assumed was the village elder. In such a small community it was unlikely to be a formal title, but she had yet to see a town, big or small, that didn't have a leader of some sort.

The elder was accompanied by another man, somewhat younger than himself, although still middle aged, and two women. Marie recognized the no nonsense air that marked them as forest women. It informed the observant that they worked as hard as any man and were used to commanding the respect they deserved.

What must it be like, she wondered, *to work alongside the men, unrestricted? To never have to consider protocol or formality.* It was an appealing thought.

"Thank you for coming to see us, Your Majesty," said the man Marie had identified as the leader.

"This is Pierre," said William. "He's the one who gave me the report on what happened in Greenwood."

"We're not ones for charity, Your Highnesses, and we wouldn't have come here if we had anywhere else to go," said Pierre.

The king nodded, but one of the women jumped in before he could speak.

"It's for your good, and the good of the kingdom, we've come." She shot a frustrated look at Pierre, and Marie guessed she would have taken a less submissive approach if she'd been in charge.

"Aye." The second man's voice was deep and rough and seemed more suited to calling through the woods than advising royalty. "It's treason the stranger was proposing, plain and simple, and we want no truck with rebellion. You treat your people fair enough, and there'll be nothing but bloodshed from that kind of talk."

He stirred restlessly, glancing toward one of the women who was hanging back from the table. Marie wondered if it was his wife and if they had lost a son or daughter to the stranger's beguiling. Looking at the group more closely she once again noted that there were very few people her own age among them. Was it because they had already relocated to the city? Or had they all joined the rebel band in the woods?

"As you say." Pierre nodded his head gravely. "It was our duty to bring these tidings to Your Majesty."

He seemed entirely unperturbed by his companions' interjections, and Marie was impressed. He clearly possessed both the strength and the calm needed to lead such independent people.

"We appreciate your warning and your support," said the king, matching the woodsman's gravity. "Clearly your loyalty has cost you your homes and possessions, and you must allow us to house and feed you for the time being. When this threat has been investigated and neutralized, we will send a team to help you rebuild your village."

The aggressive woman looked reluctant to accept such help, but the king's wording made the offer impossible to refuse. He had always excelled at such diplomacy, and Marie tried hard to emulate him.

Pierre looked merely grateful and readily accepted the king's generosity.

"Any further information you could give us might prove invaluable." The king focused his attention on Pierre. "I understand that you've already told your story to my son, but I would appreciate hearing it firsthand."

"Oh, aye." Pierre leaned back in his seat, ready to launch into storyteller mode. "There's no denying the woods are full of strange folk."

The second woman snorted in amusement, and he cast her a stern look.

"We see our fair share coming and going, and we're used to paying them no mind. So when this man turned up, I dismissed him as another strange foreigner. It was clear from the sound of his voice that he wasn't from around these parts, but, as I said, we get all types." Pierre shook his head sadly.

"If I'd had the least notion what was coming I would have barred him entry to Greenwood, ax in my hand," said the second man, his voice agitated.

"Aye, and we'd have stood by you." Both of the women nodded agreement with his words.

"I can't blame you for saying so," said Pierre, with a sigh, "though it's not our way. But none of us could possibly have guessed what was coming."

"Certainly not," agreed William, "such doings are unheard of."

"Right enough, you are, young highness," said Pierre. "And that first day he did no more than loiter round the village, chatting with anyone he could find. By nightfall he had disappeared back into the forest, and I put him from my mind.

"But the next day he appeared again, just at dusk as those of us who were working in the forest were returning to our homes. He stood in the village square and called for our attention. His behavior was unusual, and he succeeded in gathering a small crowd. I myself was curious enough until he began to speak."

Pierre stopped again to shake his head.

"Times are always tough in the forest, but they're no tougher than usual at the moment. Those of us who stay do so because we love the woods and would have it no other way. His arguments seemed weak to me, and I have no time to listen to treasonous talk. But some of the youngsters..." he trailed off as if reluctant to continue, "...well, there's no denying they got riled up by his words.

"After he left, the older and wiser heads among us talked some sense into them. They calmed down for the most part. Several of them even acknowledged that the stranger's words were empty. Overthrow the king? And who would rule in his place, tell me that? This stranger? The whole thing was about as full of holes as it could get.

"I thought the problem was past and once again dismissed the man as a not very effective trouble maker. But the next evening he was back, and while he had nothing new to say, he once again succeeded in exciting the younger folk." Pierre reached up to scratch his head, his eyes troubled.

"Bewitched is what they were!" The words burst from the second man. "My Robbie is no rebel. He's never had the least interest in politics before, but that second evening he followed the man into the woods. Came back with his eyes all aglow, telling us about the marvelous band of rebels hiding out there. We tried to reason with him, my wife even pleaded and cried, but the next night he returned to the woods again. The night after that, he didn't return to us."

The woman Marie had picked out as his wife approached the table while he was talking and stood with her hands resting on his shoulders.

"Never in all his years has our Robbie behaved so," she said, corroborating her husband's tale. "There was something strange about that man, I could sense it. I thought surely Robbie would come to his senses and return to us soon enough, once the excitement had worn off. But when several of them did return, it was only to demand that we join them." Her voice faltered, and she looked down at the ground.

Pierre took up the story again, his voice gentle.

"We refused to have any part of the rebel's plans, and the youngsters became angry. They threatened that we'd be sorry and then disappeared back into the forest. I was concerned enough—but for their safety, not our own. I didn't believe they would act against their own people." He shook his head in bewilderment.

"That night they returned, and many others were with them. They were armed with good quality weapons, far finer than anything you would normally find in the forest, and they turned us from our homes. What could we do?" He raised his arms in a hopeless gesture. "We could hardly fight back against our own children."

"I'm ashamed to say my Robbie was among them." The second man's voice was so low, Marie could barely hear his words. "I confronted him, but he claimed it was for our own good. That it was the only way. That we would see he was right in the end. I don't know what that stranger did to him, but it wasn't my boy who was standing before me last night."

"How horrible!" said Marie, the words wrenched from her by the emotion on the face of the man and his wife. "I promise we'll do all we can to help your son and the others."

The wife looked at her gratefully, but William turned a slightly raised eyebrow on her. She suspected he was less inclined to believe the tales of bewitchment.

Her father's expression gave nothing away. "As my daughter says, we will do everything in our power to get to the bottom of this matter and bring this stranger to justice."

The woman gave the king a small curtsey, pulled her husband up from his seat and led him over to the far side of the room. Marie could see her murmuring comfortingly to him.

There was silence for a moment, and then one of the remaining women spoke.

"I've known young Robbie his whole life, and I must agree, his behavior was very unlike him." She frowned with concern. "None of our young people have shown the least dissatisfaction before."

The other woman snorted at this statement, and the speaker glared at her indignantly. "None of the ones who remained, I mean. Those who were unhappy with the forester life simply left for the city. We've never tried to make anyone stay who didn't want to."

"Well, that's true enough," agreed the second.

"I believe one of you circled back to check on the village after you had left?" asked the king, his smooth voice making even his interjection seem courteous.

"Oh, aye, that was young Harrison," said Pierre, gesturing toward a gangly boy, barely into adolescence, who was somewhat reluctantly assisting with the children.

At the sound of his name, Harrison looked up eagerly and hurried over to join the group at the table.

"Your Majesty, Your Highnesses," he gave a quick head bob before gazing admiringly at William. The prince grinned easily back at him, well used to the hero worship he received from young boys.

Harrison's eyes moved on to Marie, and he paused for a moment, looking almost puzzled. Marie gave an internal sigh but put a friendly smile onto her face. She was as used to the surprise of strangers as William was used to their admiration and had long since reconciled to the fact that she did not meet people's expectations of a princess.

"Pierre tells me you were the one to return to the village," said King Richard, his voice gentle.

The boy nodded, gulping. "Some of the villagers wanted to double back. They figured the men would have left and we could return to our homes. I volunteered to go back and do some scouting." His chest puffed out. "I'm one of the best scouters in the village. I can pick out a game trail in the forest better than any of the older boys, and if a herd's moved its grazing spot, I can always find where they went."

"It seems you were well chosen for the job, then," said Marie with a warm smile. Pride shone from his face in response.

She nudged William under the table, and he grinned at her. It was a game they had played for years, Marie using wits and charm and dignity in an attempt to match the regard that William received without even trying. William found the whole thing amusing—he was always telling her that people liked her more than she thought they did.

"When I got back to the village, the men were gone all right. But they had stripped our houses of everything of worth and destroyed most of the buildings in the process. I picked through the wreckage, but there was no food, weapons or tools left for me to scavenge. I couldn't even find any blankets to take back for the elderly and the children." His face darkened. "I wouldn't have thought it of them, Robbie and Danny and the rest of them."

Marie suspected his hero worship had previously been directed at the older boys of the village and felt sorry for him. It was hard to have your illusions shattered.

"Thank you, Harrison," said the king, gravely.

Pierre thanked the lad and gestured for him to return to the children. He went reluctantly, with frequent glances back at William and Marie.

Marie leaned forward in her chair, her eyes fixed on Pierre. "Did all of the villagers who visited the stranger in the forest join him?"

Her father nodded his appreciation of her question, and Marie suppressed a satisfied smile. She was determined to prove herself useful in the investigation.

"All but one," said Pierre. He turned and called into the group of villagers at the far end of the room, and a young man emerged from the throng.

He was tall with a purposeful stride. His skin was the darker, golden tone of the south, and his eyes and hair were a warm brown. He looked exotic among the pale foresters, and Marie wondered how she had failed to notice him before.

"Greetings," he said, directing a courtly bow toward the royals, "how may I be of assistance?" His accent confirmed that he came from the south, most likely from Lanover.

"I understand that you visited this rebel in the forest," said the king. "What can you tell us of what you saw there?"

The young man paused, his expression turning thoughtful.

"I visited the rebel band only once, at the insistence of my hosts."

The king raised inquiring eyebrows, and the young man gestured back toward the group of villagers.

"I was boarding with one of the village families, and their two oldest children, Danny and Lisa, were entranced by the stranger's words. They followed him into the forest at the first opportunity, and the next evening they insisted that I accompany them. I went, out of curiosity mainly, but saw nothing particularly appealing in the rebel camp. We all returned to the village, and the next night I refused to accompany them. That was the night that none of them returned."

He looked troubled, and Marie wondered if he was wishing he had gone with them or feeling guilty for failing to persuade them not to go.

"They permitted you to visit the camp and then to return?" There was skepticism in William's voice, and his eyes were hard.

The young man smiled and raised his hands defensively. "I realize it isn't a great time to be a foreigner in these parts, but I've been staying in Greenwood for several months—well before this stranger arrived. And any of the villagers will tell you that I did all I could to dissuade the other young people from heeding his words."

"Aye, that's true enough." Pierre nodded.

"The stranger seemed very confident," said the young man thoughtfully. "I don't think he expected any of us who followed him into the forest not to return to him. He certainly didn't seem to have the concern for security I would have expected from a rebel."

Once again King Richard's expression gave away nothing of

his thoughts. "What can you tell us of their hideout and numbers?" he asked.

"They were more numerous than I anticipated." The young man frowned. "I would say there were well over a hundred. I can't be sure because I was only there for a brief time, and there might have been more out on patrol or hunting."

A quiet gasp of surprise escaped William, and Marie nudged him under the table again. It wouldn't do to let the villagers see anything but confidence from their royals.

"They were well armed," the southerner continued. "Much better armed than I expected, in fact. I can't imagine where they sourced so many fine blades and shields. The bows make sense, foresters pride themselves on their hunting, but I've been traveling through the woods for months and didn't see a single blade of that caliber prior to visiting the camp.

"They've set themselves up fairly comfortably in a series of well-hidden caves. Even Danny had never seen the cave system before, and he's always exploring the forest around the village."

"Could you find it again? Their camp, I mean," asked William. He was leaning forward in his seat, and Marie recognized the eagerness in his voice.

Her heart contracted. She wasn't entirely sure what she thought of all this talk of bewitchment, but she did know she wanted her brother nowhere near the rebel camp.

The young man hesitated. "I think so," he said, at last. "If I started at the village, I should be able to retrace my steps."

William threw their father an excited look but subsided without further comment at their father's stern expression.

"Thank you," the king said to the villagers. "Your information has been very helpful." He addressed himself to the southerner. "Please attend me at the castle tomorrow morning as I may have some further questions for you. For now, I must excuse myself as I have a meeting to attend."

Marie frowned in confusion and then remembered that her

father had an appointment with the royal treasurer. The impatience rose back up. Surely a meeting like that could be canceled at such a moment! But she knew her father wouldn't cancel it, and she had no interest in tagging along for that particular royal duty.

"William and I will stay and talk to the villagers, if that's all right, Father."

"Certainly, my dear." His warm smile suggested that he approved of her plan, and she smiled back at him, grateful he was willing to include her in the investigation.

William was quick to draw the southerner aside and bombard him with questions, so Marie drifted over toward a small knot of women. Offering what words of comfort and condolence she could, she made her way around the room. She greeted each of the villagers and assured them of her family's support. She took careful note of all their comments, but nothing seemed relevant to the capability or motivations of the rebels.

Once she had talked to everyone in the room, she dragged her brother away in the politest manner possible. William had spent the whole time talking to the young southern man and was full of praise for him.

"Yes, yes, I know, you've found a new best friend," said Marie, rolling her eyes as she led the way back to the palace. "You can tell me all about it over dinner, I'm hungry."

CHAPTER 3

Their father didn't turn up for their usual informal family meal, so Marie and William were left to fill their mother in on the news. Queen Louise was suitably horrified at the tidings, and the anxious glances she kept casting at William confirmed Marie's own concern. Her brother was showing altogether too much enthusiasm at the prospect of taking on a band of rebels.

Of course, to be fair, their mother was a timid woman who was often anxious. She had an unnerving tendency to jump at even the slightest unexpected noise, and she would cower from even a mildly raised voice. But despite this flaw, she had always managed to love her children with a ferocity that earned their undying devotion.

In many ways she was unlike a standard Northhelmian royal, and yet she always conducted herself with dignity and a regal bearing. Her warm heart extended not just to her children but also to the whole kingdom, and the people loved her for it.

Marie's father, on the other hand, was a typical Northhelmian man: undemonstrative in emotion, serious, methodical, but, underlying all of that, both naturally good and unswervingly fair.

Marie didn't always feel his love, but she never doubted it was there.

Marie had always felt fortunate in her family. And not just because they were royalty.

When William mentioned that his new friend was coming to the palace the next morning for further debriefing, Queen Louise stated firmly that she also wished to be present. William looked surprised but seemed otherwise unsuspecting that his mother and sister were both determined to put a stop to whatever wild scheme he was hatching.

It was with this thought in mind that Marie kept herself in the vicinity of the front doors of the palace all morning. When she at last heard them open, she hurried over in time to see the butler show the southerner into one of the smaller receiving rooms. When he left to inform the king of the young man's arrival, she swept into the room.

The southerner had just sat down on one of the lounges, but he jumped up at her entrance and swept her the same full bow as the day before. She surveyed him closely. He looked just as exotic in the palace as he had yesterday among the villagers, and even more handsome. She felt a slight warmth fill her cheeks and bit down on her tongue in embarrassment.

"I don't think I caught your name yesterday," she said quickly, to fill the awkward pause.

"I'm Rafe, Your Highness," he said with a second bow.

"I'm Princess Marie."

"I know." He gave her a friendly smile.

She wasn't entirely sure how to respond to his confident attitude, so she simply stood there, watching him. He watched her back.

His steady regard unsettled her in a way that hadn't happened in a long time.

"Well, what do you think?" she asked at last, throwing her

arms out as if she was on display. If she could throw him off balance, she'd regain the upper hand.

"I was just thinking that the rumors of the Northhelmian princess are true."

She raised one eyebrow. "And what do they say?"

"They say that she doesn't look much like a princess, but she certainly carries herself like one."

For a moment, Marie was offended. Or had he meant it as a compliment?

He noticed her expression and looked a little rueful.

"Sorry, I'm usually much smoother than that." The easy smile was back. "I'm told I'm quite charming, normally."

Marie couldn't help a small laugh. "I'm sure you are, Master Rafe, I'm sure you are."

"I guess I'm just thrown out of my stride by meeting a real-life princess. I promise I won't let it happen again."

She found herself as susceptible to his cheeky expression as she was to her brother's easy affection. Clearly Rafe was going to join her brother as someone she couldn't stay angry at for long.

The thought of William threw her mind back into a more serious track. Rafe quickly caught the change in her expression, and his own mood turned grave. He opened his mouth to say something, but, before he could, the door opened.

King Richard came in, accompanied by both his son and his wife. Rafe bowed to the group, and then the king gestured for them all to take seats.

Rafe was the first to speak. "I'm happy to answer any questions you have, of course, but I want to offer my services as well."

"And how could you be of service?" asked the king, in a neutral tone.

"I would like to volunteer to return to the rebel camp to gather information. I can tell my friends that I had a change of heart and decided to join them."

"And why would you want to do that?" Her father's face

remained calm, but Marie knew him well enough to know he was intrigued by the offer.

"I'm a third son," said Rafe, "and over a year ago, I decided to leave my home to seek my fortune."

Marie's family all nodded. It was a common enough thing for third sons to do.

"When I eventually arrived in Greenwood, the villagers welcomed me with open arms. It's the first time, since leaving Lanover, that I felt truly at home. I want to do something to repay their kindness."

He paused, and such a mischievous grin filled his face that Marie found herself smiling in anticipation of his next words.

"Plus, I left home to find an adventure, and this promises to turn into one."

Queen Louise gave a small laugh and shook her head. Marie knew her mother would normally deplore such foolhardy risk-taking, but she had apparently warmed to the young man as quickly as Marie had.

But her smile dropped away when she saw the way William's eyes were shining. He was leaning forward on his seat, his elbows resting on his knees, and she knew exactly what he was thinking.

"No, William!" Concern made her voice sharper than she'd intended. "You can't! It's much too big a risk."

Everyone in the room turned to look at Marie. The other three looked confused, but William merely looked guilty. Her mother was the first one to catch on, and she gasped, tears filling her eyes.

"What exactly is Marie referring to, William?" asked their father, at his usual measured pace.

"We can't send Rafe in alone." Excitement colored William's tone. "And we can't simply assign a mission like this to one of the guards. I'm the best person for the job, and I want to do it. The foresters don't exactly keep portraits of the royal family hanging in their houses. No one will recognize me."

"Am I to understand that you wish to become a spy among the rebels?" asked their father, his voice for once expressing astonishment and anger.

"Yes," said William.

"Absolutely out of the question!"

The queen drew a breath of relief at her husband's words.

"You are the crown prince and far too important to this kingdom to risk yourself in such a manner. I don't know what you're thinking!"

The king's eyes flickered briefly to Marie as he spoke, but she was too much in agreement with him to be offended. She wasn't really much of a 'spare'—William would make a much better ruler of Northhelm than she ever would.

Plus, she couldn't bear the idea of anything happening to her brother. He had always been the brightest thing in the palace and one of the few people who brought fun into her life. Northhelm without him was unimaginable.

Rafe looked astonished at the suggestion, and she was glad to see that he hadn't been in on the idea. While William tried to argue with their father, Marie got up and went to sit beside their mother. The queen took her hand and squeezed it gratefully.

The argument between the king and the prince grew more and more heated until William finally capitulated and stormed out of the room. His whole family watched him go in astonishment. William liked to bend the rules where he could, but he normally showed respect for his role and his father. The outburst was unlike him.

Richard looked toward his wife, obviously at a loss, and she went to stand beside him.

"Don't worry, I'll talk to him," she said in a soft voice. "He'll come around. He just wants adventure as much as this young man here." She smiled at Rafe who smiled back a little uneasily.

The king drew a deep breath. "I'm sure you're right, my dear."

He reached up to pat her fingers where they rested on his shoulder. "I'll leave it in your capable hands, then."

The queen smiled and followed her son out of the room.

Marie watched her go with trepidation. She was almost afraid of what William might do in this new, brash mood. Hopefully their mother would succeed in talking him down.

Rafe cleared his throat. "I apologize, Your Majesty," he said. "It never occurred to me that His Royal Highness might wish to accompany me. I have no desire to put anyone but myself at risk."

"No, no." The king waved a dismissive hand. "I don't blame you. The truth is that I rebelled a little myself at his age. It's a constraining thing to be crown prince, especially in a kingdom like Northhelm."

Marie stared at her father. She tried to imagine him doing anything rebellious and failed completely.

"If I'm to accept your offer," the king continued, "then I'll need you to draw a map to the location of the rebel camp. If we need to make a move against them, we won't have you to lead us there. Do you think you could do it?"

Rafe looked a little concerned but, after a moment, shrugged his shoulders. "I could certainly try."

The king produced parchment and pen from a small desk in one corner of the room, and Rafe sat down to draw a map. Marie forced herself to remain in her seat since she knew it would be unhelpful to lurk over his shoulder and watch every stroke of his pen.

After several quiet minutes, the door opened again, and Queen Louise came back into the room. She shook her head in response to inquiring looks from her daughter and husband.

"He needs some space. I'll try to talk to him again later." Marie was itching to go after her brother, but his mood was so unusual that she wasn't sure how he would receive her. She decided it was better to follow in her mother's footsteps and give him some space.

Rafe eventually finished his drawing and handed it over to the king. "That's the best I can do. I don't think it would be much use to one of your soldiers, but if you take along a villager who's familiar with the area, they should be able to follow it."

The king nodded his thanks, and there was a long moment of silence.

"If you do this," said the king, at last, "you'll need to go soon. I can't let this problem fester. Especially not if this rebel is building his band. The more people he lures to his cause, the more bloodshed there will be."

"I understand," said Rafe. "I'll leave this afternoon, if you like. The sooner the better anyway, if my story of a change of heart is going to hold up."

"Yes, that would be best. Do you need supplies for the journey?"

Rafe quickly shook his head. "Best not. They know we all left the village with nothing, so it might look suspicious if I turn up with a full pack. I can forage for food well enough for one day."

"Very well," said the king. "When should we look for you again?"

"I'll need a few days if I'm to be thorough in my observations," said Rafe. "I'll try to return here in a week, but if I can't make it back, I'll leave a message hidden in my host's old home."

King Richard nodded approvingly. "I can see you've thought this through. I won't hold you up for too much longer, but I did have a final question. Can you describe what this rebel looks like a little more specifically? Everyone seems agreed that there's something unusual about him, and I'd like to start some inquiries."

"It's true that he doesn't look Northhelmian." Rafe narrowed his eyes thoughtfully. "But he doesn't look Lanoverian, either. In fact, he doesn't really look like he comes from anywhere in the Four Kingdoms."

"Where else could he come from?" asked Marie.

Rafe shrugged. "I have no idea. I suppose he must come from one of the kingdoms after all, I just can't imagine which one. His accent seems unique as well."

"What does he actually look like, though?" asked the king again.

"Well, you don't notice it at first because he carries himself with so much authority, but he's very short. His hair is a strange sort of golden brown, and he wears it long for a man. But it's his skin that really looks distinctive. He has the strangest skin I've ever seen. Sort of leathery and wrinkled and a strange, bronzy color. To be honest, it barely looked human."

The queen gave a violent start and dropped the pillow she was in the middle of placing on one of the lounges. Marie turned to stare at her, but her mother didn't notice. She sat down hard on the seat and stared straight ahead of her, her eyes wide and frozen.

Rafe was still talking to the king, and neither of them responded to the queen's strange behavior. Marie rushed over and knelt at her mother's feet.

"Are you all right, Mother?"

The queen gave another small start and looked down at Marie. She forced a smile and patted her daughter on the shoulder.

"Yes, yes, dear, don't mind me." There was a slight tremble in her voice, but Marie didn't want to press her further for fear of upsetting her even more. She resolved to ask her about it later, when they were alone.

This strange man must be powerful indeed, she thought to herself. *He hasn't even left his forest hideaway, and already he has my whole family acting strangely.*

She looked across at Rafe and wondered how he would fare in the rebel camp. For some reason the thought of his being in danger was almost as upsetting as the unusual behavior of her family.

CHAPTER 4

*M*arie didn't have a chance to talk to her brother until later that afternoon when she ran into him in the corridor outside her suite of rooms.

"There you are!" He smiled at her as if he had never been angry or lost his temper with their father. "I've been looking for you everywhere."

"Really?" Marie looked at him suspiciously, mistrusting his change of mood.

He laughed at her expression and bumped his shoulder into hers. "Don't give me that look, Mare," he said. "I feel bad enough for my display this morning already."

Marie instantly softened, but she didn't want to let him off that easily.

"Do you really? You were atrocious, you know. Poor Mother was practically in tears."

William instantly looked contrite. "I feel terrible for upsetting her. I just get so frustrated being stuck here in the palace. I wish I was free, like Rafe, to go roaming the world."

Marie shook her head. "Try being me! At least you get out and about with your regiment."

William's guilty look deepened. "You're right, Marie, of course. You're the last person I should be letting it out on." He grasped both her shoulders with his hands. "Say you'll forgive me?"

She caved beneath his earnest look and nodded. He smiled in relief and, slinging one arm around her shoulders, began to propel her down the corridor.

"You've always been the best of good sports, sister of mine," he said cheerfully. "I'm quite sure I don't deserve you."

"No, you probably don't." Marie chuckled. "But you won't get me to believe you don't think you do. You've had me wrapped around your finger since you convinced me to take the blame for that pie we stole from the cook when you were five and I was three."

William gave a loud bark of laughter. "I'd forgotten all about that. How shameless of me."

"Yes," said Marie, dryly, "shameless is a good word to describe you."

"Well, it's a good thing, then, that I have a saint for a sister. Now all I need you to do is smooth things over with Mother and Father."

"Oh, is that all?"

After a moment, Marie relented. "I think you'll find they're both a lot more sympathetic than you expect. Father even admitted to Rafe that he was rebellious himself when he was our age."

William jerked to a halt, pulling Marie to a stop with him.

"Father? Rebellious!" He stared rather dreamily into the distance. "Now that's a thought to be savored."

After a moment he seemed to snap out of his abstracted musings and squeezed her shoulders. "That's decided it, then. You're a gem of a sister!"

He let go of her and raced off down the corridor.

"What in the kingdoms do you mean by..." Marie let her

words die away when she realized he was already out of earshot. She sighed and shrugged her shoulders. Cheerfulness and affection were usual for William, but this mercurial change of moods was new. She hoped it wasn't going to last too long because it felt exhausting just watching it.

Marie had no opportunity to talk to her mother, on either her own or William's behalf, because the queen stayed shut in her suite of rooms. The king was busy going from meeting to meeting, and Marie didn't see him again until the evening meal.

The king glanced at his wife's and son's empty seats but made no comment. Instead he steered the conversation toward the refugees and the threat from the rebels, and Marie was gratified to see that he was taking her desire to be involved seriously.

"I like Rafe," she said, voicing a concern that had lingered in her mind since the morning, "but I'm surprised that you were so willing to trust him with such an important mission. He's basically a stranger, after all. And not even a Northhelmian."

The king gave an uncharacteristic sigh.

"It's not an ideal situation, that's true. But the whole thing is as strange as I've ever seen, and I'm short on options. He has a natural connection with the rebels—I doubt anyone else could simply stroll into their camp—and we desperately need more information. If he doesn't succeed, then we've lost nothing. He doesn't know any sensitive information that he could give them, and if he fails, or decides to betray us, we'll be no worse off than if he'd never gone at all."

It made sense, but it also felt a little cold to Marie. The whole thing seemed unlike her careful, conscientious father.

Which just demonstrated how concerned he was by the rebels. The thought made her uneasy.

But then perhaps it wasn't such a big deal after all. Truth be told, she was worried about Rafe. And she felt sure it was wrong to place so much importance on the well-being of one individual when the whole kingdom might be at stake. A sovereign had to make those sorts of decisions and then bear the responsibility for them. It only confirmed how unready she was to be a leader.

William had better keep himself out of trouble.

"And if Rafe does fail?" she asked. "What will we do then?"

"I'm not going to pin any plans on his succeeding," said the king, a hint of weariness in his voice. "I've been in meetings with the Captain of the Guard all afternoon, trying to devise various strategies. I don't like the sound of anything we've come up with, though. If there's a chance these so-called rebels really have been bewitched, I can't go in there with the army and slaughter them all. That would be sure to turn their families against us." He sighed again. "It's an impossible situation. Which is why it would be so useful if Rafe does succeed. Any information would be better than the little we know now."

"So you think there's a chance this strange man really has been enchanting them somehow?" Marie was a little surprised that her father was taking the possibility seriously.

"Anything's possible," he replied. "Not all enchantments are good. Part of the reason we rely on the aid of the godmothers is because there are other forces in the kingdom that would harm us if they could."

Marie sat silently digesting this information.

After a long pause, her father continued. "And that's the worst part of it. Everything changes if there are enchantments at work. The best plan I've heard so far is to start placing men in all the remaining forester villages. Have them slowly infiltrate his forces as he gathers more supporters. But I'm not sure I can risk it. If he really is bewitching people, then I might not be able to trust the loyalty of my own men. I might simply be feeding his army."

He rubbed his temples and then slowly stood to his feet, excusing himself to attend yet another meeting. Marie watched his face transform into its usual calm expression before he left the room.

She sat at the empty table for some time after he had gone.

She couldn't remember ever seeing her father so vulnerable or anxious before.

She had intended to seek out her mother but decided that she would rather talk to her in the morning. One upset parent seemed enough for the night. She would have an early night and a fresh start in the morning.

As she wandered back to her rooms, she wondered how Rafe was doing and if he'd found something to eat and somewhere to shelter for the night. She felt almost guilty going into her comfortable rooms and feeling the thick carpet under her feet. They were rooms fit for a princess, with heavy brocade curtains in a rich blue and padded seats. In the bedroom she had a four-poster bed, made of beautiful mahogany and decorated with a gauze canopy in the same shade of blue as the curtains.

As she changed into her nightgown, her attention was caught by the full-length mirror, a beautiful free-standing piece framed in the same mahogany as her bed. It had been a gift from her parents on her sixteenth birthday.

She drifted over to stand in front of it and examine herself, as she'd done so many times before. The reflection made her frown.

Marie had the requisite golden hair of a princess...just.

In truth it was more white blonde than gold, and she often felt, when gazing into the mirror, that it looked almost counterfeit. As if she had put a wig on her head to try to make herself into a proper princess.

Her features were too thin for classical beauty, and her blue eyes were so pale they barely counted as blue. She was like the pale reflection of a true princess, and she was painfully aware of it. And to make matters worse, she was far too tall for a typical Northhelmian girl, let alone a typical princess.

Her mother had taught her the word statuesque as soon as she had finished her final growth spurt. Ever since then, Marie had carried herself with dignity and confidence. And it did help. But it never quite erased the pang she felt when presented to a charmingly petite princess.

Like the blue-eyed, golden-curled, rosy-cheeked Ava who had recently been crowned queen of Rangmere. Marie had needed all of her self-confidence to maintain her air of dignity on the one occasion when she had met the other princess.

It wasn't that she was ugly. Not at all. And sometimes Marie thought that was the worst thing of all. If only she wasn't a princess, if only she had been born to some nobleman of the court instead of to the king, she suspected she would have been deemed quite pretty. Certainly attractive enough to make a good marriage.

But princes had different expectations from nobleman's sons. *Everyone* had different expectations of a princess. And there was just no denying that Marie didn't live up to them.

She sighed and turned away from the mirror. She'd long ago come to accept her looks; she didn't know what had brought all these emotions back up.

And then she thought of a pair of warm brown eyes resting on her face, and a voice echoed in her head. *They say that she doesn't look much like a princess.*

Perhaps she did know, after all. She shook her head in frustration as she climbed into bed. She had trained herself away from such foolishness years ago. She would make a marriage of alliance, one that would benefit Northhelm. She had no business dwelling on a handsome face or an infectious laugh. And certainly not the face and laugh of some wandering adventure seeker.

She blew out the candle and wished she could blow out her thoughts just as easily.

CHAPTER 5

"*Y*our Highness! Your Highness!" The shrill whisper pierced Marie's sleep.

She sat up in bed and looked around her dim room. She suspected dawn had just broken because enough light was seeping around her curtains to identify the figure in her doorway. He had opened the door only part way and looked extremely uncomfortable.

She rubbed her eyes and tried to shake away her lingering dream. It had been a good one, too.

"Apologies, Your Highness." If possible, the intruder looked even more uncomfortable.

"What is it, Ferdy?" Marie's mind ran instantly to her brother, and concern made her voice more shrill than she had intended.

"William." The single word confirmed Marie's fears, and she leaped from bed and hurried to the door.

The young man in the doorway respectfully averted his eyes from her form despite the thick nightgown and robe she was wearing. If Marie hadn't been so worried, she would have grinned. As children, William and his best friend, Ferdinand, eldest son of the Marquis of Montrose, had treated her sometimes as a welcome companion and sometimes as a childish nuisance. Now that they were all grown, the two men had remained firm friends, but Ferdinand had never quite adjusted to Marie's grown-up state.

He usually treated her with excessive respect. Marie suspected he was afraid of being accused of inappropriately friendly behavior. Which was why she couldn't think of any good reason to find him lurking at her bedroom door.

"Tell me quickly," she said.

"He never showed up for patrol last night." Ferdinand's words escaped his mouth reluctantly, and Marie wondered if he was breaking some sort of male code by betraying his friend's delinquency.

But in this case, his friend was the crown prince, and Ferdinand himself was the commanding officer of William's squad.

"I went to his rooms after patrol, and he isn't there."

"But where could he have gone this early in the morning?"

Ferdinand's expression of concern deepened at Marie's question, and fear caused a sharp headache to blossom behind her right temple.

"Come on, Ferdy, tell me," she said, trying to keep her voice light. Maybe her brother was skipping his responsibilities in a fit of rebellion, and his friend knew where he had gone. She resisted the urge to massage her forehead.

"He clearly hadn't been there all night," said Ferdinand. "Apparently, he told the servants yesterday afternoon that he didn't want to be disturbed. And no one seems to have seen him since."

Marie gasped and clutched at the door frame for support.

Ferdinand nodded unhappily. "Never known him not to turn up for patrol before. I excused him to the squad but now that he seems to have disappeared...well, I was hoping you might know where he was." His voice trailed off in response to her stricken expression.

"Gotten himself into trouble, hasn't he?" William's friend sounded more sad than surprised, and Marie shot him a sharp look.

"What makes you say that?"

"Well, he's never been one to shirk his duties, but he's been increasingly restless lately. I've been a bit worried about him, to tell the truth. If he's just kicking up a lark somewhere, we might be able to cover for him, but..."

"No," Marie shook her head. "Not with everything that's going on at the moment. He wouldn't be out enjoying himself at a time like this. I'm rather afraid..." She also trailed off, scared that if she voiced her theory, it would make it real.

Ferdinand shifted his weight from foot to foot. "I suppose it has something to do with those refugees we intercepted yesterday. It was a mighty strange story they were telling."

He shot her a questioning look with a good deal of intelligence behind it.

She nodded reluctantly. "That's what I'm afraid of."

He continued to watch her steadily, but she didn't say any more. She wasn't sure how much he already knew and how much she was free to say. She would trust Ferdy with her life, but she didn't want to let her father down when he was including her in the investigation.

After a moment, Ferdy sighed and nodded. "I thought it might be like that." There was another pause. "Normal procedure would require me to report his absence up the chain of command. But normal doesn't really apply to William. I'm not sure it would be a good idea to start spreading word around the palace that the heir to the throne has disappeared."

"No, no, we can't do that. And I'm sure he'll be back soon." Marie wished her words had come out with a little more conviction.

Ferdinand sighed. He looked more downcast and worried than she could ever remember seeing him. The expression had the unfortunate effect of highlighting the slightly bulbous set of his eyes. Marie had vague memories of finding him handsome as a child and wondered what had happened to transform his features so dramatically that he was now commonly referred to by the children of the palace as Major Frog. His bow-legged gait didn't hurt him in the saddle, and he was generally considered to be an exceptional officer, but there was no denying he made a peculiar figure walking around the castle. There was a reason he was rarely seen at balls or other social gatherings.

Marie shook her head, frustrated with her mind for wandering at such a crucial moment. Ferdinand was watching her curiously, and she had to repress a flush of embarrassment.

"Perhaps if you talk to your parents, they might know where he is."

Marie nodded. William would be angry with her for running to their parents, but he had left her with no other option.

She felt a swell of her own anger warm her. *What was he thinking? How dare he leave them in this situation!*

Her emotions buoyed her up as she sent Ferdinand away with instructions not to say anything to anyone else, and quickly dressed for the day. It was only as she stood in the corridor outside her parents' suites that she deflated.

Years of sibling camaraderie and shared adventures rebelled against the idea of turning her brother in. She took a deep breath and steeled herself.

But as her hand reached up to knock on the outer door to her father's suite, her feet turned of their own accord, and she found herself knocking on her mother's door instead. *Neither of them turned up for the evening meal yesterday,* she reasoned to herself. *Perhaps Mother was having that talk with William.*

She waited a moment, and then let herself into her mother's sitting room. The familiar surroundings calmed her somewhat. The pale blue and pine furnishings were like a pastel version of her own room, and she had spent many hours here with her mother over the years.

She had expected to have to wake the queen, so she was surprised when the bedroom door opened. Her mother walked out, wrapped in a diaphanous robe of many layered blue gauze. The garment was beautiful, but Queen Louise's face looked haggard and tired. Marie's mind flashed back to her mother's near collapse in the receiving room the day before.

"Marie, dear, what is it?" Her mother's face transformed into a familiar look of anxiety.

Marie felt a rush of guilt that transformed into a fresh wave of anger at her brother. It was his fault she was here, causing her mother more worry. She should have gone to her father, after all.

Marie sat down heavily on a small sofa. She was here now, and there was no point in putting it off.

"It's William."

"William!" Her mother rushed over and sat down beside her. She took Marie's hand and clasped it between both of her own. Her hands felt clammy, and they gripped convulsively.

Marie's concern deepened. Obviously, whatever was troubling her mother wasn't to do with her brother. Which meant something else was wrong. She looked at the queen more closely. Had she slept at all? And had it really been less than two days ago that she herself had been sitting in the council room feeling bored?

A good reminder to be careful what you wish for, she thought grimly.

"Don't try to spare me," her mother continued. "Tell me at once."

Marie took a deep breath. "He's disappeared. Ferdy came to tell me that he never turned up for patrol last night. He's not in his room, and no one's seen him since yesterday afternoon."

The queen gave a muffled cry and fell back against the sofa. She covered her face with her hands and began to shake.

Marie stared at her, too shocked to respond for a moment. Her mother was acting as if she had been told her son was dead.

After a moment, Marie slipped onto the floor and knelt in front of her mother. She gently pulled down her mother's hands and gathered them into the older woman's lap.

"I'm sure he's all right, Mother. We'll find him."

"No, we won't," said the queen, her voice hysterical. "He's gone to that...that...*man*. I know he has! You heard him yesterday. Oh, this is all my fault."

Marie rocked back on her heels and stared at her mother as she began to wail. Her mother had always been anxious, but this was closer to terror. Plus, she'd never seen her hysterical before.

Weren't you supposed to throw water on hysterical people? She looked around for a handy glass or vase, but there was nothing in reach.

CHAPTER 6

When her mother showed no signs of stopping, Marie stood up and stomped her foot. "Mother!" she yelled.

The queen was shocked into silence. For a moment the two women stared at one another.

"It's been a long time since I saw you do that," said her mother at last, and Marie was relieved to hear a semblance of her usual calm control in her voice.

"Well, I've *never* seen you react like that," said Marie. She collapsed down onto the sofa again. "I think it's time for you to tell me exactly what's going on."

There was a pause while her mother looked down into her lap. "But I don't know what's going on," she said without looking back up.

"You know something," said Marie firmly. "I suspect you're right that William has gone after Rafe. But you seemed sure of it. Plus, I saw your reaction last night when Rafe described the stranger. You're the one who taught me to be poised and elegant, and yet that's twice in the last day that I've seen you lose control. There's something you're not telling me."

There was an even longer pause, but Marie waited silently for her mother to meet her eyes. When she eventually did, it was through a veil of unshed tears.

"Perhaps you're right," she said, and, surprisingly, her voice didn't shake. "There's no point in trying to hide the truth any longer. And the truth, my dearest daughter, is that I haven't told you anything."

Marie raised both eyebrows. That seemed a little extreme.

Her mother saw her reaction and sighed. "It won't make sense unless I go back to the very beginning. It might take a while."

Marie glanced uneasily toward the door to the corridor. She was burningly curious to know what her mother was hiding, but her thoughts kept returning to her brother.

"Father will be up in an hour. We can't let him go to his first meeting of the day without telling him about William. And if he has gone off after the rebels, we shouldn't lose any time in going after him."

Queen Louise shook her head and gripped Marie's arm tightly. "No!" she said. "You, of all people, can't go after him. Promise me you won't!"

"Mother! I thought you were worried about him, too. We might still have a chance to catch him."

"I'm desperately worried about him, of course I am, but it's too late for going after him. If he's been gone since yesterday afternoon, then we don't have a hope of catching up to him. And you can't go anywhere near that man. Promise me!"

If Marie thought logically rather than emotionally, then she had to admit her mother was right. It was too late to simply chase her brother down. If he'd already reached the rebels they'd be doing far more harm than good. They would have to come up with some other plan.

She eyed the door again.

Her mother squeezed her arm more tightly and pulled her attention back into the room.

"Promise me," she insisted for the third time.

Marie shook her head defiantly. "I'm not promising anything until you tell me what's going on. And as soon as you've finished, we have to tell Father."

The queen hesitated and then slowly relaxed her hold on her daughter's arm. "Yes, of course. As soon as we've finished."

She took a deep breath, and Marie waited silently for her to begin her explanation.

"When I was a child, my own mother died, and I was raised by my father, a miller. He was a good man, but sometimes he drank too much, and when he did he became boastful. He wanted to best everyone and would tell any tale to appear superior."

Marie nodded her head, impatient. The tale of the miller and his extraordinary daughter was familiar to her; she had grown up with it.

"One day, the king, that's the old king, your grandfather, called representatives from every village in Northhelm to come to the capital. My father was one of those chosen to attend from our village, and he left me to watch over the mill. One night, while in Northgate, he had too much to drink and began to boast. One of the others from our village, a man who knew his ways, thought it was amusing and goaded him on. Eventually he claimed that he would never fall on hard times since his daughter, me, could spin straw into gold."

The queen paused and shook her head. Marie had always wondered how her mother had managed to keep it a secret for so long. Especially with such a father. She had always felt that a secret like that would be a heavy burden to bear.

"There was a courtier in the tavern," Marie continued for her, "and he overheard and told the king, and the king made you spin for him in exchange for marrying his son. Yes, I know the story. Everyone knows the story." She felt a little guilty for being so rude, but it was hardly the time for rambling reminiscences.

"No." The queen shook her head again. "You only think you

know the story. No one knows the real story except your father and me."

"What do you mean?" Suddenly she had Marie's full attention.

"As you said, one of the courtiers overheard and reported the story to the king. The king was angry because he had brought the people together to discuss the bad harvest and the upcoming winter. He disapproved of seeing his people spending their time and money drinking and making such foolish boasts. He decided to make an example of my father. So he sent soldiers to my house to collect me and bring me to the palace. They arrived in the middle of the night before my father had returned from the capital. I couldn't understand what was going on. I was terrified." She shivered.

This aspect of the story was certainly new to Marie. "But you just said the kingdom had fallen on hard times. I thought that was why the king sent for you. So you could save the people."

The queen gave an unpleasant laugh. "Oh no, he never believed the story. It was far too ridiculous."

"Well, he was wrong then!" said Marie, incensed on her mother's behalf.

"No, he wasn't," said her mother, her voice dropping almost to a whisper. "I could never spin straw into gold. No one could do such a thing, except perhaps for a godmother."

Marie opened her mouth and then closed it again. She stared at her mother in confusion. "But...you did spin the straw into gold. A whole room full of gold. Grandfather used it to buy food from Lanover, and it was enough to see the whole kingdom through the winter. It's one of the reasons the people love you so much."

"That was the official story, yes, but that's not how it really happened."

"How did the kingdom survive the winter, then?" Marie was struggling to understand what her mother was telling her. The story was as much a part of her heritage as the palace itself. It seemed impossible that it could be untrue.

"Oh, the straw was turned into gold sure enough, and the gold was used to buy food. That much is true. But I didn't spin it."

"Well, who did it then?"

Her mother's voice dropped so low that Marie couldn't understand her words. She shook her head, and her mother spoke a little louder. "It was that man, the stranger in the forest."

CHAPTER 7

"What? That makes no sense. This all happened over twenty years ago!" Marie began to worry that her mother's anxiety had somehow made her delusional.

"What difference does that make?" asked her mother. "The important thing is that he's returned. Have you ever heard of anyone else with bronze skin like leather? He matches the description exactly. And I always knew he would come back. He said he would."

Marie tried to grasp what her mother was saying, but it was too much of a jumble.

"I still don't understand," she said. "Go back. What happened after the soldiers brought you to the palace?"

"The king demanded that I spin straw into gold for him. I protested that I couldn't do such a thing. But he said that, according to my father, I could. Then, of course, I understood what had happened. I pleaded with him, and so did my father, but he remained firm. He locked me in a tower room for the night and said that I had until dawn to spin the straw in the room into gold. If I did, I would marry his son and become a princess. If I didn't, he would lock me up in the dungeons for the rest of my life."

Marie gasped. "Surely he wouldn't have done such a thing! It wasn't even you who made the claim."

Her mother shrugged. "I can't say for sure, but I suspect you're right. I suspect he meant only to scare us. But I certainly believed it at the time. I was utterly, utterly desperate. Just like that, my whole life was gone."

She stopped and gazed past Marie's head and out the window. But her eyes were glazed, and Marie knew she was seeing a different room and a different window.

"I spent half the night simply staring at the straw. I even tried spinning it. Nothing happened, of course. But I was young and couldn't quite give up hope. I cried out for help and hoped that a godmother would come to rescue me." She paused. "But it was someone else who came."

She shivered and forced her focus back onto Marie.

"It was a man. A small man just like the one Rafe described. He offered me a way out, a bargain. He had a magic amulet, one that could turn anything into gold. He said he would use it to turn the straw into gold for me if I would make a bargain with him. By that point, I was willing to agree to just about anything."

"What did he want?" Despite her sense of betrayal at being lied to her whole life, Marie was finding herself fascinated by the story.

"He wanted, he wanted...no," her mother shook her head, "I'll come back to that."

Marie opened her mouth to protest, but her mother cut her off.

"After a little negotiation, I agreed to his bargain, and we made the pact. He turned the straw into gold just in time. The king couldn't believe his eyes when he returned to the room in the morning. The whole kingdom celebrated, and the king wasted no time in packing up every last bit of the gold and sending it to Lanover. I was terrified that he was going to ask me to spin again. The amulet was a one-use item, and its power was gone. It wasn't until later, when the ambassadors from the other kingdoms came to seek a meeting with him, that I understood why he hadn't.

"We were in the middle of planning a royal wedding, and the whole kingdom was celebrating, but the ambassadors were deadly serious. They came with one united demand from the monarchs of the other kingdoms. They insisted that the king immediately pass a decree outlawing me from spinning any further gold. They feared that gold would become devalued enough to destroy the economy of the entire Four Kingdoms."

The queen shook her head. "It seems so obvious now, but I knew nothing about such things then. The king agreed so quickly that I'm sure he had been thinking the same thing. I was just relieved to be given such an easy reprieve. My only remaining worry was what the king would do when he found out about my bargain."

"Yes, the bargain," Marie jumped in eagerly, but her mother ignored her.

"Thankfully my negotiations with the strange man had bought me time. And it turned out that my new husband, your father, was a kind man behind his formality. We had been married less than a year when I confessed to him what had happened.

"At first, he didn't believe me, but eventually I managed to convince him. I was terrified that he would be angry, that he would reject me for having married him under false pretenses. But he thought of nothing but me and how to shield me from the consequences of my folly."

"Your father's folly, you mean," Marie couldn't resist interjecting.

"Well, yes, my father's folly. But also my own folly in making such a pact. Your brother was born the year after that, and then your father organized for us to spend the next year in one of the remote royal properties deep in the forest. Your grandfather couldn't understand why, but Richard was determined, and he carried his own way. I was so relieved."

"That was the year I was born," said Marie. "When we were little children, I used to be jealous that William was born in the palace while I was only born in some forest lodge." She smiled at the memory.

Her mother went pale.

"Yes," she said, after a moment. "That was the year you were born. But you weren't born in the lodge."

Marie's smile fell away at her mother's tone. "What do you mean? Where was I born?"

"I'm afraid...I'm afraid I don't know."

"What do you mean, you don't know? You were there!" Marie wanted to laugh at her mother's ridiculous words, but something in her expression stopped her.

"I don't know because I wasn't there."

"What are you talking about?" The words made no sense, and Marie began to feel angry with her mother.

"The bargain I made with the strange man was that one day he would bring me a child of his, and I would raise them as my own until he came to collect them. I agreed on the condition that he wait until after I had given birth to a legitimate heir. He was angry at first, but even in my fear, I knew my duty to the kingdom, and I held firm. Eventually he consented. That was why your father took us deep into the forest. So no one would ever know you weren't ours."

Marie's mind tried to process her mother's words but failed. She couldn't possibly be saying what Marie thought she was saying. The whole thing was ridiculous and impossible.

The queen reached out and grasped both of Marie's hands in her own. "I was reluctant at first, anyone would have been, but from the moment you were placed in my arms, everything changed. You looked up at me with the most trusting expression, and I knew instantly that you were always meant to be mine. I couldn't love you more if you had come from my own body."

Marie pulled her hands free and strode over to the window. She stood there, looking out, her back to the room. Her mother wasn't her mother, her father wasn't her father, and her brother wasn't her brother. It had all been a lie. Everything had been a lie.

The queen continued talking, her voice growing more desperate. "I knew almost immediately that I could never bear to give you up, but it took me months and months to track the man down. I pleaded with him to make a new bargain with me. One where I got to keep you."

Her voice sank low again. "I think he found the whole thing amusing. He agreed that I could keep you if I could tell him his name. He gave me three days. It was utterly impossible, of course. I searched every book and talked to every teller of tales I could find, but I had no hope of finding the information. All these years I've kept searching, thinking maybe the knowledge would prove useful when he came to take you, but I've never managed to find it out."

Marie could hear the tears in her mother's voice, but she didn't turn around. *After all,* she thought, her mind strangely cold, *she isn't really my mother.*

"Every day I have lived in fear that today would be the day he came for you. But he never came. I even began to hope that perhaps he had changed his mind. Until now."

A long silence fell.

Eventually her mother broke it. "So now you know why you can't go after your brother. Now you know why you need to stay far away from the forest."

"Except he isn't really my brother, is he?"

"Don't say that! We are your true family. No one could ever love you like we do."

"I notice you didn't love me enough to tell me the truth."

Marie's voice came out as cold as the strange ice that had invaded her mind. "Does William know?"

"No, no," the queen was openly crying now. "No one knows except your father and me. We had only two trusted servants in the forest with us, and they were elderly and have long since passed away."

"How convenient for you."

"Marie!" The queen gasped. "How can you say that? We were greatly grieved by their passing."

"Why shouldn't I say it? I'm not a princess, after all, I can say what I like."

"Of course you're a princess! You're our daughter."

Marie finally whirled around. "But I'm not really your daughter. That's what you've just been telling me. All my life, I've tried so hard to be the perfect princess. And I've wondered why it was so hard. Well, now I know why. Because I'm not a princess. When I think of everything I've sacrificed in the name of duty and family! And it was all a lie."

The queen didn't seem to notice the tears streaming down her face. She certainly made no effort to wipe them away. "You are an incredible princess, and you always have been. Northhelm is lucky to have you. *We* are lucky to have you."

"Have you ever stopped to consider if I was lucky to have *you*? Maybe I never wanted this life."

Marie paced once up and down the length of the room. "And what of Father?" she asked, and then quickly corrected herself. "I mean, the king."

The queen stood up and tried to take one of her hands, but Marie whipped it out of reach.

"He's still your father, and he loves you as if you were his own flesh and blood. He doesn't know this rebel is the same man, though. I've been trying all night to work up the courage to tell him."

A white-hot fury suddenly swept through Marie, melting the ice.

"No, from what you're telling me, it's this rebel who's my true father. So maybe the forest is exactly where I need to be." Her voice was measured, but she could see each word burning across her mother's face.

For a moment, she felt guilty for causing pain, but then her anger overwhelmed the guilt, and she turned and fled from the room.

CHAPTER 8

She had fled without thought, but her feet took her back to her own rooms. For once, the familiar environment inflamed rather than soothed her. None of it was truly hers.

She had spoken to her mother without thinking, but the words had taken root in her mind. If her true family was in the woods, then that was where she needed to be. Even as she packed a bag, she hadn't quite decided whether by 'true family' she meant her birth father or the one member of her adoptive family who hadn't lied to her.

She had no way of knowing if her mother had already gone to her father or if she was still crying in her rooms. She stopped and shook her head. *Not Mother or Father*, she thought, *the king and queen.* It felt strange even in her head.

Either way, she needed to get out of the palace fast. There was no way of predicting how…the king…would react to the news of William's disappearance and her own enlightenment. It was an unprecedented situation. If he wanted to stop her leaving, he could do it.

While she'd been gone, a maid had delivered a tray of breakfast. She paused only for a few mouthfuls and packed the rest into her bag. The palace residents were only just stirring when she left through one of the side gates. The guard made no attempt to stop her, merely giving a respectful half-bow.

She wished she could have ridden her horse, a beautiful stallion, but since she wasn't exactly planning to stroll into the rebel camp and announce herself as the princess of Northhelm, arriving with a royal horse wasn't an option. She sighed. It was going to be a long walk.

She had changed into her sturdiest pair of boots, but even so, her feet were pinching by the time she reached the edge of Northgate. The Northhelmian capital wasn't as large as Rangmeros or Arcadie, the capitals of the neighboring kingdoms, but it was still a long walk from the palace in the center to the outskirts of the city.

She turned to look back at her home. The white stone made it resemble the palace in Arcadie more than the gray castle of Rangmeros, but it was more utilitarian than its Arcadian counterpart. Still beautiful, but without as many elegant towers.

She wondered if she'd ever call it home again.

While she was contemplating the view, someone jostled her. She turned, an instinctive apology on her lips, and fear shot through her. A group of four men had appeared on the street and formed a loose circle around her. They were dirty and reeked of the tavern.

She looked around wildly, but there was no one else in view. Clutching her bag closer to her chest, she tried to ignore them and continue on her way. Two of them moved to block her.

Sucking up her courage, she stood as tall as she could and looked down her nose at them.

"Excuse me," she said, her voice commanding, "you're in my way."

One of them actually fell back a step, but the other laughed.

"Well, well, well, ain't you dignified. Looks like we have a member of the upper class among us, lads. I wonder what you've got in that bag?"

He moved toward her, and Marie fell back a step. She wondered if she should try to run, but she knew there were more of them behind her, and she didn't want to turn her back on the apparent ringleader.

While she was still trying to decide, hands snaked around her, pinning her arms to her side. She struggled and kicked backward, but he was even taller than she was and much stronger. Her kicks seemed to have no effect. The leader laughed again.

Marie felt physically ill and wondered what the man would do if she was sick all over him. *What good are all my diplomatic skills and dignified bearing now?* she wondered. *How did I ever get myself into this mess?*

She was still desperately trying to think of a way to break free when a young boy strolled into the street. Their eyes met, and she opened her mouth to call for help, but he turned and fled before she could do so.

She wanted to scream after him but, truthfully, she couldn't blame him. What would she have done in a similar situation?

She had been too distracted by the boy to listen to the continued taunts of the man in front of her, but her attention was wrenched back when he ripped the bag from her arms. The strap caught around her neck, and he yanked it roughly, making her cry out.

He ignored her and opened the bag, pawing through its contents. He looked disappointed.

"Come on," he said. "With a voice like that and such fine clothes, you must have some jewels hidden somewhere. Where are they?"

He took a step toward her, and Marie had a horrifying vision of being stripped down as they searched for hidden gold or jewels. She struggled again but with equal lack of effect.

The leader was just reaching for her when the sound of a

whistle echoed up the street. All four of the men's heads shot up, and the man holding Marie released her and stepped back. She darted forward and grabbed her bag from where it had been abandoned on the street.

Looking up she saw a small troupe of city guards rushing toward her, the boy from before leading the way. She nearly cried in gratitude. She had wronged him.

The thieves attempted to flee the other way down the street, and most of the guards took off in pursuit of them. One guard, however, broke off to approach her.

"Are you hurt, miss?" he asked. He sounded genuinely concerned, and despite her shock, she felt grateful to him. For a moment she had forgotten that most of the citizens of Northgate weren't like her attackers.

"I'm fine," she said, and he looked impressed at her calm tone. "Thank you for coming to my rescue."

"That's our job, ma'am, and we're happy to help. I'm just glad that young scamp knew where to find us." He gestured toward the boy who was attempting to keep up with the other guards. "He can be a troublemaker right enough, but not like these men. He has a good heart."

"I'm very grateful to him." Marie stopped herself before adding that he should present himself at the palace for a reward. She had almost forgotten her change in situation.

The sudden memory of what she was doing alone in the street washed over her. She glanced at the guard uneasily. Was there a spark of recognition in his eye? And if not him, perhaps one of the other guards would recognize her.

She glanced up the street and saw that the guards were returning. Apparently the ruffians had managed to escape.

"Don't worry," said the guard, following her gaze. "I got a good look at one of them and have an equally good idea of who the others are. It's not the first trouble they've caused so we should have enough to make a case to the magistrates now. We'll round them up tonight when they hit the taverns."

Marie nodded her head, glad to hear they wouldn't be free long to harass other travelers. She glanced uneasily again at the returning guards.

"As I said, I'm very grateful for your assistance. But I'm also in something of a hurry..." She looked at the guard next to her nervously, but he nodded.

"We've no cause to keep you, miss," he said. "You're free to go on your way."

"Thank you," she said and gave him a small half-bow before hurrying down the street in the opposite direction to the returning guards.

She would have liked to request their escort to the city gate, but she was too afraid of being recognized. She didn't know what they would do if they realized who she was, and she didn't want to find out. It was possible they would insist on returning her to the palace.

She escaped the city without further incident, but she couldn't relax. The north road into the forest wasn't as highly frequented as the other roads out of the capital, but there was still the occasional traveler. She jumped at every noise and gave everyone she saw a wide berth.

As soon as she hit the edge of the trees, she veered away from the path and found a secluded spot to rest and eat.

"This will not do!" she said to the bushes around her.

She received no response.

"How will I fare in the rebel camp if I'm this afraid? How will I even make it to the rebels?"

She had spent her whole life making herself strong in the ways required of a princess, working extra hard to compensate for her poor appearance. But princesses were required to be dignified and elegant and diplomatic. They had to know how to disarm a foreign delegation or a visiting prince with their poise and charm. They weren't expected to know how to physically disarm a group of ruffians. That was what their guards were for.

She shook her head. No longer!

If she wasn't a princess, then she had to learn to defend herself. She had left the palace without a plan, but she had one now. She would join the rebel training camp and learn to fight.

That would also give her a chance to observe the strange man who was apparently her father. She hadn't decided yet if she wanted to own the connection. Finding out her family wasn't really hers had been enough of a shock. She hadn't even begun to process what it meant that her father was some strange, barely-human-looking rebel leader. She wanted the chance to examine him before she decided what to do about it. Regardless of her feelings toward the family that had adopted her, she didn't wish any harm on Northhelm.

William wouldn't like any of it, but with any luck she could use that charm and diplomacy to convince him to sneak straight back to the palace. Surely, after some reflection, he would realize how important he was to the kingdom.

She smiled. It felt good to have a plan.

Now she just needed to find the rebels. She tried to picture the map that Rafe had drawn and could recall only a vague image. Her heart sank.

CHAPTER 9

*M*uch to Marie's dismay, she made it all the way to the abandoned village of Greenwood without seeing anything that prompted her memory of the map. The village looked just as she had imagined, small and sad with its hollowed-out homes and broken-down walls.

She peered listlessly into each doorway as she walked past but saw nothing of particular interest. She had already consumed every last scrap of the breakfast she'd brought with her and would have been glad to see some food, but she knew better than to expect it. And sure enough, just as the young Greenwood scout, Harrison, had reported, there was no sign of food, tools, weapons or blankets. Overturned and damaged furniture littered the empty rooms, and the occasional ripped garment hung over them. Nothing else was in sight.

The empty village felt eerie, but night was starting to descend, and the houses of the village, even damaged as they were, offered better shelter than the open forest. Marie had spent nights in the open before while traveling, but she had always been part of a larger, well-supplied group.

She walked through the village a second time, this time

looking at the houses with an eye for the night's accommodation. She had almost chosen one that looked slightly less damaged when a house near the far end of the town caught her attention. It was still fairly intact, although its door was lying on the ground several feet from its frame. She found it hard to pinpoint why this home felt different from the others, but its air was somehow less abandoned. Even without a door, it would provide reasonable shelter for the night.

Marie marched inside and righted the table, which had been thrown against the far wall. She retrieved the broken leg and carefully balanced the table on top of it. As long as she didn't lean on it too heavily, the leg should stay in its place. She carefully placed her bag down on its surface and looked around to see if there was any other salvageable furniture.

None of the chairs had survived, but the beds in the second room looked reasonably undamaged. She smiled. Without food, she had no real need to sit at the table anyway. A bed was far more important.

The weather was only starting to turn cold, but it was still a chilly night with nothing but her cloak to wrap around her. The walls of the cottage offered protection that was more than welcome—it would have been worse outside. She tossed and turned for most of the night, trying to keep her mind from circling endlessly between her adoptive parents in the palace and her apparent birth father in the woods.

As soon as light began to seep into the structure, she rose and completed a limited morning ritual. Without food or any real way to wash, there wasn't much to be done. On the other hand, she also didn't know where to head next.

Returning to the palace in defeat was entirely unpalatable, but if she couldn't find the rebel camp, she wouldn't have much choice. She couldn't last long in the woods without food, tools or weapons.

Poking idly around the house, her eye was caught by a large

stone that had been tucked into one corner of the main room. Various items from the cottages had been strewn around outside, but she couldn't think of any reason why the looters would have carted a heavy stone *into* the house.

She examined it more closely, but nothing about it seemed unusual. Her height and breadth gave Marie more strength than most of the other girls at court, but she was barely able to lift it. In the end, she settled for rolling it over.

Hidden underneath was a sheet of parchment.

She snatched it up with interest and found herself staring at a roughly drawn map. It was a functional rather than beautiful illustration, and her eye was immediately drawn to a spot clearly marked 'rebel camp.'

She gasped.

A quick inspection revealed the town of Greenwood also sketched on the sheet. The area south of Greenwood, toward the capital, had been left blank, but several hazards between the town and the camp had been marked.

She was holding a far more detailed map to the rebel camp than Rafe had given them at the palace. She stared at it.

Had a villager left it here? Or a rebel? If so, who? And why?

She looked around the house again, but nothing else caught her eye. She paced up and down, staring at the map in her hand. It was exactly what she needed, but could she trust it?

On her fifth turn, she was hit by a sudden memory. *Rafe!*

He had said that if he couldn't get back to the capital, he would leave a message hidden in his host's home. Perhaps he had realized the weakness of the map he had drawn previously and had snuck out early to leave a new one. Even if he provided no further information, this map made his spying efforts worthwhile.

A smile spread across Marie's face.

If she was right, then this map really was exactly what she needed. And she even had her answer as to why this house had felt less abandoned. It had received a visitor more recently than any of the others.

She picked up her bag and stepped out of the house, the map held out in front of her. She only made it three steps before she paused. Staring down at the map, she bit her lip.

The map hadn't been made or left for her. If she took it, the house might be empty when the king's men came looking. There was no telling when Rafe would make it back.

A night's sleep hadn't changed her own position. Despite the upheaval to her personal life, she had no interest in aiding the rebels to destroy Northhelm. She turned back into the house.

Retrieving paper and pen from her bag, she carefully laid them out on the rickety table. Bending over to begin copying the map, she paused again. How exactly would she explain it, if the rebels caught her with a map to their camp?

She frowned and nibbled on the end of the pen. After considerable thought, she sighed and packed the paper and pen away into her bag. She would have to memorize its contents.

She studied it closely and then tried drawing the map in the dirt floor of the cottage without looking at the original. When she compared them, she had several things wrong. It took five attempts before she could perfectly reproduce the image from memory.

Satisfied, she returned the parchment to its hiding spot and looked around the cottage. With the help of the villagers, the king would know which cottage to examine. They didn't need any sign to set this house apart. If the next visitor to the village was a rebel, however...

Marie returned the table to its overturned state and carefully restored everything else to its original level of destruction. Last of all, she smoothed out the floor and then traipsed back and forth across it several times to create a realistic level of disruption.

Surveying the cottage from the doorway, she felt certain there was no sign of her visit. Shouldering her bag, and calling up her new mental map, she set off back into the forest.

The villagers' story had made the camp sound quite close to Greenwood. But it quickly became obvious that the local youths must be able to traverse the forest much more quickly than Marie. She had been hoping to reach the camp by mid-morning, but at lunchtime, she was still some way off according to the landmarks she had passed.

She stopped to rest but, without any food, it was an unsatisfying break. She was hungrier than she could ever remember being and hoped the rebels would be willing not only to accept her but also to feed her as quickly as possible.

CHAPTER 10

*R*afe had been right about the low levels of security. As Marie approached the expected location of the rebel camp, she kept a close eye out for sentries. No one challenged her, however, and she arrived at a large, open clearing without hindrance.

She hesitated on the edge of the trees, examining the space before her. She could see a distant cave mouth and assumed that must be the beginning of the cave system Rafe had reported. As she watched, several people came in and out of the opening, calling greetings or questions to each other.

The overall tone of the camp seemed light-hearted, as if the young foresters were on a camping trip rather than engaged in rebellion. The mood surprised Marie almost as much as the lack of security.

Only the small group practicing sword play in the clearing marked the group as militant. Even from a distance, Marie could see the quality of their blades. It was much greater than their skill in wielding them.

Once again, Rafe proved his reliability. The swords were not forester weapons.

Marie chewed her lower lip. She had only been observing the rebel camp for less than a minute, and already it seemed a strange mix of contradictions.

With a shake of her head, she threw off her hesitation. She hadn't come all this way to back out at the last moment. Her stomach grumbled to remind her of another reason for continuing into the camp.

She cast one last look around, hoping to see the rebel leader, but there was no sign of him. Sighing, she stepped forward.

A sharp whoosh and a puff of air made her jump. She whirled around to stare at the arrow embedded in a tree trunk next to her ear. Whipping her head back to follow its path, she saw a young man perched in a tree on the other side of the clearing.

He had nocked another arrow but wasn't aiming it at her. She looked back at the arrow next to her head and then met the eyes of the archer. He held her gaze with a calm, serious expression. He didn't look like someone who missed. It must have been a warning shot.

So there was some security, after all.

While she had been examining the sentry, the group practicing in the clearing had broken off and rushed toward her. She drew a deep breath and held her ground as they quickly formed a ring around her.

She scanned their faces, but neither William nor Rafe was among them. Facing the ring of sword points alone brought memories of the previous morning's attack rushing back. She squared her shoulders and stood tall.

She had been grateful for rescue then, but she refused to look for one now. She would rescue herself.

"And who do we have here?" The amused drawl provided yet another juxtaposition when compared to the serious face of the sentry in the tree.

Marie glanced between the archer and the speaker, a young

man who clearly considered himself a leader among the trainee soldiers.

"He never misses, you know," said a young woman a little way round the circle. Her eyes remained fixed on Marie, but the princess knew she referred to the archer.

"I guessed as much," said Marie calmly.

A small smile flitted across the other girl's lips, and Marie wondered what sort of relationship she had with the boy in the tree.

"Yes, yes, but who are you?" The leader's impatience with the interjection colored his tone. Marie had to refrain from rolling her eyes. Clearly he didn't have as much control over the group as he thought he did.

She opened her mouth and then quickly closed it again. *Stupid, stupid!* The hours of traipsing through the forest should have given her ample time to prepare for such an obvious question. And yet she had nearly announced herself with her full name and title.

The speaker's eyes narrowed, and she quickly blurted out an answer.

"Marie. I'm Marie."

Internally she kicked herself for her stupidity, but externally she maintained a calm façade. Marie was a common enough name in Northhelm, and they would hardly be expecting the princess to turn up alone at their camp.

Sure enough, no one reacted to her announcement or gave any sign of recognition.

"How did you find us and why have you come?" It was the girl again, and she kept her eyes glued on Marie despite receiving a glare from the pseudo-leader.

Marie met her eyes with a smile. She had prepared for this part.

"I'm an old friend of Rafe. He told me all about the camp here and how to find it. I wasn't sure I wanted to join him at first, but the more I thought about it, the more it made sense. So I decided to come." She flashed her smile around the group. "Is he here?"

Marie was pinning her own safety on Rafe's credibility with the rebels, but she hadn't been able to think of any other believable explanation for her appearance. She was hardly going to announce that she was possibly the daughter of their leader. She wasn't quite ready to accept that herself.

"Oh! Rafe." The girl's tone suggested acceptance, but underlying tension remained.

Marie examined the group as subtly as possible and noticed an interesting phenomenon. The majority of the young men were smiling and nodding, the main exception being the original speaker who still looked angry at losing control of the proceedings.

The tension emanated mostly from the girls. She repressed a smile.

Rafe must be popular in camp if an old friend of his was so unwelcome. *No,* she thought, *not an old friend, an old* female *friend.*

The reaction of the other girls was almost enough to make her forget her gnawing hunger. All of her life she had been judged by the highest of standards and had failed to measure up. But now that she was just ordinary Marie, she was clearly considered pretty enough to count as a rival. It was a nice feeling and new enough to be appreciated. She had thought that she'd risen above caring about such petty things. It turned out she wasn't so elevated after all.

For the first time, she wondered if no longer being a princess would turn out to be the best thing that ever happened to her.

"He was out hunting this morning, but I think I saw him return," said one of the boys. "I'll go see if I can find him."

He broke away from the group and ran off toward the cave mouth.

Marie watched him go, careful to hide her nerves. She wished there had been some way to warn him of her arrival. His reaction could put them both in danger.

The group around her had relaxed and all of the sword points had dropped. The foresters whispered among themselves, but no one addressed her. Apparently, they remained at least a little wary of the new arrival.

The girl who had spoken to Marie ran off to converse with the boy in the tree, and the pseudo-leader of the group turned to face the cave entry, his arms crossed and back stiff. He, at least, was clearly unwilling to take her word for it.

The rest of the group contented themselves with frequent glances across the clearing.

Marie's stomach gurgled loudly, and she hoped the young man who had gone to fetch Rafe would hurry up.

After several minutes that dragged into forever, the boy reappeared with a familiar figure in tow.

"A friend of mine? Are you sure? What did you say her name was?" Rafe's voice drifted across the clearing, and Marie fixed him with a look that was just short of a glare.

The boy's response was too quiet to hear, but Rafe looked up at his words and met Marie's eyes across the clearing.

He started, and Marie could have sworn she saw a look of fear cross his face. It was gone too quickly for her to be sure, however, and the smile that transformed his expression left no room for negative emotions.

"Oh," he said loudly, "that Marie! Of course! How stupid of me."

He hurried across the open space, and the ring around Marie melted in front of him. He pulled her into a friendly embrace.

"Thank you," she whispered into his ear and felt the slightest squeeze in response.

He let her go quickly but kept one arm slung across her shoulders in a companionable way. He beamed around at the rest of the group.

"So who have you met so far?" he asked.

"Well, unless you count a close encounter with an arrow, I wouldn't say I've actually met anyone yet." Marie tried to match his jovial tone. She knew the situation was still fraught, but she found herself strangely fixated on the warmth of Rafe's arm across her shoulders.

She had spent years training herself to meet any situation with poise and dignity. It had taken her a long time to build up the necessary internal reserves, but it was the price of being a princess.

Except suddenly she wasn't a princess anymore. She still wasn't really sure how she felt about that, but she hadn't expected it to be such a relief to rely on someone else to carry the situation. Thankfully, Rafe had the sort of presence that seemed capable of seeing them through more difficult circumstances than these.

He scanned the surrounding area, his eyes fixing first on the arrow still lodged in the tree and then on the young man perched on the other side of the clearing. He laughed and waved the archer over.

For the first time, Marie saw the young man's serious expression break into a grin. He swung himself down from the tree and, slinging an arm around the girl, led them both over to the group.

Despite the contact between the two, the girl's focus was on Rafe. Marie examined the approaching faces and decided that the pair must be related.

"Marie, this is Lisa and Danny," said Rafe, confirming her assessment.

"Of course, your forester hosts," she said, eager to lend credibility to her 'old friend' status. "It's a pleasure to meet you."

She held out her hand and received a warm handshake from Danny and a slightly less enthusiastic one from Lisa.

"Where are you from, Marie?" asked Danny.

"Northgate." She didn't want to make things more complicated for herself than necessary. "Nice shooting, by the way."

Both siblings smiled at her last comment, and she smiled back as warmly as she could. As flattering as it felt to know that the foresters found her pretty, she didn't want to make enemies of all the girls.

"And this is Robbie," continued Rafe, pointing at the boy who had fetched him from the cave system.

Robbie was another Greenwood name. Marie wondered how many of the young people surrounding her were from the small village.

"I'm Peter." The gruff voice belonged to the pseudo-leader of the group, and Marie suspected he was offended at not being introduced first. "And I don't like this business of people just walking into camp. First Rafe and now all of his friends, apparently."

Marie tensed but tried not to show it. She felt a similar bristling all around her. Only Rafe seemed unaffected.

CHAPTER 11

"Oh, come on, Peter. I'm not that bad, am I?" Rafe released Marie to clap a hand on the other man's back.

Peter opened his mouth to respond, but Danny got in first. "It's funny, no one seemed too worried about camp security when I tried to set up a sentry roster. If you're so concerned, maybe you should take watch tonight."

Peter looked uncomfortable and shut his mouth again.

Seemingly emboldened by Danny's words, Robbie also spoke up. "Yeah, you leave Rafe alone. He's the best hunter in camp and I've never noticed you complain when you're eating a nice venison stew." The younger boy glared at Peter.

Hearing the general murmurs of agreement, Marie concluded that Rafe's charm worked as well for making friends as it did for winning admirers. The thought brought her a momentary twinge of discomfort. While she was grateful for the protection his popularity bought for both of them, she hated the idea that he might have noticed how easily she herself had succumbed to his charm. The last thing she wanted was to be seen as another one in a long line of easily-manipulated acquaintances.

She might have had the strength to walk away from a palace,

but she couldn't give up her pride quite so easily. She took a half-step away from Rafe and tried not to think about the missing warmth of his arm.

"Funny you should mention venison stew…" said Rafe, letting his smile convey the rest of his message.

Several of the young men let out whoops of approval, and the group broke up, most moving toward the cave entrance.

"Come on, Marie, I'll show you around," said Rafe.

"We'll come, too," said Lisa, and once again an expression flashed across Rafe's face so quickly that Marie almost missed it. She hoped Lisa hadn't seen the momentary disappointment. None of the possible reasons for Rafe wanting to be alone with Marie were likely to win favor with Lisa.

Danny fell into step without comment, and Marie took the opportunity to examine the young forester more closely. His hair and eyes were dark, like his sister, although their skin was fair. Most of the foresters were even paler than the rest of the kingdom because they spent so little time in the sun. The contrast worked well for the brother and sister and they made a good-looking pair.

Her eyes strayed toward Rafe and Lisa, who were chatting amiably, and she had to suppress a twinge of jealousy. She knew her own pale coloring wouldn't show to best advantage next to the striking darker features of the other girl.

She shook her head and rejected the thought. She hadn't come to the camp because of Rafe—a reminder she clearly needed.

Inevitably, her mind shifted to thoughts of the rebel leader—she could no more bring herself to think of him as her father than she could now assign that title to the king. The lack left her with a strange sort of hole, one she had never expected to have.

"Is your leader here?" she asked Danny. "Rafe told me a lot about him, and he sounds fascinating." She hoped she had pulled off the correct level of nonchalance.

Rafe threw her a sharp look, and she almost grimaced. Obviously not quite as casual as she had hoped. She wondered what she would say if they ever did get a moment alone, and he asked her about her interest in the rebel.

"No, he's off on a recruiting trip," said Danny.

Marie wasn't sure if she was more disappointed or relieved.

"R left before Rafe showed up," added Lisa. "So he should be back soon."

"R?" asked Marie.

"Short for Rebel," said Lisa. "But most of us just call him 'R'. No one seems to know his real name although there are plenty of guesses."

Marie's mind flashed back to her mother's story. How different her life would have been if the queen had managed to discover his name.

"I wonder how many new recruits he'll bring with him." Danny sounded thoughtful, reminding Marie of his earlier words in the clearing. He had tried to set up a sentry roster. Obviously, he was taking the whole thing more seriously than his comrades.

"Whoever they are, they should be grateful to us," said Lisa. "They'll be arriving to much better fare than we got at first."

Marie's stomach rumbled again at the mention of food.

"And even better since Rafe arrived." She smiled up at him warmly.

"I do my best," said Rafe, his modesty so clearly faked that they all chuckled. "But truth be told, Danny here is a much better hunter than I am. We'd eat even better if he'd agree to go out occasionally."

Danny smiled, but it didn't quite reach his eyes. After a moment, he sighed. "Maybe I will come with you next time you go out. I don't like to leave the camp when no one else seems interested in keeping watch, but there's only so much one person can do. And in all the time I've been on duty, no one's turned up but the two of you." A smile crept across his face. "And, no offense, Rafe, but you're hardly threatening."

Rafe put his hand to his heart as if wounded, but the ready smile was already turning up the corner of his lips. Marie marveled at his acting skills. He was clearly born to be a spy. *Or a diplomat,* she thought a little wryly. She only hoped she could live up to his example.

She hadn't thought about it when she was formulating her plan but, by tying them together, she had placed his safety in her hands as much as the reverse was true.

When they stepped into the cool darkness of the cave system, Marie immediately noticed the scent of roasting venison. The resultant gurgle from the direction of her stomach was loud enough that all three of her companions turned to stare at her.

Lisa giggled, and Marie shrugged apologetically. "I haven't eaten since yesterday afternoon. It took me longer to find you all than I anticipated."

Lisa's expression changed to one of sympathy. "Oh, you poor thing. We should take you straight to the dining cavern."

Rafe's face mirrored her concern, but he shook his head. "The food won't be ready yet, we should take her mind off it in the meantime with a tour."

As much as she was drawn toward the smell of food, Marie knew he was right.

"This place looks amazing," she said, trying to make her voice brighter than she felt.

Rafe smiled at her approvingly, and she almost flushed, instantly berating herself and wishing she wasn't so affected by his opinion.

"Yes, it is," said Danny, "I'm amazed we never found it before. It's not that far from our old village." He sounded disappointed in himself.

Marie smiled at both of the foresters. "Not to you, perhaps! It felt like a long way to me."

"Oh, did you come via Greenwood?" Lisa sounded curious.

"Yes." Marie glanced at Rafe. Should she have kept her visit to Greenwood a secret?

"I didn't know how to give her directions straight from the capital," said Rafe, "so I told her to start at Greenwood."

The siblings nodded their heads.

"What did it look like?" asked Lisa.

"Umm…empty," said Marie, unsure what she should say. She glanced at Rafe again, but his face gave nothing away.

"Oh." Lisa looked down at her feet. Danny nudged her with his shoulder, and she looked up at him with a reluctant smile.

Were they regretting their actions in attacking their own village? Marie wondered. It had definitely been the strangest part of the whole business.

Rafe's eyes narrowed slightly as he watched the pair, but he didn't say anything, merely gesturing for Marie to precede him into the next cave. Marie hoped she would get a chance to talk to him alone soon and find out what he had learned.

The extensive cave system glowed in the late afternoon sun, which surprised Marie until she noticed the many ventilation cracks that dotted the walls. Their presence also explained the lack of stale air.

"What's it like when it rains?" she asked.

"Surprisingly dry," said Danny. "Some water runs down the walls, but nothing too substantial. The ventilation holes are so well placed, it's almost hard to believe they're natural."

"A lucky find. I wonder how our illustrious leader stumbled upon it." Rafe's voice held just enough mockery to concern Marie.

Danny and Lisa, however, seemed unfazed. Lisa even laughed.

"He's certainly an extraordinary man," she said. "I've never met anyone like him. It's hard to believe he's not a forester sometimes."

"Where is he from?" asked Marie.

"Lanover, I think." Danny didn't sound too sure.

"Oh, no." Lisa rejected the idea with a dismissive wave of her hand. "I'm sure I heard he was from Rangmere."

"He doesn't look Rangmeran," objected Danny.

The brother and sister began to bicker light-heartedly, and Marie seized the opportunity to sidle closer to Rafe. She had a lot of questions, although none she could ask him openly. One query couldn't wait, however.

"Peter mentioned all of your friends turning up. Does that mean I'm not the first one?" She put as much meaning into her expression as possible.

Rafe, however, looked merely confused. "That was just Peter, exaggerating for effect. Why? Should I be expecting more 'old friends'?"

"I'm not sure…I would have thought…" Marie bit her lip and tried not to let the worry overwhelm her. She had been certain she would find William at the rebel camp.

"Marie?" Rafe gripped her hand.

His concern felt like a warm blanket settling on her shoulders, but it wasn't enough to stave off the fear.

William is a good fighter; he can take care of himself. It should have been a heartening thought, but the uneasiness lingered. If he wasn't here, where was he? Plenty of dangers awaited the heir to the throne if someone were to find him alone and unprotected.

"Is something wrong?" Lisa looked genuinely concerned although her eyes flashed briefly down to Rafe and Marie's clasped hands.

Marie quickly pulled her hand from Rafe's and shook her head.

"Nothing a good meal won't fix," she said as lightly as she could.

"It should be ready soon," said Danny. "Let's move a bit more quickly."

The rest of the tour was completed at a much faster pace. The foresters-turned-rebels showed her a large meeting cavern, a small cave that had been turned into an armory and then a long passage that continued on into the dim distance. Smaller caves opened off on either side at regular intervals, and many of the openings were covered by makeshift curtains or planks of wood.

"These are the sleeping rooms," explained Lisa. "I've got a roomy one just here, you can share with me, if you like." She pulled back a brightly-colored curtain to reveal a large, clean cave.

"Thank you," said Marie, pleased to be so easily accepted. "That would be perfect."

"You can share my pallet tonight, and tomorrow we can make you your own."

"Thanks Lisa," said Rafe, and Marie suspected, from the smile Rafe received, that the offer hadn't been made for her sake.

She was once again glad to have Rafe as entrée into the camp.

In perfect timing for their completed tour, a gong rang out through the caves.

"Oh, excellent. Food!" Danny led the way back through the rebel hideout toward the entrance.

The dining cavern was a large cave just off the main entry. Lisa explained that a second, smaller cave opening visible on the far side of the cavern led to the kitchen.

"It's got its own exit, as well as a large opening for the smoke to escape. Apparently, everyone used to have to take turns cooking." She wrinkled her nose in distaste. "But thankfully Rebel managed to recruit a couple of good cooks from the village he visited before Greenwood, so we escaped that duty."

"A good thing for all of us!" said Rafe with a cheeky grin.

"Hey!" Lisa elbowed him and tried to look offended.

"The man speaks only truth," said Danny solemnly, although a laugh lurked in his eyes.

"Well!" Lisa put her nose in the air and linked her arm through Marie's. "Come on, Marie, let's go find somewhere where we're better appreciated."

Marie let herself be led into the dining cavern by the other girl. She grimaced apologetically at Rafe over her shoulder, but he waved her on with a smile.

It felt good to be treated like just another one of the girls. As long as she was careful not to think of her old family, and particularly of the missing William, it was surprisingly easy to enjoy no longer having royal status.

CHAPTER 12

*M*arie was thankful to discover that Lisa didn't kick in her sleep and her full belly made her own sleep surprisingly easy. Dawn came quickly, but the inevitable moment of disorientation on waking was thankfully short. She eased out of bed, trying not to disturb Lisa, and headed out of the caves to complete her morning wash.

When she had finished, she stood next to the small stream that ran past the clearing and stared at the burbling water. She had left the palace—the only home she'd ever known—with two purposes: to find her adoptive brother and to meet her real father.

She had found the rebel camp but the only person she'd managed to locate was Rafe. She sighed. Her heart told her to go searching for her brother, a desire motivated in part by her love for him and in part by her reluctance to meet her supposed father. But she knew that it would be foolish to leave the camp now. She had barely made it this far with the aid of a detailed map. With no idea where to even begin looking, she would be far more likely to die in the forest than find William.

She turned her mind determinedly away from thoughts of all

the disasters that could have befallen him. Perhaps he had been unable to find the rebel camp and, realizing his foolishness, had returned to Northgate. Given her own troubles until she found Rafe's map, it was a real possibility.

Which left nothing to do but wait around for the rebel leader to return to camp. She sighed again. What would he be like? A charismatic rebel, as Danny and Lisa clearly saw him? Or a monster, like her mother described? And what were his intentions in amassing such an inexperienced and poorly trained army? The whole thing made little sense and seemed as much of a jumble as her own life had become.

She nearly bit one of her nails until she remembered that she'd beaten the habit years ago. She was determined not to fall apart now.

A rustling behind her told her that someone else approached the stream. She looked up, hoping it would be Rafe.

Instead, it was Peter who emerged from the trees, and he wasn't alone. She examined the faces behind him but could see no sign of Rafe, Lisa, Danny or even Robbie. She recognized a couple of them from the clearing the day before and a couple more from the dining cavern.

No one was smiling.

"Good morning," she said, pasting a smile onto her face.

Peter crossed his arms and examined her.

"Is something amiss?" she asked, after a protracted moment of silence.

"That's what we'd like you to tell us," said Peter. "We know Rafe, but we don't know you."

Marie scanned the faces of the small group, looking for any sign of sympathy. A couple of them looked away, as if embarrassed to meet her gaze, but the rest met her eyes with the same grim expression as Peter.

Her heartbeat sped up. So she wasn't as safe as she had thought.

She looked around, hoping Rafe or Lisa would appear, and then remembered her determination from the day before. It was time to start rescuing herself. She stood taller and took a deep breath.

"How many of you knew each other when you first came to camp?" she asked. "I have as much reason as any of you to be dissatisfied. I spent my whole life serving this kingdom, only to find out that my own family has lied to me and betrayed me. I want the chance to see what alternatives this stranger offers, and I have as much right to be a part of his cause as any of you."

She stopped to take another deep breath and noticed several nodding heads. She wasn't exactly sure where the words had come from, but they had been convincing. She'd nearly convinced herself.

"What skills do you bring?" asked Peter, his voice still hostile. "Can you hunt or cook or fight?"

"I can't fight yet," said Marie, suddenly remembering her third reason for searching out the rebel camp. "But I'd like to learn. I'm strong and a fast learner. I saw you all training yesterday, and I'd like to join you."

Peter looked reluctant, or possibly disappointed at her reasonable answers, but the rest of the group had relaxed.

"That's reasonable enough," said one of the girls, directing her comment at Peter. "How many of us came here knowing how to fight?"

He looked around at the rest of his group and then capitulated, nodding his head reluctantly. Marie felt like congratulating him. A wise leader read the mood of his group and worked with it rather than against it.

Still, I'd better keep an eye on him, she thought. *If he's a better leader than I think, he'll find another way to turn them against me. And if he's as poor a leader as he appears, he'll resent this, and by extension me.*

She wondered why he seemed so set against her.

As the group wandered back toward the caves, she considered the matter further. *Or maybe it's Rafe and the others from Greenwood that he dislikes.*

It made sense that there would be factions in a group like this one. With their true leader gone, they seemed directionless. They certainly lacked the discipline and structure that turned recruits in the royal army into a united whole.

She chewed on her tongue in substitute for her fingernail as she wondered again what the rebel's plans could possibly be.

As they approached the dining cavern, Marie's thoughts turned toward food. She quickened her pace so that she entered the caves in the midst of the group who had ambushed her at the stream.

Lisa, Danny, and Rafe were just exiting the sleeping corridor, and their looks of concern when they saw Marie and her companions confirmed the idea of factions. She smiled at them to let them know she was fine.

Rafe smiled back, but concern lingered on his face.

Marie began plotting how she could arrange a private conversation with him.

As it turned out, however, no opportunities presented themselves. The combined group ate a quick breakfast, and then Peter announced the morning training session. After her words at the stream, Marie could hardly miss it.

Some of the young people stayed behind to clean up the food, and Marie assumed these must be the new kitchen volunteers. Everyone else streamed past the armory and then piled outside into the fresh air, chatting and laughing as they went.

Marie stuck close to Rafe, Lisa, and Danny and picked up a bow and quiver of arrows when Rafe signaled for her to do so. Outside in the clearing, a small group of archers broke off from the rest and headed toward the forest. When they reached the trees, they paused, one of them glancing inquiringly toward Rafe.

He grinned and shook his head, gesturing toward Marie. The

archer, clearly part of a hunting party, shrugged and disappeared among the trunks.

The rest of the rebels divided up into two groups. Those with swords followed Peter to one side of the clearing where they began to pair off. Lisa waved and joined them, the only one of their small band to have chosen a sword from the armory. Marie remembered that she had been practicing with Peter the day before.

Everyone who remained held a bow, and Danny was clearly the training master of this portion of the camp. He arranged them in short lines before a number of targets and then began moving among them, offering advice and assistance.

Marie was unoffended to be placed at the back of the line that waited in front of the easiest target. Her only surprise was that Rafe joined her.

"Don't tell me you can't shoot a bow?" she asked.

Danny, who was assisting the girl at the front of their line, looked up and grinned. "He likes to pretend he's pretty useless, but all those deer he brings back from the hunting trips suggest otherwise. In fact, I suspect he could easily take over from Peter or myself in training this lot." He gestured at the foresters around him.

"Perhaps," said Rafe, his easy grin surfacing readily. "But that sounds a lot like work."

The girl receiving Danny's help giggled and flashed Rafe a flirtatious look. The girl behind her elbowed the giggler, but Marie noticed that she was stealing glances in Rafe's direction as well.

In fact, most of the short line in front of her was female, and none of them seemed to object to Rafe's joining them, despite his evident skill.

The majority of the archers were clumped around the most difficult targets, which made sense. Many foresters were trained in the use of a bow from a young age since hunting formed an important part of their livelihood.

Glancing toward the other group, she noticed the same thing she had seen the day before. The quality of the blades far outweighed the quality of the swordplay. Growing up in a palace, Marie had spent plenty of time watching the guards train. While she had little skill with a sword herself, she knew what it was supposed to look like. Only Peter appeared to have received any training. It made her wonder about his background.

She wasn't sure whether to be relieved that this army didn't look like much of a threat or concerned for the safety of the young foresters. So far, despite Peter, they seemed like a decent group. Marie could see why their families suspected bewitchment. She had no desire to see them all slaughtered by Northhelm's royal guard.

As a child, Marie had convinced William to teach her the basics of archery, but she'd had little opportunity to practice in the last few years. Her first shot didn't even hit the target.

Rafe laughed, but Marie found it as impossible to be offended with him out here as it had been at the palace. She sighed and frowned. "I thought I was a little better than that."

"Don't worry, we'll whip you into shape in no time." Rafe handed her another arrow.

She looked behind her to see if anyone else was waiting to use the target and saw that the others from her line had all moved up to the next target. Obviously, they had only been warming up. She tried not to feel embarrassed.

Turning her attention back to Rafe, she took the arrow and fitted it in place. He stepped closer.

"Here, let me help you." He placed his hands lightly on her hips and corrected her stance before reaching up to take each of her hands in his.

She tried to focus on his instructions but was instead overwhelmed by the warmth of his arms around her and his smell, a mix of soap and leather and green, growing things.

She fought an insane desire to tip her head back the short distance required to rest it against his shoulder. He made her feel short and small, and for someone who had always been too big and too tall, it was a heady feeling.

She closed her eyes for the briefest moment to revel in the sensation, but her mind immediately conjured an image of the giggling girl who had been first in line. Her eyes flew open and her spine stiffened. She might not have been born a princess, but she had been raised as one, and she wasn't going to melt into a puddle at the feet of a charming boy.

She tried to ignore the way his breath felt against her ear and instead focused on his words. She adjusted her grip and, this time, when she let the arrow go, it lodged itself half way toward the center of the target.

"Yes!"

Rafe grinned at her victory cry. "You do know it's supposed to land on the circle in the middle, right?"

She glared at him. "Don't disparage my achievements, thank you very much." She let one side of her mouth creep upward. "After all, people might say I had a bad teacher."

"We couldn't have that!" he agreed with mock solemnity. "I guess I'll have to show you again."

When his arms wrapped quickly around her, Marie wondered if he had been looking for an excuse to repeat the exercise. It was an appealing thought.

But she hadn't known Rafe long enough to know if he flirted with all the girls. They certainly all seemed willing to indulge him in such activities. Plus, she couldn't forget that as far as he knew, she was a princess. Perhaps he was simply seizing an otherwise impossible opportunity to embrace royalty.

She wondered what he would think if she told him she wasn't really a princess. For some reason, she found the idea appealing.

She was dreading telling William the truth, but she was suddenly gripped by an urgent desire to know what Rafe would think of her as just Marie.

Emboldened by the memory that she was, after all, just one of the girls, she momentarily abandoned her pride. When he leaned in closer to correct her grip, she leaned slightly into his light embrace. At the same time, she let the feeling of warmth he gave her fill her eyes and threw him a sideways smile.

He drew in a sharp breath and stepped backward mumbling something about her being ready to try another shot.

She stared straight ahead at the target, fighting embarrassment. Apparently, she did dignified better than flirty.

She concentrated fiercely on the arrow and let it fly. It hit the target dead center.

Rafe congratulated her, his voice light and friendly, but she barely glanced at him. Walking forward to retrieve her arrows, she resolved to focus. She was here to learn to fight and to discover who she really was. The last thing she needed was a handsome and charming distraction.

CHAPTER 13

*H*er renewed determination produced excellent results, and by the end of the morning session, Rafe and Danny agreed that she was ready to move up to the next target. Lisa, who had re-joined them, was profuse in her congratulations, and Marie hoped the other girl hadn't seen her inept attempts at flirting with Rafe.

After the midday meal, there was a rest period which the two girls spent constructing a pallet for Marie. Lisa also used the time to convince Marie that she should try out a sword.

When Marie announced that she was joining Lisa at the afternoon training session, Rafe seemed less than enthusiastic about the idea. He offered no protest, however, instead following the lead of the two girls and selecting a blade from the armory.

Danny made no comment when he saw that they had all abandoned him, merely raising one eyebrow in Rafe's direction.

"I can pair with you, Marie," said Lisa, but Rafe was already shaking his head.

"I've seen how much you've been progressing," he said to the forester girl. "It's kind of you, but you won't learn anything paired with a beginner like Marie. I'll do it."

Lisa glowed at his praise, any resentment she might have felt at his choosing Marie clearly mollified by his words. Marie, however, felt embarrassed again. He clearly felt the need to look after her and was probably wishing her far away.

She wondered if her presence interfered with his spying efforts. So far, private conversations seemed nearly impossible in the rebel camp, and she wondered again how she could create an opportunity for them to talk.

By the end of the afternoon training session, however, she was too tired and sore to think about anything but her exhaustion. She had excellent stamina as a rider, but the sword was heavy, and her arm muscles were already strained from her unaccustomed efforts with the bow. Weariness overtook her long before Peter called a halt and only pure determination kept her going.

Peter had attempted a few verbal jabs at her complete lack of skill, but Rafe had been ready with an easy retort each time, so Peter had quickly decided to simply ignore them. Marie was glad for his absence and grateful to Rafe. He was an excellent teacher.

They returned their weapons, and Lisa invited her to join the rest of the girls down at the stream.

"Don't worry," she said, correctly reading Marie's expression. "This is our time and the boys all have strict instructions to stay away."

"Does that actually work?" asked Marie, joining the stream of girls heading out of the caves.

Several of the girls heard her and grinned.

"It probably wouldn't," one of them admitted, "except that lots of us have brothers here. They keep the rest in line."

"Not that anyone needs to keep that Rafe in line as far as I'm concerned," another one said with a dreamy sigh.

Several of the girls laughed, but none of them contradicted her.

"He's easily the most handsome man here," agreed a third.

"And the most charming." Clearly Rafe's popularity was universal.

"You're so lucky to be an old friend. I wish he'd spent the day helping me to hold a bow." The last comment was directed at Marie, and it took all of her poise and self-control not to blush bright red at the memory of her earlier foolishness.

"He isn't spoken for, is he?" asked one of the girls.

"Um, not that I know of," said Marie, taken off-guard.

She looked a little helplessly at Lisa, and the other girl laughed at her.

"Don't mind us," she said. "We're harmless, really. Most of us come from small villages, so we're just appreciating the opportunity to mingle."

"And admire some new men—yum!" said the first speaker. "Although Lisa here is probably annoyed more than anything. Didn't Rafe board with your family in Greenwood? And now you have to share."

Marie watched Lisa closely to see her response, wondering how attached the other girl felt to Rafe. She liked Lisa, and she didn't see how it could end well for the forester. Not given Rafe's real role in the rebel camp.

But Lisa seemed unbothered by the comments. She shrugged and laughed and said it was worth it for a bit of excitement.

Her comments went down well with the other girls, who were quick to point out some of the other desirable young men in the camp. The conversation lasted all the way down to the water, and Marie noticed that Danny's name came up more than once.

As the group splashed in the shallow stream, Marie reveled in the opportunity for a full wash, as well as the unexpected joy of the company. With every minute that passed, she felt freer. The bored girl in the royal council room seemed impossibly far away.

It only took until the next morning for Marie to realize that the attitudes of a lifetime aren't so easily abandoned.

She had passed a surprisingly good night on her new pallet and was just rising from the morning meal. Laughing with Lisa and Danny, she turned around and nearly ran into Peter. His arms were crossed, and he watched her with a calculating expression.

"You won't be joining us for training this morning," he said.

"Excuse me?" asked Marie, too surprised to be offended.

"With the camp expanding, the kitchen volunteers need some help. Since you're the newest recruit, you need to do a morning shift in the kitchens. Unless you think you're above such work?" His tone clearly indicated that if she did have any such notion, she would be wrong.

Marie's entire body stiffened, and she almost opened her mouth to tell him that, as a princess, she was indeed above such work. Then she remembered she wasn't a princess.

In the next half second, she felt ashamed. Even if she had still been a princess, it shouldn't have mattered. In Northhelm, royalty were raised to understand their role as one of service to their kingdom, not superiority.

"Oh really? I don't remember anyone putting you in charge, Peter!" Lisa's indignant voice cut through Marie's thoughts.

"Well, someone has to be." Despite his bold attitude, Marie could read a hint of uncertainty in his face.

Peter's expression, coupled with her friend's words, reminded her what was really going on. This wasn't about whether Marie was willing to serve in the kitchens—this was a power play. And gaining the upper hand in such situations was exactly what Marie had spent her life learning to do.

Her mind instantly began to consider what it would take to bring the entire rebel camp under her influence. After all, she had come to the one place where her true parentage meant more than her adoptive one. She was as close as it could come to rebel royalty, wasn't she?

But the plans had no sooner formed when she discarded them just as quickly. She hadn't come here to lead the rebels. She still didn't even know if she wanted to acknowledge her birth father. It would be weakness, not strength, to let her pride push her into a role she didn't even want.

She reached out and placed a hand on Lisa's arm. The other girl turned to look at her, clearly winding up for an argument with Peter.

"It's all right, Lisa," she said, "I'm happy to help out. Who knows, maybe I'll manage to claim an extra serve of that delicious breakfast." She winked at the two siblings and earned a smile from Danny.

Peter turned and marched out of the cavern.

"What's his problem?" asked Lisa, clearly still annoyed with him. "You'd think he'd be happy to have someone fall into line so easily."

"He was probably hoping for a bit of a fight. Or at least for Marie to look upset about it," said Danny.

"Upset about what?" Rafe strolled up to them, tossing an apple into the air and catching it lightly.

"Apparently, Marie's been reassigned to kitchen duties. By the high and mighty Peter, no less." Lisa made a face and turned to Marie. "I bet when you get there, the head volunteer will have no idea what you're talking about and claim she never asked for extra help."

Danny let out a snort of laughter. "It wouldn't surprise me." He shook his head. "It's just too bad we don't have a clearer hierarchy outside the kitchen. There's no question who's in charge there. I'm sure the rest of camp would run more smoothly with that kind of authority structure in place. Especially given how often R seems to be away on recruiting trips."

Rafe had been watching Marie with concern while his friends

spoke, but Danny's comment made him grin. "Have you ever spent any time in a large kitchen? I can assure you, absolute order is essential."

"Oh, you've spent a lot of time in large kitchens, have you?" asked Marie.

He slung an arm around her shoulders. "Never underestimate me, my dear Marie, I'm a man of many talents."

His easy assurance made her smile, and she tried not to focus on his touch—the first since her bungled attempts at flirtation the day before.

"You know, you've never given us any details of your history, Rafe." Lisa put her hands on her hips. "Except for those outlandish stories you like to tell which I'm sure are entirely made up."

Rafe began to protest his innocence, but she brushed his words aside and continued. "You're going to have to tell us all about yourself one day, you know."

"All shall certainly be revealed...one day," agreed Rafe. His tone remained light, but he dropped his arm from Marie's shoulders, and she noticed a shadow in his eyes.

Lisa's words were clearly meant jokingly, but they reminded Marie of how much the kingdom was relying on Rafe. And how little they actually knew about him. She watched her three friends leave for the morning training session with a heavy heart.

Just before he exited the cavern, Rafe turned and met her eyes. His considering expression matched her own mood, and she could feel the weight of unspoken words between them.

In another moment he was gone, and Marie was the only one left standing in the dining cave. She rubbed her hand across her eyes. The light-hearted foresters made it easy to forget that none of this was a game.

CHAPTER 14

*L*isa's prediction turned out to be accurate. The efficient and authoritative young woman in charge of the kitchens seemed bemused at receiving an extra volunteer.

"Not that I'm one to turn down help," she said. "You look strong enough to be of use."

Marie decided to take the words as a compliment and was soon laughing with the other volunteers as they scrubbed dishes and prepared the midday meal.

The kitchen rebels seemed a cheery bunch, and it was even easier to forget the true purpose of the camp in their light and airy cavern than it had been with the rest of the rebels. The hard work made her muscles ache, and she was sure that between archery, sword practice, and the kitchens, she'd managed to use every muscle in her body in the last two days. She could only hope she would harden up soon. The foresters certainly seemed unaffected by it all.

She helped serve the meal and then took a plate for herself. Winding her way through the crowd, she looked for her friends' familiar faces. She quickly latched on to Rafe, who was waving her over to sit with him, but was surprised to see no sign of

Danny or Lisa. She recognized one of his companions, though, the hunter who had signaled him the day before.

Rafe introduced her to the group, and it quickly became clear that they had all just returned from a successful hunting expedition. Guiltily, Marie felt glad that her shift in the kitchen was over. She wouldn't have to help prepare the deer they had brought back.

Rafe wolfed down his food so fast that Marie kept expecting him to choke. As soon as he'd finished, he leaped to his feet. One of the other young men raised his eyebrows at this strange behavior, but none of them commented on it. Rafe signaled to Marie with his head, and she quickly abandoned her half-full plate to follow him.

A quiet chuckle chased them out of the cavern, and Marie flushed slightly at what the hunters must now be thinking. But she also applauded Rafe's skillful maneuvering. She wondered if he had joined the hunting expedition with this in mind. They would certainly never have been able to escape from Danny and Lisa so easily. And if it meant they had a chance to talk alone, it didn't matter if a few of the young men thought they had snuck out for an assignation.

Rafe led her out of the cave system without comment and didn't stop until they were well into the forest, past the stream. When they reached a small clearing, he whirled around so quickly that Marie almost collided with him.

"What are you thinking?" She had never heard him use such a harsh tone before, and for a moment she was too taken aback to think of a response. "Do you have any idea how dangerous it is for you to be out here? I know your brother had some crazy ideas, but I didn't suspect it of you!"

The mention of William released an unexpected swell of anxiety and before she could stop them, Marie's eyes misted over. She blinked hard and repressed the tears before more could follow.

Rafe had already seen them, though, and his expression softened. He stepped forward, as if he meant to take her in his arms, but instead he ran both hands through his hair and turned to pace the short length of the clearing.

"I'm sorry, I'm just going a little mad with worry here," he said when he faced her again. "I'm only one man. I'll do my best, but I can't protect you against a camp full of rebels."

Marie softened at his words. Despite her resolution to learn to survive without a protector, her heart liked the idea of having one. She had been debating for days about how much she should tell Rafe, and she had nearly decided to tell him the whole truth. But now that it came to it, she couldn't quite get the words out.

She liked the idea of the two of them against the world. It was exactly the sort of excitement she'd been craving. And who knew how he would react once he found out the truth about her and her connection to the rebels?

"It's William," she blurted before she could overthink it any more.

"William?" He froze, his brow furrowed. Whatever he'd been expecting her to say, that clearly wasn't it. "If you're about to tell me that your brother talked you into coming out here then don't bother. I won't believe it."

"Of course not! He would never do that!" Marie's vehemence seemed to convince Rafe.

"All right then, what about him?"

"He's gone!"

"Gone?" Rafe's question held more unease than shock.

"He disappeared the same afternoon you left. We didn't realize he was gone until the next morning but, given how he was talking, I was sure he'd decided to come after you. We couldn't risk sending guards in case they exposed him. So, I snuck out and followed him myself."

She hung her head and tried to look shamefaced. It wasn't hard when she remembered her blunderings through the forest.

"I nearly didn't make it, to be honest. I definitely wouldn't have got here if I hadn't found your map."

"My map?" For a moment boyish pleasure peeked through Rafe's concern. "I did think it was a good one. And I'm impressed you found it. What did you do with it?"

"I left it there for the royal guard to find, of course."

"That was well done." Rafe nodded approvingly before his expression darkened. "I don't like the thought of you wandering around the forest alone and starving, though. Anything could have happened to you!"

"That's been exactly my fear, ever since I arrived and discovered William wasn't here. What happened to him in the forest?"

Rafe returned to pacing, a crease between his eyes.

"I've been hoping that he couldn't find the camp," Marie continued. "He didn't know about your plan to leave messages in Greenwood. Maybe, when he couldn't find it, he decided to return to the palace."

"Yes." Rafe hesitated but then continued. "I'm sure you're right. Or maybe you guessed wrong, and he never came into the forest at all." Rafe clearly intended his words to be reassuring, but Marie could still see the crease.

"What is it?" When he didn't answer, Marie stepped forward and gripped his arm, holding him in place. "And don't try to tell me it's nothing. I can see you know something."

"I don't know anything for sure," said Rafe, quickly. "It's more of a suspicion, really. When I came here from Northgate, I couldn't shake the feeling I was being followed. I couldn't see anyone, and the feeling finally went away just before I arrived at camp, but still..."

"William's been training as a soldier since he was young." Marie bit her lip. "He's very good at it."

"Yes, his patrol were the ones to find us after we were forced to leave Greenwood. The other men clearly respected his skills. I can't help but wonder if it's possible..."

Marie's hand on his arm tightened convulsively. Rafe gently pried it off and held it between both of his.

"Try not to worry, Marie. This is all supposition. And even if the prince did follow me, he may have just noted the location of the camp and then returned to report it. Quite a smart move if he wasn't sure I was trustworthy."

Rafe's smile and self-deprecating words were almost as warming as the strong clasp of his hands. Marie found herself surprisingly reassured. Following Rafe just to learn the location of the camp was exactly the sort of thing she could imagine William doing. Enough activity and excitement to relieve his boredom without the same unconscionable risks. She smiled at Rafe.

"You're probably right. Sorry for letting myself get carried away."

He shook his head. "You've shown more courage and strength than most of the people I've met on my travels. Obviously, my first assessment about you was right. You've got all the qualities that make a good princess...and then some."

His words should have encouraged her, but Marie couldn't help remembering the other half of his original statement: that she didn't look like a princess. And now she knew why. It didn't matter how hard she had always worked to become a good royal, her true heritage was written across her face.

"I'm not a princess," she said, forgetting herself for a moment.

Rafe laughed but cut himself off when she didn't smile back. "What's that supposed to mean?"

Marie cursed silently and cast around for a response. "Not here. Here I'm just Marie. And I don't want you even thinking anything else. If you slip up, we'll both be in major trouble."

"Oh, of course. You should have more faith in me." Rafe's grin returned, and he patted her hand, still gripped in his. "Don't worry, Just Marie, I won't be the one to betray us."

Marie nodded, pushing away the thought that it was she who

was betraying him. "Talking about the rest of the camp, we should get back. I'm sure Lisa and Danny are wondering where we are."

"Not so fast," said Rafe, dropping her hand and turning serious again. "Now that you've established that William isn't here, you need to get back to the palace yourself."

Marie bit her tongue and thought quickly. She should have seen that suggestion coming.

"No." She shook her head. "I almost died in the forest on the way here and…" She tried to think of something convincing. "I got attacked by thieves before I even left the capital. The guard only just arrived in time to save me, and it was only luck they were called in the first place. Despite the dangers, I'm safer here."

"What?" Rafe cursed and looked thunderous. He paced the small clearing again, his hands balled into fists. "Are you all right?"

"Yes, I'm fine."

He calmed down slightly, but the murderous look didn't entirely leave his face. "That decides it. We're leaving right now and I'm coming with you."

"What? No! We can't do that! Unless you've found out all about the rebel plans." Marie put her fists on her hips and stared him down, one eyebrow raised.

Rafe groaned and ran his hands through his hair again. "This is an impossible situation!"

"No, it's not." Marie tried to smile encouragingly. "There are two of us now—think how much more we can learn. Once we have the information we need, then we can leave together."

Rafe sighed and seemed to deflate. "All right then. But at the first sign of danger, I'm taking you and running."

"Whatever you like," agreed Marie, relieved to have won his acquiescence so easily. "Tomorrow morning while I'm working in the kitchen, you should go hunting again, but see if you can sneak off to Greenwood and leave an update."

"I'll see what I can manage," promised Rafe. "They must be worried sick about you."

"Talking of worry, we really do need to get back."

Marie led the way on their return, pleased at her improved sense of direction. She took them directly to the cave system but stopped, just before stepping out of the trees, to throw Rafe a triumphant look. He was watching her, a strange light in his eyes.

Her look turned quizzical, and he stepped in close to whisper in her ear. "You may be Just Marie for now, but you'll always be a princess to me."

His warm breath against her ear sent delicious chills through her, but his words produced a more mixed response. Was he trying to let her know that he wouldn't truly forget her real station? What would he think when he discovered the truth?

She let him step into the open ahead of her, giving her a moment to suppress the flush in her cheeks. Still pondering his words, she failed to notice the increased movement around the cave mouth or the excited chatter that filled the air.

By the time she looked up, Rafe had already been swallowed by the crowd. She looked around, trying to understand what was happening, and then sucked in her breath sharply.

A whole new group of young men and women had arrived at the camp, and standing in their midst was a man who stood out, despite his short stature. His presence was undeniable and was clearly responsible for the almost manic undercurrent to the camp.

Taking in his bronzed skin and strange appearance, Marie had to agree with both Lisa and Danny. This 'R' didn't look either Lanoverian or Rangmeran.

It was an unimportant point, really. A way of putting off more personal reflections. She glanced down at her own pale arms. He didn't look like her, either. Could he really be her father?

She hung back on the outskirts of the crowd, almost wishing she had taken up Rafe's offer to flee immediately. Now that he was in front of her, she couldn't imagine confronting such a man with their supposed connection.

At least no one knows who I am, she thought. *I just need to keep a low profile and avoid attracting his attention. Rafe and I will be gone soon enough.*

Even as she was thinking it, the stranger looked up and met her eyes through the crowd. His face transformed instantly, assuming an expression she couldn't quite read.

"Well, well, well," he said, his voice cutting though the noise. "There's a face I haven't seen around here before. It seems I haven't been the only one doing some recruiting."

PART II
LOYALTY

THE PALACE

The queen paced up and down Marie's empty sitting room. Her eyes fell on the two trays of food that had been left in the room an hour earlier by a maid who had slipped in and out without speaking. A single tear slid down her cheek.

In a little while, she would force herself to at least pick at some of the food on both trays. She needed to keep up the façade that both her children were confined to their beds due to illness. She glanced over at Marie's closed bedroom door and shuddered. If only her daughter really were safe in bed.

Not that she wished her sick, of course. But how many times over the years of Marie's childhood had Queen Louise crept into her room to listen to the sweet sound of her daughter's peaceful breathing? Just checking that she was still there—that she hadn't been stolen from her bed by the nightmare that haunted the queen's dreams.

An almost overwhelming compulsion to cross the room and open the door swept over her. She suppressed it. There was no comfort to be found in the empty bed that awaited her there.

At least her children's supposed illness provided a reasonable explanation to the palace staff for the queen's anxiety. Despite a lifetime of trying to suppress her fears, she felt entirely unable to hide her turbulent emotions now. She only wondered how long the trusted few who were in on the secret could keep up the illusion.

Louise hated the necessity of deceiving the people around her, many of who had served her faithfully for decades. But she would not put her children at risk. Their safety came first. In that, she and the king were in complete agreement. They couldn't afford for word to get out that both the prince and princess were alone somewhere in the forest, unprotected. Not when the forest was teeming with enemies of the kingdom.

The door opened behind her, and she spun around. Who would enter without knocking? Could it possibly be...?

King Richard entered, and the queen only just managed to restrain a sigh of disappointment. Logically she knew that if Marie chose to return, the scouts, who had been positioned between Greenwood and the capital, would find her long before she reached her rooms.

Except that the familiar environment evoked such a strong image of her daughter. It seemed only natural to look up and find her walking through the door.

Even without the sigh, the king seemed to know what she was thinking. He crossed the room and wrapped her in his arms. She sighed and sank against him, trying to absorb some of his strength. He had always handled the worry better than she did.

"The scouts?" she asked, wishing her voice didn't sound so small.

She could feel his head shaking without moving her cheek from where it rested against his chest.

"I'm sorry, my dear, they haven't found either of them." He paused. "But you know we can't get too near the camp, not until we're ready to make a move. It might put them at risk."

"I know." Louise took a deep breath and stepped back. She had to be strong for the sake of her children.

She glanced up at her husband's familiar, dependable face. "Do you blame me? For telling her?" She rushed the words out before she could lose her courage. She had been working herself up to ask for the last two hours.

"Oh, my dear, no!" Richard stepped forward and took both her hands. "I think events have shown us that we should have told her a long time ago." He squeezed her fingers and smiled. "She'll come back to us. I really do believe that. William, too. We'll find them."

Louise smiled back at him, forcing herself not to question his optimism. They made a good team—the stoic king intent on his duty and the gentle, emotional queen. With an arranged marriage, it could have turned out very differently.

She moved toward him, meaning to embrace him again, when a knock on the door startled them apart.

"Come in," called the king, as calm as ever.

Ferdinand entered the room. He grimaced when he saw that he had disturbed a private moment between them but saluted sharply anyway.

"I was told I would find you here, Your Majesty."

His words were directed at the king, but it was the queen who answered. "Have you heard something? Have they found them?"

Ferdinand had been trusted with choosing the scouts. He had sent them out, as quietly as possible, to search for the missing royals with instructions not to venture past Greenwood. Louise knew they could trust William's childhood friend implicitly. And it would have done no good trying to hide the truth from him anyway, since he had been the first to discover the prince's absence.

"I'm sorry, Your Majesty, but it isn't that. The scouts have had no success so far." Ferdinand's face looked drawn and tired, and the queen felt certain he was doing everything he could to find William and Marie. She couldn't blame him for the failure.

"It's Rangmere."

The king raised his eyebrows, but his voice remained measured. "Not causing trouble again, are they?"

The queen closed her eyes and drew a deep breath. Trouble from their eastern neighbor was the last thing Northhelm needed right now. The new Rangmeran queen had promised peace, but it was hard to know if she was trustworthy. Her reign was still so new.

"I hope not," said Ferdinand. "A royal delegation has arrived from Queen Ava and are seeking an immediate audience with you."

"It could just be a new monarch looking to re-establish and strengthen diplomatic ties." King Richard paused. "But I must admit the timing is interesting." He turned and offered his arm to his wife. "There is, of course, only one way to find out. Shall we go to greet them, my dear?"

Queen Louise placed her hand on her husband's arm and turned her gentle smile on Ferdinand. "Thank you for coming to find us, Ferdy. Will you accompany us?"

The major saluted again and fell into step behind them. Minutes later, the three of them entered the main receiving room.

The queen regarded the small group gathered there with some surprise. The old king had always sent large delegations, expensively dressed, with numerous ceremonial guards. Only six people confronted her now and, although dressed well, practicality had clearly been their primary wardrobe concern. She hoped it was a good sign.

At the announcement of the monarchs' arrival, the whole delegation gave deep bows. When they straightened up, one of the men stepped forward.

"Greetings, Your Majesties, from Her Royal Majesty, Ava, Queen of Rangmere." His friendly smile softened the formality of his words and confirmed the queen's impression that this was a very different delegation.

"My name is Jacques, Count of Anhalt, and Her Majesty has entrusted me with not only her greetings but several important messages to you."

Queen Louise regarded him closely. He looked serious, concerned even, but not agitated. Hopefully whatever Queen Ava wanted could wait until they had resolved their current crisis. The count introduced his companions, but only one stood out to the queen.

Ava had sent one of her personal guards with the delegation, a young woman named Evelyn. The name was familiar to the Northhelmian royals thanks to the regular reports from their ambassador in the Rangmeran capital. Evelyn had been a merchant caravan guard until recently but had been instrumental in helping Ava win the throne away from her brother. The ambassador's reports of the merchant girl had been highly complimentary.

The queen examined Evelyn and had to admit that she gave a favorable first impression. Tall and athletic, the guard held herself with confidence. If Louise remembered correctly, Evelyn was also a close friend of the new queen. Sending one of her personal guard was already an unusual move; sending one of her innermost circle was a statement.

The queen's scrutiny had not gone unnoticed. Evelyn stepped forward and gave a small half-bow in her direction. "I think you'd better hurry up and get to the point, Jake," she said. The queen gathered she was talking to the count. "Their Majesties must be wondering what brings us here in such a hurry."

Straight to the point. Queen Louise smiled. She had been right, she liked this girl.

"Of course," said Jake, his expression turned serious. "I would have preferred to give you warning of our impending arrival, but Her Majesty heard word of strange doings in Northhelm and decided to send us without delay." His concerned expression deepened. "Although, I must admit that we were already planning to come with minimal fanfare. If there are forces working against the Northhelmian crown, it's best to keep word of our arrival as quiet as possible."

Evelyn snorted and then looked apologetic.

Jake raised one eyebrow at her, but the queen could see the smile in his eyes.

"Sorry, Jake," said Evelyn. "But this is a palace, and at least twenty servants have seen us already. I suspect that word of our arrival has already made it to half the inhabitants."

Queen Louise held back a smile of her own. "I'm afraid Evelyn is right. But I confess to being very curious to learn the reason you desire so much secrecy."

All trace of humor dropped from Evelyn's face. "I'm afraid that's no joke, Your Majesty."

"No, indeed," said Jake. "There's a reason Queen Ava sent Evelyn and me. We were recently involved in defeating a threat against Rangmere. Unfortunately, we only managed to chase it into Northhelm."

Evelyn stepped forward. "We realize that your relationship with Rangmere has been strained in the past. Ava sent us to assure you that it wasn't our intention to cause any harm to Northhelm. We're here to pass on the information we have, find out what's happening and then take any requests for assistance back to Rangmere. Whatever you need, Rangmere will stand with Northhelm."

The queen looked between Jake and Evelyn. She was usually a good judge of character, and the pair seemed entirely genuine. It hadn't occurred to her that the new Rangmeran queen might be a help rather than a hindrance in their current difficulties. She looked at her husband. He was steadily regarding the delegation.

"What sort of threat have you chased into Northhelm?" he asked.

Evelyn made a face and exchanged a look with Jake. "You see, there's this jewel…"

CHAPTER 15

$\mathcal{M}$arie found herself transfixed, mesmerized by the stranger's gaze. Part of her hoped that he had truly only recognized her as a newcomer. But the rest of her knew the truth. A man who could plan so carefully would know what his own daughter looked like. She should have foreseen it.

For a wild moment, she wondered what he would do if she turned and bolted back into the trees. Before she could decide on any action, however, Lisa appeared and grabbed her hand, pulling her forward.

"This is Marie," she said to R. "She's already proven to be very helpful around camp."

"Has she indeed? I'm so glad to hear it." The stranger's lips were smiling, although Marie still couldn't read the look in his eyes. "But I must profess myself surprised. Where did you spring from, Marie?"

He said her name in such a familiar way that Marie had to repress a shiver. This man was a stranger to her, regardless of what her mother had confessed. She hated the feeling that he knew more about her than she did about him.

Lisa opened her mouth, presumably to answer his question,

but Marie quickly jumped in. If he knew her true identity, then she had to do her best to keep Rafe out of the conversation.

"I recently found out that after spending my whole life working hard in the service of my kingdom, my own family have been lying to me." She met his eyes, attempting a nonchalance she didn't feel. "After that bit of news, a rebel camp seemed very appealing." If she was right, and he knew her identity, then her words would make perfect sense to him.

Sure enough, his eyes lit up, and he smiled.

"We provide a welcoming home for anyone who finds them-selves dispossessed," he said. "Come walk with me, Marie." He gestured for her to fall in beside him.

Lisa gave her an excited look and squeezed her arm, clearly considering the invitation a great honor. She gave Marie a slight push, which almost caused her to stumble.

Reluctantly, she began to move toward the cave system at the stranger's side. Just before they entered, her eyes found Rafe among the crowd. His gaze was locked on her, his expression sending a clear warning, but she knew there was nothing he could do.

She tried to send her own warning back. She could only hope he would stay out of it. After all, he had no idea what he was really mixed up in, and she didn't want him putting either of them in unnecessary danger.

Rebels were still emerging from the various parts of the cave, but none of them stopped their leader. They did, however, throw many curious glances at Marie. Clearly any hope of anonymity among the crowd was long gone. Had she made a terrible mistake?

Glancing sideways, she tried to assess the man walking beside her. She was normally good at judging people's ages, but his strange face defied her. She eventually decided that he was a little younger than her father. *The king,* she corrected herself, still not accustomed to her newly discovered lineage.

She could feel the strange pull of his presence even more strongly at close range and could hardly blame the villagers for their claims of bewitchment. Something about this man seemed unnatural.

She shivered.

"Are you cold?" R's response to her small movement was immediate. "These caves are drafty, I'm afraid."

"Yes," agreed Marie, deciding to be bold. "I'm not sure they'll be suitable for habitation come winter."

It was clearly a leading comment, but she figured she didn't have much to lose at this point. This stranger had been the one to set up the elaborate ruse that was her life. Undoubtedly, he had done so with a purpose. Which meant he was already predisposed either toward or against her, and she was presumably about to find out which one. She couldn't imagine that anything she said at this point would affect the outcome.

He laughed, the high-pitched giggle at odds with his appearance, and smiled at her.

"No, I don't suppose they would be. It's a good thing I have no intention of still being here at wintertime."

Marie repressed any outward sign of her surprise. She hadn't expected such an open answer.

Despite her effort, he seemed to pick up on her emotion.

"There's no need to dance around things, my dear Marie," he said. "I have no desire to withhold information from my own child."

Marie's eyes flew to his, this time unable to keep the surprise from her face. He regarded her steadily, an enigmatic smile curling up his mouth. She glanced around, wondering if anyone had heard his words, but they had entered a smaller cavern she hadn't seen before, and they were completely alone.

"You seem surprised, daughter. But I assumed from your words outside that your adoptive family had finally told you the truth."

"Yes," said Marie slowly. "They did."

"Then let me assure you that I couldn't be more delighted that you've come to find me. I've been watching you for years, and you've grown into exactly the sort of child I always dreamed of having."

Marie hadn't been sure what to expect, but it certainly hadn't been this. His frank and complimentary comments threw her completely off balance. She scrambled to think of an appropriate response.

"I can only imagine how many questions you must have," he said. "Please, ask me whatever you want."

She had certainly never imagined being offered such a carte blanche. And now that it was before her, she didn't know where to start. Looking around wildly, she spotted a small stool and half collapsed onto it.

"Yes, yes," said R, smiling, "please make yourself at home. This is my own personal cavern, and you are always welcome here."

Marie examined the space curiously, her mind eager for any distraction. Several small stools dotted the floor and a simple pallet lay in one corner. A large wooden chest stood at the foot of the bed, its dark wood matching the dark wood of the single small table. There were no adornments or personal touches to give her any indication of the personality of the inhabitant.

R sat down on one of the remaining stools and gave her a bright smile that seemed more creepy than friendly on his bronze, leathery face. She successfully suppressed another shiver.

It seemed she had been given the perfect opportunity to discover the rebels' plans, but her thoughts kept turning toward more personal questions.

"Why did you do it?"

Even as she said it, she realized it was a pretty nonsensical question. Apparently all of her hard-won poise had deserted her.

The man across from her raised his eyebrows. "I'm afraid you'll have to be a little more specific. Do what, exactly?"

Marie took a moment to consider exactly what it was she wanted to know. "Make a deal with my mother. Give me away. Set up my whole life to be a lie. Take your pick."

R looked down at his hands, which he had clasped between his knees. After a silent moment, he looked back up at Marie. His stance read penitence, but she wasn't sure she could see it in his eyes.

"My dear girl, I never wanted to give you away. I merely desired for you to have the best possible life. And I saw a way to make that happen. Can you blame me for taking it?

"And as for turning your life into a lie—that wasn't me. Your adoptive parents were free to tell you the truth at any point. It was they who chose not to do so."

Marie watched him closely, wondering how much of what he said was true. Admittedly, her adoptive mother had said nothing about being constrained to lie to Marie. So perhaps he was telling the truth.

Thoughts of her adoptive mother brought another question to the front of her mind.

"Who is my mother? My real mother, I mean. I want to meet her."

R looked down again and, when he looked up, Marie thought she could read real sadness in his eyes.

"Unfortunately, that will not be possible. Your mother died giving birth to you. If she hadn't, I don't know if I could have gone through with my bargain. She was a wonderful woman, and she loved you very much, even before you were born."

Marie digested the news silently, wondering if she should feel grief for the death of a woman she knew nothing about and had only recently learned existed. She couldn't muster up the emotion. If anything, she felt relief. One less emotional complication to deal with.

Perhaps she was becoming a horrible person now that she was no longer a princess.

"But who was she?" Marie asked after a significant pause.

"She was my wife, for all too short a time," he replied. "But before that she was a tradesman's daughter."

"From Northhelm?"

"Certainly." He sighed. "When it came to choosing a bride, I couldn't help but be drawn back to my home."

"*You're* Northhelmian?" Marie wondered if he would find her incredulity rude.

If he did, he didn't show it. "I am indeed." He chuckled. "I don't look it, I know, but I was born here as surely as you were."

"Then can you tell me..." she paused, suddenly unsure what to call him. "What's your name?"

"I would be honored if you would call me Father," he said.

She was shaking her head before he'd finished the word. "I'm sorry but, no, I'm not ready for that." Her head kept shaking, seemingly of its own volition, while she spoke. "In fact, I'd rather that you didn't tell anyone else about our...connection yet, either. This is all very new for me, and I'm just not ready."

"Very well." He sounded disappointed. "In that case, it would be best if you called me Rebel or R like the rest of the camp does."

Marie noticed that he hadn't answered her question, but she didn't like to press him about something so unimportant. Especially not when she had so many other questions.

"How were you able to spin straw into gold? You're clearly not a godmother."

R giggled, strangely amused by her comment. "Certainly not! Of course, as you know, all power resides with the High King. But he dwells in his Palace of Light and dispenses it through the godmothers. And sometimes the godmothers use...tools...objects of power to assist them in their work. I discovered that it is sometimes possible to acquire such items and turn them to my own purposes. For a price, of course."

"Bewitchment," Marie breathed.

R shrugged. "If you will."

Marie tried to keep the discomfort off her face. Although she didn't know of any rulers of Northhelm who had actually met the High King, they had always given him their allegiance. Her own father had told her, only days before, how much they relied on the assistance of the godmothers. The High King's messengers had never brought anything but good to the kingdom.

"Is that...wise?" she asked.

"Wise?" R's face twisted with bitterness. "I have always paid the price for my use of power. How did you think I came to look like this?" He gestured at his face. "And I have always made the price clear to others who would seek to use it, too. The present queen understood the pact she was making with me."

Marie stared at his strange appearance with renewed intensity. The idea that his appearance had been twisted by magic only made him seem even more unnatural.

"And you shouldn't just blindly believe what you're told about the godmothers. For every 'worthy' young person gifted with riches, position and love, there are others who are deemed to be villains. And for them, the godmothers have no mercy and will gladly take from them everything they have."

Marie weighed his words. Many of the tales included villains, of course. But they were always deserving of their fates. They always had the option to choose another path and rejected it.

Or did they? What if the stories were wrong? Was it so terrible of this man to use the power he had acquired to make tales of his own?

She frowned. "And who am I in this story you're creating? The hero or the villain? Because it seems to me that everything I had has been taken away."

He leaned forward, his expression earnest. "My dear Marie, you are the hero. Nothing has been taken from you that was not illegitimate to begin with. Everything I have done has been done for you. To give you the position that is your birthright."

Marie looked around the empty cave. "And what position is that?" She tried to keep her own bitterness out of her voice.

"Why, that of queen, of course!"

She whipped her head back around and found him staring at her with burning intensity.

"For centuries, I have worked and bargained, and it has all led to this. That you, my daughter, should have the position that should have been mine. Ruler of Northhelm."

CHAPTER 16

*R*afe had clearly been waiting for her. He pounced on her as soon as she re-entered the main caverns.

"Are you all right? What happened? What did he say to you?"

She looked at him and, for a mad moment, wanted to blurt out the truth. *Oh, I've just been chatting with my father, who is apparently centuries old. He claims that more than four hundred years ago, a godmother took Northhelm away from him, the older son, and gave it to one of his younger brothers. And he's been working all those years, interfering in people's lives, to acquire the power he needed to reclaim the throne for the true bloodline. So now he wants his child, which would be me, by the way, to lead his army of rebels and take my place as queen. So, you know, nothing of any particular importance.*

It sounded mad, even in her own mind. And she was afraid that if she opened her mouth, she would either laugh hysterically or cry.

This is not where I pictured my life going, she thought.

Rafe was still staring at her, his expression concerned, so she pulled herself together enough to answer.

"Oh, he just interviewed me, asked me what skills I brought to the camp, things like that."

Rafe's brow furrowed, but she was saved from further questions by the arrival of Lisa and Danny.

"So?" Lisa sounded almost breathless with excitement. "What did you think? He's great, isn't he? You're so fortunate that he singled you out like that!"

Marie smiled weakly.

"Did he say anything about camp security?" Danny looked concerned. "I've been worrying that he might think us slack when he returned."

"No, he didn't mention it," said Marie, glad to be able to give one truthful answer. She glanced between the siblings. She would have to remember to ask R exactly what 'object of power' he'd used to ensnare all the young foresters to his cause. It seemed like the sort of knowledge that would be useful to have.

She looked at Rafe a little guiltily. If he was in her position, he would probably have thought to ask.

She had come out of the unexpected meeting with plenty of new knowledge but not a lot of extra insight into her own situation. On the face of it, the decision should be easy: lead a group of bewitched and untrained rebels against her own adoptive family to take a throne she'd never wanted; or remain loyal to the family who had loved and raised her, gather intelligence against the rebels and remain a princess, however illegitimate.

But it turned out that nothing about the situation was simple. Her family might have raised her, but they hadn't loved her enough to tell her the truth. And to remain with them would be continuing to live a lie. Even her role as the 'spare' would be a sham since her parents, knowing the truth of her birth, could hardly allow her to ever take the throne. No wonder they had always been so protective of William. She wondered why they had never had any more children of their own. Was that part of the enchantment, too?

Her birth father, however strange, had at least greeted her with openness from the first moment of their meeting. And he certainly seemed to value her for who she was. His welcome affected her more than she would have anticipated after her other family's deception.

All their lives, the king and queen had believed that she was a nobody—worse than nobody since she was the daughter of a monster. (And why did they believe him a monster, anyway? It was the old king who had made the unreasonable demand. It was he who had threatened death. R had merely come to the rescue.) She could almost taste the satisfaction of informing them that actually it was she who had the truly royal blood.

These thoughts consumed her as they all made their way toward the dining cavern, Lisa chatting about the new recruits. Marie wasn't listening to her friend, but eventually the sound of Lisa's voice filtered through into Marie's consciousness. And thoughts of Lisa and Danny were all it took to cause her to reject her foolish and selfish thoughts. What did her pride matter in the face of all these poor, bewitched foresters? Why should they be put in danger in order to put her on the throne? She had always said, and believed, that William would make a far better ruler than she would, anyway.

Of course, R said that the foresters weren't in any danger. That he had never planned for them to actually fight...*That's why I'm gathering an army of untrained youngsters,* he'd said. *Northhelm will never go to war and slaughter their own children. Once I've gathered young people from the city, the army will have no choice but to stand down. And it won't be such a great step, in their minds, for you to take the throne. It's why I made sure you were raised as a royal. You have all the training and respect that you need.*

It made sense, in a twisted sort of way. But it still seemed wrong to Marie. And that was even before she considered William. She truly had no desire to take the throne from her brother. And what exactly did R plan to do with her father and brother to make way for her ascension?

Her mind went round and round in circles, twisting itself into knots. She needed time to absorb and to think. Which is exactly what she'd told R. Thankfully, he seemed willing to give her the time she needed. He wasn't done recruiting, after all.

Rafe clearly noticed her abstraction. The worried look didn't leave his face throughout the evening meal, and every time she looked up from her food, he was watching her. When Lisa announced she was heading for bed early, Marie eagerly joined her. She wasn't ready for a proper conversation with Rafe yet.

The night brought little clarity but, with the dawn, Marie made a decision. She wouldn't decide anything immediately—she would wait and watch. Regardless of which path her future took, she didn't want to be helpless ever again. She wanted to be able to defend herself. So she would use the time to train, and she would observe.

If R really had been wronged, and if he really had impossibly extended his own life, waiting hundreds of years for the perfect opportunity to right the wrong done to him without bloodshed, then he deserved that she at least give him a chance. However much her instincts rebelled against the idea, he was family.

While it wasn't an answer, really, the decision did bring a measure of peace. It at least allowed her to face Rafe at breakfast.

He was quick to take the seat beside her and to whisper in her ear. "Did he seem to suspect anything? Do we need to run for it?"

She shook her head, smiling to throw off Lisa and one of the other girls who were watching them from the other side of the table.

"No, no, we're safe. At least for now. He was very welcoming. Apparently, I remind him of his daughter." It was as close as she could come to the truth.

"He has a daughter?" Rafe sounded incredulous.

Marie shrugged. "Apparently."

Danny arrived and took the seat on Rafe's other side, so he was forced to abandon the conversation again.

After the meal, Marie returned to the kitchen. She was sure

R would have released her from kitchen duties, but she liked the friendly group who prepared the food. Plus, a kitchen was the perfect location to gather information and gossip and, if she did ever wish to take a leadership role among the rebels, her hard work now would prove that she was not above serving them.

In the afternoon, she joined the group practicing archery. Peter cast her a contemptuous look, but she ignored him. If she only had time to practice one weapon, it was an easy choice. She hadn't liked wielding the heavy sword. Lisa smiled a little ruefully at her but didn't seem surprised.

Once again, Rafe acted as her personal tutor, but this time he took care not to actually touch her. Marie wondered if his careful avoidance was a response to her clearly unwanted flirting, or if he sensed that she was keeping the truth from him. She couldn't decide which option was worse.

Unsurprisingly, her archery suffered from her mental and emotional distraction, and she shuffled off toward the stream with the rest of the girls in a dejected mood.

Lisa sidled up beside her and offered a sympathetic smile. "Don't worry, it wasn't that bad."

Marie gave her an incredulous look. If Lisa had noticed from the other side of the clearing, her efforts must have been pathetic indeed.

"I've never been much of an archer myself," Lisa admitted, "which is a bit of a disgrace when you're a forester."

Marie smiled at her new friend, grateful for her support. Clearly the emotion didn't reach her eyes, however, because Lisa leaned in closer so she could whisper her next words.

"And don't worry about the other thing, either. In my experience, when someone tries that hard *not* to do something, it's because it's exactly the thing they most want to do."

Marie blushed and looked at the ground, too embarrassed to meet the other girl's eye. Transparency wasn't a good quality in a diplomat, and she'd thought she was better at hiding her feelings. What else had Lisa picked up on?

Lisa laughed at her. "I'm pretty sure that's twice now I've just told you not to worry. I'm sure no one else even noticed—it's easy to pick up on things when you're very tuned into them."

"I'm sorry," said Marie, looking up quickly, genuinely sad to think she might be causing pain to someone who had welcomed her so openly.

Lisa shrugged. "I have no claim on him. And I never thought I did." She sighed. "Hoping something isn't the same as having it, and I know that well enough." She managed a small smile. "You have to be tough to survive in the forest. We're a strong breed."

"I knew that even before I came here," said Marie, gripping her friend's arm. "And I could hardly doubt it now that I've met you and Danny."

Lisa flashed her a grateful smile and then shook her head. "Enough about us, though. I've been meaning to ask you all about your friendship with Rafe. I meant what I said about him the other morning. He's always got some story to tell of his travels, but he somehow always evades talk about his family and his home. So, of course, I'm dying of curiosity." She fixed Marie with an expectant gaze.

Marie felt relieved she and Rafe had taken the chance to get their stories straight on their walk back to camp the day before. Not that he'd given her that much information about himself, now that she thought about it. Still it was enough that she shouldn't get herself into trouble now.

She assumed a guilty expression. "I may have slightly overstated it when I first arrived."

Lisa put her hands on her hips and gave the other girl a mock glare. "Marie! I'm shocked!"

Marie grinned at her new friend's playfulness. "Well, 'old' is all a matter of perspective really."

"You sound just like my grandmother." Lisa grinned back

at her.

"The truth is that I only met Rafe when he came through Northgate. We kept in contact after he continued up north into the forest, and he invited me to join him when he decided to come out here. I wasn't sure at first." She shrugged. "But here I am now."

"Oh, of course. I was so sorry to hear about the way your family treated you." Marie could easily read the curiosity in Lisa's face and knew the forester wanted to ask about Marie's situation. But she didn't have to fake her look of pain in response to the mention of her family and, after a pause, Lisa let the topic drop.

"So, you've never met this big family of his then, I suppose?" She said instead.

"Unfortunately not. Although, like you, I'm filled with curiosity over what sort of family would produce Rafe."

There was a moment of silence as the two girls contemplated this question.

"Nope," Lisa said at last with a single shake of her head. "I simply can't imagine a family full of Rafes. Although…" she gave Marie a cheeky, sideways glance, "if his brothers look anything like him, I wouldn't say no to meeting them."

Marie giggled. "Well, it *is* supposed to be a big family. And he does have brothers…"

"Oooh, enough for all of us, I hope," said one of the other girls who had just wandered over to join them.

"As long as I get first pick!" said Lisa with a giggle of her own.

They arrived at the stream before the newcomer could reply and both abandoned the conversation to launch eagerly into the water with the other girls. Marie joined them more slowly, trying to stop her mind from revolving around Lisa's earlier words.

Could her friend be right? Was there a different possible interpretation of Rafe's avoidance of her? And did it matter, anyway? He would never trust her again once he discovered her double role in camp.

CHAPTER 17

*L*ife in the forest camp settled into a routine. In the mornings, Marie helped in the kitchen; in the afternoons, she practiced archery; and, at all times, she attempted to avoid R. At first, he sought her out frequently, but he quickly picked up on her reluctance and seemed content to give her space.

She observed him from a distance and tried not to attract unnecessary attention to herself around camp. Word had quickly got out, however, that she was a favorite of R's, and many of the rebel foresters treated her with deference. It hadn't been her desire, but neither did it seem disconcerting. She had been raised a princess, after all.

Only Rafe, Lisa, and Danny treated her in the same way as before, apparently blind to the changed perceptions of the other foresters. Marie was grateful for their friendship. They brought fun and light to her days in the camp, marred only by her constant chafing desire to go searching for William. She had to keep reminding herself he was almost certainly safe back at the palace after scouting out the camp. It was nothing but foolishness to let baseless worries about him overwhelm her when she had enough real worries of her own.

With R back in camp, Danny had resumed his role as head hunter. On days when game was scarce, he didn't make it back for the afternoon training and Rafe stepped in to take his place. Marie's skills slowly improved, and she moved up to one of the middle targets.

Despite her pride in her new ability, Marie was conscious that it wouldn't have helped her during the attack in Northgate. She mentioned the thought aloud one mealtime and Lisa quickly agreed.

"It's why I was so eager to learn to fight with a blade," said the other girl. "Arrows are extremely effective in their place, but they won't help you defend yourself in close quarters. Foresters are a fairly egalitarian bunch, but my parents never wanted any of their children, boys or girls, to learn sword fighting. I think they were afraid we would run away to join the army or become city guards or something."

She paused for the briefest moment and met her brother's eyes across the table. The emotion they shared was difficult to read. Grief? Guilt?

Marie glanced across at Rafe, who raised his eyebrows the slightest fraction. So, he'd noticed as well.

Was there a limit to R's powers? Were her friends starting to question their decision to turn against their own families?

But in another second, the moment was gone, and Lisa was continuing to speak. "So as soon as we arrived here, I joined the sword training. Putting up with Peter is a small price to pay for learning such a valuable skill."

"Archery isn't so limited," said Danny, his brow creasing as he considered his sister's words. "A bow can be drawn quickly, and an arrow loosed at a short range. And, if necessary, an arrow can be used as a sort of knife."

"Yes," said Lisa, smiling in affectionate exasperation, "if

someone is as skilled as you are. But how many of us can say that? You know I never had any aptitude for it."

"That much at least is true," said Danny, his serious expression breaking into a grin. "Not even my excellent tutelage was enough to turn you into an archer."

Lisa laughed and threw half a bread roll at him. He made no move to avoid it, but the roll sailed straight past him anyway and hit Rafe in the chest.

"Hey!" complained Rafe, before rescuing the abused bread and stuffing it into his mouth.

"Case in point," said Danny, "she has no sense of aim at all."

Marie scooped up her own half-eaten roll and lobbed it at Danny, hitting him squarely in the face. Lisa crowed in triumph.

Danny seemed unfazed. "And that," he said, "is why Marie, on the other hand, is turning into a fine archer. It's all about natural skill."

"Well, the two of us will just have to stick together, then. Between us, we'll have you all covered."

The two boys smiled at her words, but they gave Marie a brief pang. Whenever she started to relax, a simple moment like this one would remind her about her complicated position in the camp and her uncertain future. She wished she were simply another forester, free to smile and agree that she would stick with her friend.

Rafe, who always seemed quick to pick up on her changes of mood, turned thoughtful also.

"You know, it's a good point, though," he said. "If you really want to learn to defend yourself, some skill with a blade would be a good idea."

Marie made a face. "But did you see me that first day with a sword?"

"Swords aren't the only blades, you know. I think a bit of training with a knife might be a good idea. You have better reach and strength than many girls. A knife can be a handy thing to have in a tight spot."

"Hmmm, that's not a bad idea," agreed Danny. "Do you know enough to teach her, Rafe?"

Rafe shrugged. "Enough, I think."

"Oooh, that's a good idea, I want to learn, too!" said Lisa, clapping her hands.

Marie looked between the three of them, wondering if she was going to have any say in the matter.

Rafe caught her eye and smiled at her. "If you'd like to, that is, Marie."

She immediately realized her desire to be consulted had nothing to do with any reluctance to learn knife fighting.

She nodded her agreement while silently resolving, yet again, not to allow herself to get so emotionally wrapped up in Rafe's opinion of her. She was setting herself up for inevitable disappointment—he could hardly think anything positive about her once he discovered her double life.

"You know, I have some questions for you before I take the very serious step of putting myself under your guidance." Lisa's mock serious words pulled Marie's attention back to her friends.

Rafe matched her assumed gravity. "Of course, of course," he said. "As long as you assure me that you posed the exact same questions to Peter before placing yourself under his excellent supervision."

Lisa threw the other half of her roll at him, and he reached out and grabbed it from the air before it could fly past him. This piece followed the previous one into his mouth.

"Don't tell me you're afraid of a few questions, Rafe!" Danny joined the conversation with a lazy smile.

Rafe leaned back and spread his arms wide. "I assure you I am without fear. Ask away."

"I want to know about your family. Tell us something about

them." Lisa propped her elbows on the table and her chin in her hands and gave Rafe her full attention.

"Ah, of course," said Rafe. "A question that naturally springs to mind when considering the skills of a potential knife fighting teacher."

"Oh, go on, Rafe, you can't stay a secret forever," said Marie.

He shot her a look that she couldn't quite interpret and then broke into a smile.

"Very well, then. I do aim to please after all." He looked up at the roof of the cavern, considering. "I have a great many brothers and sisters—far too many for any particular attention to be paid to me. I can assure you that it's no mean feat to stand out among such a mob. My sisters like me well enough, with the exception of the eldest who has always found me far too frivolous." His broad grin suggested he found this assessment amusing rather than offensive. "Thankfully the rest of them find me entertaining. My brothers on the other hand..." He shrugged. "Well, the only way I could ever get them to pay me the least heed was to join them in their weapons practice. And then I found I was good at it, so I worked all the harder." He shrugged again. "You have to be good at something, if you want to stand out among so many."

"Very neatly done," said Danny admiringly. "You brought it back to knife fighting after all."

"Did I not just tell you that I aim to please?"

Lisa snorted at the boys' antics before opening her mouth to ask another question. Unfortunately, however, they had lingered too long for the kitchen volunteers' liking and were chased out of the dining cavern before she got the chance to ask it.

The next day, the four of them began using the free time slot after lunch to practice knife fighting. The first day they drew quite a crowd of spectators, but interest seemed to dwindle when the small group returned each day to do the same exercises. Only the contingent of girls who followed Rafe and Danny around whenever possible continued to linger. None of them were brave enough to ask to join, however. Or else, they had no interest in participating and were simply satisfied with the frequent friendly smiles Rafe sent their way.

Only two other people showed a continued interest in their activities, and both seemed content to observe from a distance. One was R, and he informed Marie when he cornered her alone in the corridor one day, that he heartily approved.

"As always," he said, "you demonstrate how hard you are willing to work and how well you deserve to rule."

Marie wished she didn't feel so flattered by his approbation. She forced her mind toward her brother in an effort to fight the feeling.

"And what about William, doesn't he deserve to rule?" she asked.

"William certainly has many excellent qualities." The sentiment didn't quite seem to reach R's eyes. "But everything has always come so easily to him. You have had to work for everything you have, and it makes you stronger and more resilient."

Marie wondered how he always knew what words would best tap into her deepest emotions. She wished he didn't have such power over her.

"That may be so," she said, "but I won't see him harmed."

"Of course not, of course not." R's voice was as smooth as glass. "It is you who will be queen, and you who will decide how best to handle the family that adopted you."

It was a nice sentiment, but a small warning voice in Marie's head suggested it sounded too good to be true.

"Do you know where he is?" she asked R, a question she hadn't been able to bring herself to ask before.

"Why, in the palace, I assume." His surprise seemed genuine.

"You've never seen him in the forest?" pressed Marie. "Around the camp?"

"No indeed, why would he come here?"

"No reason." Marie watched him with slitted eyes but couldn't see any dissimulation in his face.

Rafe had left a report in Greenwood days ago but had only been able to slip away to check on the town once since then. He had reported that his map and subsequent missive were gone, but no response had been left in their place.

So Marie was still left to hope that William had simply returned to the palace.

~

The other person to watch them from a distance was Peter. Marie often saw him lurking, his disapproving gaze fixed on them. And, once she started paying attention, she noticed that his eyes were often turned their way during training and meals as well.

She had no desire to confront him merely on account of a sour expression, so she did her best to ignore him. She commented on it once to Rafe, but he turned her concerns away with a light answer. He certainly seemed to have no problem laughing and joking despite Peter's lurking presence.

Lisa seemed similarly unconcerned, and only Danny took Peter at all seriously. But then Danny always took their situation at camp more seriously than the others around him, and even he dismissed Peter as any serious threat.

Marie wondered if she was being paranoid, or if her life had trained her to be more observant than her friends. She was, of course, weighted down with the guilty knowledge of their duplicity, so it might have been her imagination that Peter's eyes lingered on her and on Rafe.

When days passed without even a harsh word from him, she decided it must be paranoia, after all.

And then R left on another recruiting trip.

CHAPTER 18

R had tried to corner Marie before he left, but she had managed to evade him. So, she had no more warning than the rest of the camp when he left one evening.

The next afternoon, Peter was waiting for them in their usual practice spot. Even the most unobservant person could have sensed the coming confrontation, and he had already gathered quite a crowd before they arrived.

The circle parted at their arrival, letting them through to the empty space in the center. Marie tensed at the sight of Peter's angry face, but Rafe, who was standing beside her, remained completely at ease. He even grinned around at the watching crowd.

"I know I'm an expert teacher," he said, "but even I don't normally draw such enthusiastic admirers."

Many of the gathered spectators chuckled, and several of the boys called out joking encouragements to him. Peter glared at the assembled group, his face turning red and his eyes narrowing to slits.

"You think you're so special," he hissed, his eyes darting between Rafe and Marie. "Well, I say you're nothing special at all.

You're not even foresters, and I'm getting sick of you lording it over the rest of us. I've seen you with your group of archers. Thinking you're so much better than us swordsmen."

Marie shook her head at his overactive imagination. The small movement focused his attention on her again, and she felt Rafe stiffen beside her. Peter opened his mouth to direct some comment at her, but Rafe spoke first.

His light voice betrayed nothing of the sudden tension she could feel radiating from him. "I can assure you, I have nothing but the greatest respect for anyone who can wield a blade. I myself actually prefer a sword to a bow. I merely seek to help where I am most needed."

His words only further enraged Peter, and Marie had a sneaking suspicion that he was purposefully drawing Peter's ire away from her.

"Don't think I haven't heard the comments," spat Peter. "That you think you could teach swordplay better than me."

Rafe spread his arms wide, a disarming expression on his face. "I can assure you I've never said such a thing."

"But you think it, don't you?" Peter crossed his arms.

Rafe just grinned at him. "My thoughts are entirely my own, and I don't feel the need to own up to them, whatever they may be."

Another titter of amusement ran through the gathered foresters. Once again, the crowd's response fueled Peter's rage.

"We'll see who's the better swordsman," he said, drawing the sword strapped to his side.

Rafe merely watched him silently, the amusement still lingering on his face.

"Draw your sword!" demanded Peter. "Or are you too much of a coward to face me?"

"Not at all, if you insist," said Rafe. He drew his own sword.

Danny stepped forward and spoke quietly in his ear. "Are you sure this is a good idea, Rafe?"

Rafe's reply was equally quiet. "I don't see what choice I have. He won't be satisfied until he's had the chance to fight someone, and I'd rather it be me than..." His eyes flicked toward the girls.

Danny followed his gaze and then bit back a curse. "Very well, then." He stepped back, ushering the girls to join him.

Marie appreciated Rafe's gallantry but also his practicality. She'd been making a lot of progress, but she wasn't proficient enough with her knives to fight a duel with Peter. She bit her lip, wanting to protest but knowing it would be pointless. She just hoped Rafe didn't get hurt.

The two young men crouched into fighting stances and began to circle one another. Peter, clearly impatient, was the first to lunge forward, but Rafe easily parried his attack. Frustrated, Peter danced backward, repositioning himself for another strike.

But however often the forester attacked, Rafe easily blocked him. The Lanoverian was obviously the more skilled swordsman. And even Marie, who had witnessed very few duels, knew that Rafe's refusal to counter-attack made a clear statement. His forbearance only further enraged Peter, whose attacks became more and more frenzied.

Finally, Peter made a particularly wild attack and Rafe, with a flick of his wrist that Marie couldn't follow, sent the forester's sword flying across the open space in the center of the crowd. He lowered his own blade and stepped back, silently inviting Peter to acknowledge the end of the match.

Peter stood still, breathing heavily and staring at Rafe. Rafe shrugged and started to return to his friends, when Peter suddenly lunged at one of the watching rebels. Ripping the sword from the young man's scabbard, he attacked Rafe, who had turned most of the way away from him.

His desperate blow caught Rafe unaware, knocking the sword from his hand.

Marie gasped and stepped forward. Instinctively she wanted to intervene, although she had no idea how to effectively do so.

Danny gripped her arm and pulled her backward, shaking his head.

Marie glanced at him for the merest second, but by the time she had returned her eyes to Rafe, he had two knives in his hands. She hadn't realized he carried knives and had no idea where he had drawn them from. They were long and looked wickedly sharp but still inadequate against the length of Peter's sword.

Peter smiled and attacked again.

Marie opened her mouth to call out a useless warning but shut it again in shock. Instead of seeing Rafe cut down in a pool of blood, she watched Peter fall back, his expression changing to one of desperation.

Rafe moved so quickly that she couldn't even follow his two flashing knives. Somehow, he was not only holding back the longer blade but also going on the offensive. Once, twice, three times, he cut long slits in Peter's shirt, skillfully avoiding piercing the skin underneath.

The spectators fell away and Rafe drove the other man all the way across the clearing to the edge of the trees. Marie still couldn't see how he was doing it, but she now suspected he had been holding back the entire time he had been in the camp. His skill with weapons clearly far exceeded any of the foresters. He had already proved his mastery with the bow and arrow and sword, and she had never seen someone use knives so effectively.

When he disarmed Peter this time, the other man bowed his head and made no attempt to go for another weapon. Rafe stepped even closer to him and said something, but they were too far away for Marie to hear the words.

She did, however, see Peter's head come up, and his eyes focus on her.

When he had finished speaking, Rafe once again secreted his knives and then strode back to the group.

"Show's over, everyone," he called, but he was smiling to take any sting from his words.

Slowly the crowd began to disperse, many of the boys stopping to pat Rafe on the back or shake his hand. Rafe accepted their congratulations with his usual good cheer, but Marie could tell that he was uncomfortable.

When he finally reached Marie and the others, he sighed. "Well, that didn't go exactly to plan."

"Rafe, you've been holding back on me," said Danny, shaking his head.

Rafe shrugged.

"What did you say to Peter?" asked Lisa, her eyes huge and her expression curious.

"That's between me and Peter," said Rafe, but his eyes drifted toward Marie.

"I'm glad you're all right," said Marie, quietly. "But somehow I don't think Peter is less angry with you than he was before."

Rafe smiled at her, the expression lighting up his face. "I can take care of myself."

"Evidently." She looked across the clearing, but Peter had disappeared. She sighed. There was nothing to be done about it now. "Shall we go inside? It doesn't seem like a good moment for practicing." She gestured at the many rebels who still lingered in the clearing.

Her friends were quick to agree and the four of them retreated into the caves. Admiring eyes and whispers followed them.

Peter made no further attempt to challenge them or interrupt their practice, but Marie could still feel his burning eyes following them whenever they were in the same vicinity. Both Danny and Rafe seemed to feel that the matter with Peter was settled, but she couldn't feel the same assurance. The fight had only increased the admiration and respect that the rest of the camp gave to Rafe, and she could imagine how much Peter must resent it.

Even R, who usually seemed distanced from the goings-on of the camp, noticed the change when he returned. He sought Marie out in the kitchens one morning to ask her about it and listened with rapt interest to her story.

"Interesting," he said, his face thoughtful.

Marie wished she were better at interpreting his strange expressions. She had downplayed Rafe's skill, not wishing to draw attention to him, but she still felt uneasy.

As it turned out, she should have saved the concern for herself. Two days later, R interrupted the evening meal to announce yet another trip. It was the first public announcement he had made since Marie had joined the rebels. She nibbled on her tongue, wondering what was coming next.

"As our group grows," he said, holding everyone's rapt attention, "I no longer like to leave you all leaderless in my absence. I have, therefore, determined to appoint someone to act with my authority while I am gone."

The uneasy feeling returned to Marie's stomach.

"I have chosen Marie as my deputy and expect you to show her the same respect and deference you show to me." His eyes turned hard, although Marie could see no rebellion in the faces around her. Even Peter looked acquiescent, lulled, no doubt, by the enchantment of R's presence.

She glanced at her friends. Lisa looked thrilled and reached over to give her arm a quick squeeze. Danny looked approving, he had been wanting a better authority structure from the beginning. Rafe looked thoughtful.

He alone had never shown any signs of falling under R's thrall, and Marie wished she could read his mind even more than she wished she could understand R.

He raised his eyebrows at her, and she shrugged in reply. What could she say?

R gestured for her to join him at the front of the room, and she reluctantly made her way forward. He placed a warm, approving arm around her shoulders, and she had to force herself not to cringe away. Despite how much time had passed, it still felt wrong to receive such a fatherly gesture from him.

She mumbled a few words of gratitude to the crowd for their trust and then quickly fled the room. R followed her.

"What are you doing?" she asked him. "I didn't ask for this."

"No," he said, and there was a hint of steel in his voice that she hadn't heard before. "I've been very patient with you. Indeed, I understand and applaud your desire to get to know the camp. But you also need to learn how to lead it. I'm giving you the chance to do so and also to protect your friend from any further attacks. Surely you want that?"

She stared at him, silenced by his words. What had he meant? Were his words merely a reference to Peter, or had that been a threat against Rafe?

"Very well," she said, her words reluctant and her voice heavy.

R giggled. "That's the way, my dear." He smiled, patted her on the shoulder and was gone.

Marie sighed and returned to the dining cavern, trying desperately to think of what explanation she could give her friends.

CHAPTER 19

$\mathcal{B}$ut to her surprise, no one questioned her appointment as leader. Lisa and Danny seemed entirely approving and not the least bit curious as to why she had been chosen. She could only assume it was a side effect of the enchantment.

Rafe, on the other hand, clearly wanted to know what was going on between R and Marie, but he couldn't ask around the others.

Marie felt guilty about leaving him in the dark, but she also made sure to stick close to Lisa and give him no opportunity to talk to her alone.

She gave up working in the kitchens in the mornings and dedicated herself instead to learning all about the running of the camp. She interviewed as many of the rebels as possible, searching them out at their regular tasks and joining in where possible.

Everyone seemed happy to talk to her and enthusiastic about R, but they all seemed a little hazy on what exactly was going to be required of them as rebels. It didn't help that they all gave her a different reason when she inquired as to the purpose of the rebellion. Almost as if they had each heard something different in R's words. Once again, it made no sense except as a consequence of the enchantment. She had never heard of rebels with so little ideological cohesion or interest in fighting. Only a small handful even seemed to have a significant grievance against the crown.

Everything she saw led her to agree with Danny. For a rebel camp, the security and organization were sorely lacking. She also had no trouble thinking of ways to improve the situation.

Her dilemma lay in the fact that she wasn't sure she wanted to do it.

It surprised her to learn that she liked being in charge, and she had no doubt that bringing the camp into order would be supremely satisfying. But she couldn't forget what the purpose of the camp actually was. Truly taking leadership would put her one step closer to defying her family and setting herself up as queen.

A part of her wanted to forget consequences and just do it. Whipping the camp into shape and uniting it under her leadership would be a challenge, a worthy test of her skill. After all, she had trained all these years to be the perfect royal, and now that she had discovered the truth of her heritage, all her effort might go to waste. Unless, of course, she seized the chance that R was offering her.

But still, she hesitated.

On the third day of her leadership, Rafe failed to appear at breakfast.

"He's gone out hunting." Danny shrugged, as if disclaiming responsibility for his friend's strange actions. "He wanted to get out early, so he's gone alone."

Marie chewed on her tongue again. So he'd given up trying to catch her alone, then. She knew she should be glad, but she felt disappointed instead.

Now that she was in no immediate danger of bumping into him, thoughts of Rafe continued to dominate her mind. Eventually she gave up trying to focus on any of the tasks before her.

Shaking her head at her own contrariness, she collected her bow and arrow and left the camp.

While it would be a triumph to surprise her teachers with success, she didn't really expect to catch any game. She merely wanted a chance to get away. To clear her head.

The solitude of the forest was soothing, but it didn't bring answers to her troubled mind. Waiting and watching had seemed like a wise plan, but she was starting to realize that it was getting her no closer to a solution. She suspected that the answer wasn't going to drop down from the sky merely because she waited long enough. She was simply going to have to make a choice, however distasteful.

It was an unappealing thought.

Still trying to put off the inevitable, she focused her attention back on the forest as she looped back toward the camp. Perhaps it wasn't too late to flush out some game.

Hearing a noise, she froze, trying to track its direction. Easing back behind a tree, she stared toward the sound. Whatever it was, it sounded big. Perhaps a deer?

A deer did emerge from the trees, but it wasn't walking on its own legs. Instead they bobbed well above the ground, slung across broad shoulders. She mentally kicked herself. No wonder she'd barely survived in the forest—she couldn't even tell the difference between a human and a deer.

Rafe looked cheerful, pleased perhaps with his catch, and she debated whether she should step forward and reveal her presence. She wished she could tell him the whole truth, explain her dilemma, and ask his advice.

But she didn't dare. She was too afraid of what he would think of her for lying to him for so long—for being tempted in the first place.

While she hesitated, the forest around her erupted. Shocked, she watched several of the young rebel men pour from the trees and rush toward Rafe.

Outnumbered six to one and hampered as he was by the deer, he had no chance to even draw a weapon. The rebels leaped on him, pinning him to the ground, and Marie recognized Peter in their midst, his eyes shining and fists flailing.

After a brief scuffle, Rafe was hauled to his feet, firmly clasped by three of the foresters. Peter placed himself in front of them.

"Not so high and mighty now, are you?" he asked.

His triumph made Marie sick.

She assessed the situation, trying not to focus on the blood trickling down from above Rafe's eye. She glanced toward the camp, but the distinct thump of a fist hitting flesh pulled her attention back to the group before her. Rafe was bent slightly forward, curled, as much as he was able, around his stomach. Peter's hand was still clenched into a fist.

Marie sucked in her breath and abandoned any thought of going for help. Instead she quietly selected an arrow and drew her bow. Taking a deep breath to steady herself, she took aim and fired a shot into the tree next to Peter.

All seven of the men in the clearing looked up, first at the arrow and then back toward her position. She took the opportunity to nock another arrow and step forward.

Her hands were steady, and her voice was calm.

"The next one goes into you, Peter," she said, keeping her aim on him.

One of the others took a hesitant step toward her. She shook her head without taking her eyes off Peter.

"I wouldn't try that, if I were you. An arrow will move much faster than you will." She paused to let her words sink in. "I will not have such doings in my camp. I suggest you all stand down—right now!"

Out of the corner of her eye, she could see Rafe watching her. His expression was half admiration, half fear. He hadn't looked fearful before, so she could only assume his concern was for her.

She knew that even with the bow and arrow and the element

of surprise, the odds were against her. But she was relying on the authority R had bequeathed to her. Hopefully it carried some weight, at least with Peter's five companions. None of them had shown any desire to flout their leader before, and she trusted that they weren't as blinded by hate as Peter.

For a long moment, no one moved. Marie began to feel nervous. Perhaps she had miscalculated.

Then one of the rebels holding Rafe let go and stood back. The other two were quick to follow his lead. After that, it only took seconds for the rest of them to melt away toward camp.

Rafe stood up and shook himself off, and Marie lowered her bow. She wanted to run to him and check if he was wounded, but she restrained herself.

Her eyes remained focused on him, however, so she didn't see Peter rush toward her. He wrenched the bow and quiver from her grip and tossed them aside.

She had the briefest second to wonder what exactly he intended to do, before he was suddenly gone. Looking around, she found him lying on the ground. Rafe was standing over him, both fists clenched.

"I warned you," said Rafe, his breathing heavy. "I warned you what would happen if you ever touched her."

Peter looked up at the other man, and Marie could read the fear in his face. She could understand the emotion. She would have been terrified if Rafe had ever looked at her like that.

"You need to leave, now, and never come back," Rafe continued.

"But I…" Peter's voice died away.

"I gave you a chance," said Rafe, his face and voice implacable. "I won't be giving you another."

Peter opened his mouth again but shut it without saying anything. After a moment, he scrambled backward, putting distance between himself and Rafe. Once he had room to move, he stood slowly upright before turning and walking away.

"You saved me," said Marie and then bit her lip at the stupidity of the obvious statement.

Rafe flashed her his usual cheerful grin, all trace of his earlier icy rage gone. "Then I guess that makes us even. I seem to remember you started this encounter by saving me."

"I did, didn't I?" A delighted smile spread across Marie's face. "I guess all your training paid off!"

For a moment, they grinned at each other a little foolishly.

"Do you truly think he'll leave?" Marie hardly dared to believe that Peter might be gone from their lives for good.

"I do," said Rafe. "His pride was hurt, and he let his anger blind him, but he's not suicidal. I suspect, once he has some distance, and if he can shake off R's enchantment, he'll be embarrassed by his own behavior."

"Enchantment?" Marie latched onto the word. She had never confirmed the villagers' suspicions to Rafe. "So you believe R's managed to bewitch them all?" She wished she could confirm it to him and discuss the implications, but how would she explain her own knowledge? What reason could she give for R confiding so openly to her?

Rafe gestured at the deer now lying on the forest floor. "Hunting was just a cover. I've been to Greenwood."

"Oh, of course." Marie felt stupid for not having guessed it.

"This time there was a note left under my stone."

"What did it say? Can I see it?" Marie wondered if it had been written by her adoptive father, and if she would recognize the handwriting. She felt suddenly lonely for her old life and her family. The unexpected, desperate longing for some physical connection to them took her by surprise.

Rafe shook his head, looking apologetic. "I didn't want to risk bringing it back with me. I read it three times and then burned it."

Marie nodded reluctantly. She had come to the same conclusion with Rafe's map, after all. "What did it say?"

"It was a warning." Rafe sighed and ran a hand through his hair. "Apparently they've received an emissary from Rangmere."

"Rangmere?" It was the last thing Marie had been expecting. "From the new queen? What does that have to do with the rebels?" She chewed on her tongue. Northhelm's relationship with their neighboring kingdom had been rocky for some time. And although Queen Ava had promised that the aggression would stop under her reign, Marie's old distrust still lingered. Hardly surprising given she had personally been a part of foiling a previous attempt by Ava, when she was only a princess, to annex their other neighbor, Arcadia.

She hoped it wasn't some new threat to Northhelm. An image of her parents, at home in the palace in Northgate, rushed into her mind. Guilt clawed at her. She could vividly conjure up a picture of her mother's anxious face—she would be sick with worry for Marie. The last thing either of Northhelm's rulers needed was further stress.

"The Rangmerans came with a warning from Queen Ava. Several of her subjects recently uncovered a plot against her throne. It involved the use of an enchanted jewel that one of her nobles used to enthrall the people around him. Apparently, it overpowered their loyalties and made them follow him without question." Rafe paused to give her a significant look. "Sound familiar at all? The king certainly thinks so. And, unfortunately, the culprit got away. They believe he fled into Northhelm."

"An enchanted jewel?" Marie spoke slowly, considering the information. It lined up with what R had told her about the source of his powers. "Was there a description of what it looked like? We should try to find it!"

"Queen Ava described it as large and blood red. But the noble in question apparently wore it on a thick gold chain around his neck. If R has somehow acquired this gem, I'm sure he'll keep it on his person as well. I can't imagine we'll just find it lying around."

"No, I suppose you're right…" Marie wondered if she could ask R to show it to her. At least then she'd know where he kept it. She could excuse her interest as a desire to learn about ruling the camp.

"Was there any information about the enchantment?" she asked. "Does it have any limitations?"

"According to the Rangmerans, it starts out like a gentle suggestion, but the more time the person spends around it, the stronger the compulsion to obey its owner becomes. Thankfully, if a person is removed from the jewel's influence, they should recover after a few days. One of the bewitched described it as waking up from a dream."

"Hmmm." Marie considered the information. "R must take it with him on his recruiting trips since it's how he convinces the foresters to become rebels in the first place. Which explains why he's never gone from camp for too long. And how an incident like this is able to happen." She gestured at the forest around them, which still showed signs of the earlier struggle. "Discipline starts to disintegrate the longer he's away."

"Yes." Rafe sighed. "It does seem to line up. In lots of ways, Danny and Lisa are just like their old selves: as long as I've known him, Danny has been serious, conscientious and an excellent hunter. And Lisa has always been friendly, fun and incredibly loyal to her brother. But they both always seemed intelligent and I found it odd from the beginning that they never questioned R. Certainly, when he's here, they seem to hero worship him. Particularly Lisa. But when he's away, I've noticed occasional changes. As if they're not really sure what they're doing in the camp."

Marie nodded. "I've noticed the same thing. It's subtle, but it's definitely there. Which means we can break his hold on them if we can only get them away from the jewel for long enough. Or somehow get our hands on it." She frowned as she considered the matter further. "If the enchantment's so powerful, though, how come it didn't affect everyone in Greenwood? For that matter, how come it isn't affecting us?"

She paused, suddenly struck by a horrible thought. "You haven't been feeling any strange compulsions to join the rebellion, have you?" She wouldn't put it entirely past R to have enthralled Rafe but then instructed him to test her loyalties.

Rafe shook his head. "Not a one. But then I wasn't affected like Lisa and Danny were when R visited the village, either." Marie nodded, relieved to remember that Rafe had resisted the jewel's effects from the beginning.

Rafe continued. "The Rangmerans reported that they were able to damage the jewel, thus disrupting its influence over those who had been enchanted. Unfortunately, the perpetrator fled with the jewel before they were able to examine it further. It's possible, however, that it was permanently damaged in some way."

"Well, that would be something at least." Marie sighed. "It's an overwhelming enough task without starting to doubt ourselves."

Rafe said nothing, but she could feel the intensity of his gaze. She tried to ignore it.

"Was there anything else?" A sudden thought struck her. "Did it say anything about William?"

Rafe's expression twisted, and Marie's heart sank.

CHAPTER 20

"*I* wasn't sure whether to tell you or not." He stepped forward, as if to comfort her, then seemed to think better of it and stepped back again. "He never returned to the palace. They were very concerned to hear that he never arrived at the rebel camp, either. They've begun searches for him, but they have to be very discreet. At the moment, the official position is still that you're both sick in bed."

Marie stared at him, aghast. She had been occupying herself by learning to fight and laughing with the rebels while William was missing, in danger, possibly even dead. She felt a sudden need to vomit.

It must have showed in her face because this time Rafe did approach her, laying a concerned hand on her arm.

"I'm sure he's all right," he said, although his face remained worried. "He's highly capable."

"I only hope you're right," Marie whispered. Her eyes filled with tears, although she fought them back before they could fall. "But I should be doing something, looking for him, not spending my time here—learning to fight and worrying about people like Peter!"

Rafe's grip on her arm tightened. "You're not responsible for your brother. And it wouldn't do anyone any good for you to go missing as well. You've learned a lot, but you still have no chance of finding him by simply wandering around the forest and hoping you trip over him."

His voice softened. "And you can't blame yourself. We're doing important work here." He shook his head. "This camp is a strange place. It's all too easy to forget its true purpose. But we can't allow ourselves to be sucked in by it. We can't let ourselves forget who our true enemy is." He paused, as if giving a chance for his words to sink in. "And it's not Peter."

He was right, of course. Only it wasn't so simple for Marie. She wished she could really know, for certain, who her enemy was. The news from Northgate had only increased her inner conflict.

She could feel Rafe's concerned gaze, and she appreciated his support and good sense. But she'd also spent too long in the world of diplomacy not to read the undercurrent to his little speech.

He wasn't stupid. He knew that there was something strange going on with Marie, something she wasn't telling him.

She drew a deep breath and forced a smile. "You're right, of course, on all fronts. And speaking of R, he's already been gone for several days on this latest trip…"

"Which means he'll be arriving back at any moment." Rafe looked grim. "Which also means we should be getting back to camp."

Marie nodded her agreement, and Rafe let her go in order to retrieve the deer. They made their way back to camp in silence. There was plenty to think about, but none of it was safe to say out loud where they might be overheard.

~

Marie had been gone longer than she had intended, and people were already trickling out of the dining cavern when they arrived back in camp. Marie picked up her pace, hoping she still had time to get some lunch before everything was packed away. Rafe followed behind her, calling return greetings to the rebels, who responded to the sight of his catch with jubilation. There was no sign of any of his attackers.

Marie and Rafe had been right about R's timing. He returned partway through their afternoon training session, and everyone quickly broke off their activities to cluster around him.

He must have visited one of the larger villages, because he had a decent number of young foresters with him. Marie concluded that he must have cleared out the villages in range of the camp by now. What would he do when he needed to go on a longer trip? He could hardly cart them all with him.

She and Rafe mingled with the enthusiastic crowd, not wanting to draw attention to themselves. While Marie examined the new recruits, another thought occurred to her. Had all of the villages been pillaged like Greenwood? If so, was there a flood of refugees pouring into the capital? Once again, an image of her anxious mother and overwhelmed father flashed into her mind. She began chewing on her tongue.

Despite the fawning group surrounding him, Marie could see R trying to catch her eye. She avoided him studiously. She couldn't avoid him forever, though, and she sensed that their next meeting would be a pivotal one. He would want to know how she had done as camp leader, and she would have two options. She could embrace a new future with the rebels and give him her recommendations for improvements, or she could ask to see the enchanted item he used to bewitch the foresters and start plotting how to get it off him.

Normally, Marie prided herself on her courage, but it seemed to have gone missing. She turned and slipped back into the sanctuary of the forest. What did R think of her escape, and had Rafe noticed her exit? She didn't turn back to see.

An hour later, Marie sat on a fallen log, her arms wrapped around her legs and her chin propped on her knees. She was chewing determinedly on her tongue and staring at a strange patch of moss on a tree in front of her.

If only I didn't have to make this decision alone, she thought. A laughing, brown-haired face popped into her mind, but she ruthlessly suppressed it.

Another minute passed.

"My goodness," said a voice beside her, "that's a serious expression."

Marie gasped and half-jumped, losing her balance on the log and nearly tumbling off. When she recovered her position, she found she had acquired a companion.

The older, gray-haired lady didn't look like the sort of person who commonly spent her time sitting around on logs. Despite this, she seemed entirely unruffled by her surroundings. She shifted her position slightly, and Marie gasped again. Wings.

She swallowed, rose to her feet and gave a half-bow. "Godmother," she said, respectfully.

The godmother smiled in a grandmotherly sort of way and patted the log beside her. Slowly, Marie sank back down onto it. She waited for the godmother to say something, but the silence continued. As a princess, she had always known she had a godmother, but she'd never actually met her before.

"I'm sorry," said Marie, at last, when her patience ran out. "I wasn't expecting you."

She cringed and wished she had thought of something more intelligent to say.

"Weren't you?" The godmother sounded mildly surprised, although not in the least put out. "I thought you called me."

"Called you? No…"

Being rude to a godmother was never a good idea. Marie tried again. "I *was* just thinking that I wished I wasn't alone...?"

"Oh yes, that will be it, then." The godmother looked pleased. "The High King warned me a crisis point was coming and to be on the lookout. I'm not usually so sensitive, but I was particularly tuned in."

"Oh. Well, thank you." Marie tried to think of all the lessons she had ever learned about godmothers. Thankfully, this one didn't seem inclined to be offended.

She wondered if her godmother had known from the beginning that she wasn't a true princess. It probably wasn't a good thing to bring up, either way.

"You were at my Christening." Her curiosity overwhelmed her good sense.

"Yes, dear, of course."

"Did you know then that I wasn't truly a princess? Did you mind?"

The godmother raised her eyebrows. "Goodness me, I can see why the High King thought I might be needed."

Marie wasn't quite sure what the godmother was referring to, but she flushed anyway.

Her godmother regarded her steadily for a moment. "Identity issues are always hard ones to overcome. But I find that most people already know the answer—they just need a little help finding it." She smiled at Marie. "I suggest that you start by thinking back on all the old tales."

She paused, apparently to give Marie time to reflect.

Marie tried to think of every tale she'd ever heard that involved a godmother and a prince or princess. It didn't take her long to see the godmother's point.

"Oh, right." She flushed again. It seemed obvious now.

"Don't worry, dear." The godmother patted her hand. "I like to feel needed." The twinkle in her eye caught Marie off-guard. She hadn't expected her godmother to have a sense of humor.

"You're worried because you weren't born a princess. But it's my job to make sure that people end up where they're supposed to be—and it's surprising how often those born in a palace don't deserve to be there while those born in a woodcutter's hut do. The High King cares about the choices you make, not where you were born."

"So, you think I should go back and pretend to be a princess. Just forgive everyone for lying to me my whole life?" Marie tried not to sound petulant.

The godmother paused, considering Marie's words.

"Or...wait!" Marie felt a sickening rush of panic. "Are you saying my decisions since I found out about my birth mean I don't deserve to be in a palace?"

"I hate to be the one to tell you..." The godmother looked at her with sad eyes.

Marie paled.

A sudden chuckle broke the tension. "Good gracious, girl! So you ran away from home—hardly the actions of a master villain! If we had to discipline every youngster who got a bit agitated with their parents and ran away for a while we'd be busy all day long."

Her expression slowly turned grave. "Your next decisions do matter, though. That's why I'm here now. And they'll matter to more than just you. The whole kingdom will stand or fall based on your actions over the coming days."

"No pressure!" muttered Marie.

"Sorry, what was that, dear?" The godmother turned to her with an innocent expression.

"Nothing," said Marie hastily. She went back to chewing on her tongue. "When you say 'fall'...?" she asked uneasily.

"Fall to darkness." The godmother's tone was matter-of-fact. "There's a reason the High King rules from the Palace of Light. He holds the darkness at bay. Bad things happen in kingdoms that choose not to offer him their allegiance. We do what we can, of course, but our efforts can only go so far." She sounded sad. "People, such as yourself, have to make their own choices."

Marie could feel a weight settling around her shoulders. She'd wanted help in making the right decision, not a massive increase in pressure.

"And how am I supposed to know what the right choice is? Do I support the king and queen because they raised me? I always believed they were good people— and then I found out they lied to me their whole life. What else don't I know about them? And my real father says their ancestors stole the throne from him—that they don't even have the right to rule." She put her head into her hands. "What am I supposed to believe?"

"That's the thing about beliefs, ultimately it's up to you to choose what you believe."

"That's not helpful!" Marie felt sick of being responsible. She wanted someone to just tell her what was true.

"I could tell you what to believe, of course. That would be easy. But then they would be my beliefs, not yours."

Silence descended on the clearing while Marie silently acknowledged the truth of the godmother's words. She felt an overwhelming weariness.

"So how do I know what to believe, then?" she asked after a long moment.

"Well, in this case it comes down to people. Determining who you can trust. And, fortunately for you, you've spent most of your life learning exactly that skill. You call it diplomacy. So, go through everything, step by step. You can start with me."

"You?"

"Your birth father says that he, and his heirs, are the rightful rulers of Northhelm, doesn't he?"

Marie nodded.

"Well, how did they lose the throne?"

"Apparently, a godmother...oh." Marie pondered the implication of her words. She remembered hearing her father's story for the first time and how it had made her question the interventions of the godmothers.

"There's nothing wrong with questioning us." Could the godmother read minds? "Just as long as you keep questioning and searching until you reach the truth. Don't just blindly believe your birth father, any more than you should blindly believe me."

Marie shrugged and hugged her knees more tightly. "That's all very well, but I wasn't there, I didn't see what really happened. In fact, all the other people involved must be long dead by now."

"Do you need to know the particulars of this specific instance? What about all the other tales? Are there any about godmothers getting it wrong?"

Slowly, Marie shook her head.

"Of course, you might not be able to trust the stories. What if we somehow made them up? Suppressed the ones about our failures? You've studied history, consider that instead. What does it tell you about the state of the kingdom whenever it's followed the promptings of the godmothers? What has been your own experience with us?"

Marie frowned as she considered her godmother's words. The history books were clear—a kingdom ruled by love was a place of peace and prosperity. The High King himself had dictated that it be so. And the godmothers did his bidding—working hard to ensure that princes and princesses found true love so that their kingdoms might prosper. And removing those who showed themselves incapable of true love.

Marie had to admit that Northhelm had always prospered when the godmothers got involved.

As for her own personal experience...she'd never met a godmother before. At least, not since she was a baby.

But she had been involved in the business in Arcadia the year before. A godmother had given the queen a magic pea to help her find the right bride for her son. The right bride had turned out to be a woodcutter's daughter and, with Marie's help, she'd saved the kingdom even before she married the prince.

Marie still kept in contact with Alyssa, the new princess, and she was certainly reporting a period of widespread peace and prosperity in Arcadia. In that case, the intervention of a godmother had favored a woodcutter's daughter over several princesses, but there could be no question it had turned out for the good of the kingdom.

She spoke slowly. "So maybe the godmothers were right when they took the throne away from my father."

"Perhaps. Of course, people change." The godmother spoke lightly, her tone giving nothing away. "Maybe he has changed in the many years since then."

Marie wanted to think so. He had certainly been welcoming to her.

But he had set himself up as a godmother, of sorts. Which meant he had to be evaluated by the same standards.

The power he used was stolen—he admitted as much himself. And the use of it came with a price—she had lived her whole life with the anxiety that plagued her mother. The very jewel he now used had been used previously in an attempt against the Rangmeran crown. Where the godmothers sowed love, her father sowed fear. She thought of Lisa and Danny, caught in his snare, and shivered.

"I don't think so," she said, sadly. But then a streak of stubbornness welled up in her. "But just because he's in the wrong, it doesn't make my adoptive parents right! They didn't have to lie to me."

"No, they didn't." The godmother sighed. "But even good people can make bad decisions." She threw a wry glance at Marie. "Wouldn't you agree?"

Marie flushed again. She was starting to be glad she'd never met her godmother before. The grandmotherly figure made her feel like a small and somewhat foolish child. A far cry from the dignified and poised princess she had fashioned herself into.

"True love gives without thought of return," continued the godmother. "Both your adoptive parents and your birth father have claimed to love you. Both have shown you kindness and consideration. Ask yourself this—what, if anything, do they seek to gain by such behavior?"

Marie wobbled slightly on the log. She felt as if the breath had been knocked out of her. The answer was so blindingly obvious.

CHAPTER 21

*N*othing. Her adoptive parents had nothing to gain. All this time she had been feeling betrayed, and she had never once stopped to consider her parents' motives.

They had taken her in and loved her, despite believing she was the daughter of a monster. They had never made her feel inferior. She had been the one who felt like she failed to measure up to the standards of a princess. Her mother had always assured her that she was more than enough.

They had done all this without knowing the purposes of the man who gave her to them. Believing that she would one day be taken from them. And they had done it for her sake. Because they loved her.

Tears silently streamed down her face.

Her birth father, however, had chosen to give her away. To force her on a couple who had never asked for her. He claimed it was to give her a better life, but he couldn't have known how they would treat her in private, the unwanted addition to their family.

In fact, his own words betrayed him. He had later said to her that he had ensured she be raised as a royal so that she would be perfectly positioned to seize the throne. Everything he had done had been to further his own plans of revenge and power, not to ensure that his daughter had a happy and fulfilled life. In fact, his plans forced her into a position of choosing between her birth family and the one who had raised her. What loving father would ask such a thing of his daughter?

It all seemed so obvious now, and she almost wished she had been susceptible to the power of his jewel, after all. It certainly felt preferable to simply being a fool, caught up in her own insecurities and hurts.

An arm wrapped around her shoulders, and she turned blindly into the comforting shoulder being offered. Healing washed through her as she cried, a warmth and peace that seemed to flow from her godmother and fill her body.

When the tears dried up, her indecision and insecurity had disappeared with them. Of course she wouldn't betray her family. She would use everything they had ever taught her to defeat R and defend the kingdom.

Lisa's and Danny's faces appeared in her mind. She just hoped she could do it without any of the rebels being hurt.

If she could save Northhelm, then she would have earned her place in the palace. She wouldn't be living with her family as an impostor but as a loved and loving family member—just as she had lived all the previous years of her life. If the High King didn't care where people were born, why should anybody else?

The decision felt invigorating and left Marie ready for action. She stood and stretched, wiping the remaining tears from her face. Smiling, she turned to thank her godmother and found her place empty. She scanned the clearing, but there was no sign of her. She hadn't even thanked her. She could only hope her disappearance meant the godmother's task had been completed successfully. Hopefully Marie had been shepherded toward the right decision.

The thought of facing R no longer intimidated her, so she turned back toward camp.

As soon as she approached the cave system, she was hailed by an unfamiliar face. Obviously one of the new recruits.

"Are you Marie?" the girl asked.

Marie nodded.

"R wants to see you. In his personal cave. He said you know the way." The girl looked impressed.

After Marie's recent revelations, the sight of the girl's blind loyalty sickened her.

She forced a smile and nodded. "Of course, I'll go find him now." She could feel the girl's eyes watching her retreating back and had to fight down the urge to turn around and tell the girl to run home as fast as she could.

As she approached R's cavern, she took several deep breaths and carefully assumed her 'diplomat' demeanor. She couldn't risk any part of her true feelings peeking out.

R welcomed her with enthusiasm and made no mention of her earlier defection into the woods.

"I can see you've done an excellent job ruling in my absence. Tell me, how did you find it?"

Marie tapped into her earlier feelings of enthusiasm and allowed her face to break into a grin. "It was nice to actually use my skills. Fun as it's been to learn to shoot, archery isn't what I was raised to do."

R giggled. "No, indeed. It is my earnest desire to see you using your skills to their fullest extent. You will make a great queen."

It was a loaded statement and R's eyes said he knew it, even if his voice remained light.

Marie kept her smile in place. "It would be a pity to waste so many years of training."

"That it would, that it would." R came forward and gripped her hand warmly.

She forced herself not to flinch or pull away.

"I knew you only needed a chance to see yourself in action. You were born to rule and I will not have it otherwise."

The fervor in his eyes made Marie uncomfortable. There was something uncanny about him that always put her on her guard. The high-pitched giggle and light-hearted tone never quite seemed to match the dangerous and almost manic light in his eyes. She would do well to remember that this man was no fool, despite his odd mannerisms.

His words brought her brother, the rightful future ruler, to mind. He had never shown up in camp, but he hadn't returned to the capital either. Was it possible R knew more about his fate than he was telling Marie?

The thought made it even harder to play along, but Marie controlled herself.

"They can be a fractious lot while you're away, these rebels," said Marie. "It makes me wish I had an object of power such as yours. It certainly does simplify things."

"You shall, my daughter, you shall," said R. He rubbed his hands together, visibly warming to the idea. "When I find you the right one."

"May I see yours?" Marie forced her face to betray nothing but idle curiosity. "I'd like to know what such an item looks like."

R paused for the briefest moment before letting her hand go and swinging around to check the entrance of the cave. "Of course you can, of course. Natural enough, I'm sure. Although it isn't the look of the item that counts."

Having established that they were alone, he reached down the front of his shirt and drew out a thick gold chain. A large, red gem winked from the end of it. The jewel caught the light and reflected it back in every direction, making the cavern appear bathed in blood.

A small shiver escaped Marie, but she hoped R would attribute it to excitement.

He stroked the jewel lovingly. "I loaned it to a young fool

from Rangmere recently." He shook his head. "The idiot used to wear it outside his clothes, as if he wanted to advertise its presence."

He looked over at her. "I know you would never treat one of my gifts so lightly." Once again, she detected the faintest trace of warning beneath his affectionate tone.

"Of course not…Father," she said.

A brilliant smile broke across his face. "It gives me great joy to hear you say so, my daughter."

Marie let out a small breath before smiling back. "What happened to him?"

"Who?"

Marie noted how well her strategy had worked. R's delight at her use of his title had completely distracted him from the conversation.

"The fool from Rangmere."

"Oh." R waved a dismissive hand. "He died, as most young fools tend to do. But not before he had returned my jewel."

A dark cloud passed across his face, and Marie wondered uneasily how much of a hand R had played in his death. What had made the young man so desperate that he had bargained with R in the first place? And what price had he agreed upon?

Whatever the stated price, the arrangement had apparently cost him his life. How had she ever even considered that R might be in the right?

She examined his face, which was focused back on the jewel. What had R wanted from the young man that would make it worthwhile to give up ownership of the jewel, even for a short time? Could he be convinced to make such a bargain again?

Even as she thought it, Marie rejected the idea. R's bargains brought darkness and death. She would have no part in them. There had to be another way.

She turned her own attention to the gem and noticed a large crack running down the center.

"Oh," she said. "It's damaged!"

The dark cloud on R's face turned thunderous. "Twice a fool!" he said. "He let his enemies crack the jewel." Slowly his face settled back into its usual lines. "Thankfully, it still retains much of its power. Don't worry, daughter, it will be sufficient to place you on the throne."

"Are you sure?" Marie faked alarm. "What sort of damage has been done to its enchantment?"

"There is no cause for concern." R grinned. "My current plans have been built around its new limitations. You will notice that I gather only young people around me. Once its powers could reach anyone, now they seem to touch only the young. And even then, there are a few who seem unaffected by its enchantment. They are protected somehow."

He furrowed his brow but then shook his head, shaking away the expression. "But the young are more than enough. We shall easily conquer with them at our side."

Marie nodded and matched his smile. Inside, her thoughts whirled. She wished she knew what made her and Rafe immune.

That question led to another that had been itching at her mind for a while. "It's fortunate that I decided to come here to join you," she said. "I have to admit to being curious about what you would have done if I hadn't turned up."

"Your arrival was certainly an unexpected help." He looked pleased. "But I never make bargains unless I have the power to follow through with them. The queen had agreed to my deal. She always knew that one day I would come for you, and she could not have stopped me when I did."

Marie wanted to ask if she would have had the power to stop him herself, but it wouldn't have fit with her new cooperative persona.

"I'm so pleased to have you by my side, Marie." R tucked the gem back into his shirt. "I believe it is time for the next phase of my plan. I will leave tomorrow for Northgate to win the hearts of the city's youth." His sharp gaze focused in on her. "You'll need to settle the new recruits in yourself. And I'll be gone longer than usual. I trust in your abilities, however."

"Thank you, Father," said Marie, transforming her face into an expression of pride and determination. "I won't fail."

CHAPTER 22

*A*ll Marie wanted to do was find Rafe and tell him everything. But she forced herself to wait until R had actually left the camp.

Except, after that happened, the newcomers needed what seemed like an endless amount of assistance, and Lisa and Danny stuck to her side like burrs. However hard she tried, she couldn't get time alone with Rafe.

She could have used her authority to order everyone else away, but that was just the sort of attention that they didn't want to draw. Instead, she forced herself to be patient and to ensure that everyone had a pallet and some kind of chore around camp to keep them busy.

It didn't help that Rafe had taken to hunting every afternoon. He had admitted to her, in the one brief, whispered conversation they had managed, that he was doing it to avoid being asked to take Peter's place at training.

"I don't mind helping them learn to shoot," he said. "That's a helpful skill for any forester and will keep food on their plates. But I won't teach them just enough about swordplay so they can get themselves killed by a real soldier."

Standing watching the rebels' attempt to integrate the newcomers into their afternoon training sessions, Marie considered his words. He was right, of course. It was one thing to make sure everyone had a bed to sleep on. Helping them turn into an army, however, didn't fit with her new plans.

What she needed was a distraction. Something other than warfare to occupy the minds of the foresters and, hopefully, something that would give her a chance to talk to Rafe.

For some reason, while she pondered the question, her mind wandered back to her visit to Arcadia the year before. She had been there so that she could both examine, and be examined by, their prince, Maximilian. She had liked him, but it had been obvious to her that he and Alyssa were already in love. And she had no interest in getting in the way of true love.

Of course, the Arcadian court and the Northhelmian delegation had all pretended that it was an ordinary diplomatic visit of state. And how had they distracted themselves from the true purpose of the visit? With parties and balls and picnics and any other entertainment the Arcadians could devise.

The rebels themselves were hardly dedicated to the business of war. They already acted as if they were all on some kind of camp out. She thought of the girls' comments at the creek each day and smiled. A dance would probably be very well received.

She announced the projected dance at the evening meal and, sure enough, the foresters greeted the news with great excitement. She had decided to hold it in two nights' time since R had guaranteed he would be away for a longer trip. But from the reaction that followed her words, this still left little time for preparation.

She allowed herself one secret smile and then got to work on all the necessary organization.

~

The kitchen staff were surprisingly willing to prepare extra food for the evening. One of the assistants that she had befriended during her time in the kitchen confided that they were all looking forward to showing off with their specialty dishes.

She asked Lisa to put together a group to decorate the main cavern, and Lisa had soon roped in Danny and several of his friends. She instructed them to gather large boughs covered in leaves varying in shade from deep green to bright red.

"Which only leaves the music," Marie said to Danny while she watched him place a particularly large branch bright with orange leaves.

"I can play," said a voice from behind her, and she turned to see one of the newcomers. He smiled at her. "If you'd like, that is. I even brought my fiddle with me."

"And I brought my flute," added another of the young men. Marie recognized his face this time. She thought he was one of the rebels from Greenwood.

"That would be excellent," she said. "But I don't want you to have to play all evening. Some of the girls might be disappointed if you don't have any chance to dance." She gave them her most winning smile, and they both looked away, embarrassed but obviously pleased at the idea that they might be an object of interest to the girls of the camp.

"I know some others who brought their instruments," said Danny, watching his friends with a twinkle in his eye. "I'll set up some sort of roster so everyone has a chance to relax and enjoy themselves."

"Thank you, Danny," said Marie. "That would be perfect." She hoped Danny's willingness to abandon the training and throw his efforts into the dance indicated that R's grip on him was slipping a little.

"There you are, Marie!"

Marie turned to see Lisa peering into the cavern.

"Oh, good job, Danny, it looks completely transformed," she said approvingly.

"Always the tone of surprise," said Danny with his usual grin. "Good to know you had complete faith in me when you assigned me the task."

"I know *I* always have faith in you," said a familiar voice behind Lisa. Rafe strolled into the cave, still dirty from his hunt. "What exactly are we talking about?"

"Lise assigned me the job of decorating the cavern for the dance and is pleased to discover I actually managed to do it," said Danny.

Rafe looked around the cave. "I was wondering where everyone had got to when there was no one practicing in the clearing. Now I see. A masterpiece like this would have taken all afternoon."

Danny punched Rafe lightly in the arm. "Watch and learn, my friend," he said, "watch and learn. The girls will be flocking to dance with me when they see my skills on display."

"Is that a challenge?" Rafe's eyes lit up.

Lisa rolled her own eyes at Marie. "It was actually you I came to find. Let's leave the boys to their displays of manhood." She grabbed Marie's arm and began to haul her out of the cavern.

"Don't worry, Lise," Danny called after her, "I'll make sure Rafe saves you a dance."

Lisa made a rude noise in her throat but didn't turn around. Danny's chuckles chased them out into the passageway.

"You were looking for me?" asked Marie.

The sparkle returned to Lisa's eyes. "All the girls think this dance is a great idea, and we know you've been too busy organizing it to think about yourself."

"Myself?" Marie had no idea what she was talking about.

"What you're going to wear, I mean," said Lisa.

"Oh." Marie considered the matter. She'd left Northgate in a hurry and certainly hadn't packed any dresses suitable for a dance.

"What are all the other girls doing?"

"Oh, most of us packed dresses," said Lisa.

"Really?"

"Foresters are always prepared." Lisa grinned at her friend cheekily. "And luckily some of us like to be extra prepared. So, once we pooled our resources, we had enough dresses for everyone. Even for you."

"For me?" Marie couldn't help the smile that spread across her face. Until a sudden doubt assailed her. "Will it fit me, though? I'm quite tall." She looked down at the plain, serviceable clothes she was wearing. Hardly dance-worthy.

Lisa just laughed at her. "I had noticed, you know."

Marie still looked skeptical.

Lisa shrugged. "Some of the girls are pretty handy with a needle. We modified where we needed to. Everyone is going to look their best tonight. We're determined."

Interesting, thought Marie. *Even with the influence of the jewel, they find it easier to come together and unite for a dance than for weapons training. It looks like the enchantment might be even more damaged than R thinks.*

It was an encouraging thought.

Lisa led the way to their shared sleeping cavern, which was now crammed full of girls. Many of them were from Greenwood, but Marie recognized several other faces. They all broke into applause when she entered, and she felt her cheeks redden with pleasure.

Lisa gestured for the small crowd to part, revealing Marie's pallet. A blue dress lay there, decorated with a large blue bow. It was made from a rougher material than Marie's usual dresses and the pattern of the material was dotted in bunches of colored flowers. It was a classic forester design and very different from the dresses Marie had worn to the Arcadian dances. And yet she had never been more delighted by a garment.

"Thank you," she said, putting as much feeling into the words as she could. "It's beautiful."

Lisa smiled around at all the other girls, clearly happy with their efforts. "The design will leave your shoulders bare," she said. "We thought it would show off your beautiful, pale skin."

Marie's eyes actually filled with tears. She had always hated her excessively pale coloring, and she appreciated Lisa's attempts to turn it into an asset.

She felt a little less sure of herself when she stood with Lisa outside the meeting cavern that evening. The music had already begun, and she could hear laughter and the sound of dancing feet. She paused and took a slightly panicked breath.

Lisa looked back at her. "Come on, Marie!"

Marie didn't move.

Lisa came back to her. "Don't worry," she said. "It fits perfectly, and you look beautiful. And I guarantee he'll think so, too."

"Lisa! That's not...I mean..." she sputtered to a stop, aware that her thoughts had indeed turned to Rafe. After all, he was the only one here who knew that she was a princess. The only one who had seen her in her usual dresses.

Don't be so vain, she told herself.

Her thoughts spun back to before she had discovered William was gone and her whole life had fallen apart. This wasn't the first time the thought of Rafe had brought up her old insecurities. She determined it would be the last.

She felt beautiful because she was dressed in the love of her friends. And if that was enough for her, it was enough for everyone else, too. It didn't matter what they all thought, as long as she felt happy with the way she looked.

She squared her shoulders and stepped forward.

"That's the way!" said Lisa with a cheeky grin.

Marie swatted her shoulder and led them into the dance.

CHAPTER 23

*H*ours later, she looked around with a contented sigh. Most of the food had been consumed, and they were onto their third shift of musicians, but the dancing continued unabated. The smiles she saw all around her told her that romance was much higher on everyone's minds than rebellion. Just as she had hoped.

If R stayed away long enough, and enough of the foresters were distracted by romance, she might even be able to convince them to return home before he reappeared. She looked around for Rafe, wanting to share the thought with him.

He was dancing with great enthusiasm, so she positioned herself on the edge of the dance floor, ready to catch his attention at the end of the song. He had asked her to dance as soon as she and Lisa had appeared, and the invitation had given her a secret glow that had lasted all evening.

She had refused it, however, telling him, with a significant look, to ask her again later. He had appeared to understand her meaning. If they danced together toward the end of the evening, they could dance their way out of the party altogether and finally have a chance to talk. Their absence would be too obvious at the beginning of the dance.

Watching him dance with another girl, Marie had to squash an uncharitable feeling she was rather afraid might be jealousy. *He asked me to dance first,* she reminded herself and basked again in the glow the knowledge gave her.

Without meaning to, she began to follow the conversation of three girls who were standing not far from her. She vaguely recognized them as being newcomers from the last batch of recruits.

"He's definitely the best-looking here," said one of them.

Marie followed their eyes and saw that they, too, were watching Rafe.

"And the most fun," agreed another.

"I wonder where he's from?" asked the third. "Have you all heard the story about when he fought that other boy? The one who disappeared? Probably too embarrassed to show his face!"

They all giggled.

"I'm determined to have another dance with him," said the first one.

"Hey!" said the third. "You've already danced with him once, let the rest of us have a turn."

"He's danced with that Lisa twice," said the first. "We can't let someone from *Greenwood* get the better of us."

Marie frowned. She knew that Greenwood was one of the smaller villages, as well as being located closest to the capital, but she didn't like hearing it referred to in such scathing tones. There was obviously a lot she didn't know about the inner dynamics of the foresters.

"Psst, careful," said the second in a quieter voice. "Isn't that Marie over there? She seems to be great friends with the Greenwood group."

There was a moment of silence during which they presumably all examined her. Marie kept her eyes carefully trained on the dancers.

"So what if it is?" said the first one, although she also spoke more quietly than before.

Marie gave a small sigh. Her eyes were still following Rafe around the dance floor, and she couldn't help a swell of a different type of jealousy. Rafe was just like her brother—everything came more easily to them. It was effortless, the way they won people over; there was just something about them that people liked. Her mother was the same.

Marie, however, was more like her father. They had to work hard to earn respect and gain liking. These girls had been here for mere days, and they already loved Rafe. Marie, however, they were willing to dismiss, despite her position in camp. She clenched her hands within the folds of her skirt.

Slowly, however, she relaxed them again. She looked down at the blue material. The feel of it had reminded her that she had friends here in camp. The foresters who had been around long enough to get to know her had come to like her. She was literally clothed in their acceptance and affirmation. She smiled, her eyes still fixed on the dance.

"Look at her." It was the first girl again. "I bet she's planning to claim the next dance with him. Just because she's in charge." Their voices were coming closer.

The three girls crossed between the dancers and Marie, and one of them jostled her on their way past.

"Oh, excuse me!" she said, her voice sweet. "I didn't see you there."

All three paused and slowly looked Marie over. She met their eyes calmly.

"You know, that's a hideous dress," said the jostler.

Marie had to use all her training to suppress her gasp. She didn't like to admit it, but the words hurt; she had been so proud of the dress just moments before. Their expressions seemed to

MELANIE CELLIER

mirror the hundreds she had experienced in the past. The ones that showed surprise when they first saw her—the princess who didn't look like a princess was supposed to look.

"I'm only telling you as a friend, so you don't make the mistake of wearing it again," the girl continued, her friendly tone obviously false.

Marie held her ground. She was familiar enough with this sort of unprovoked antagonism. There were always a small number of people who responded to a princess with jealousy, or who tried to assert their own power by bringing her down. It was simply a part of the job.

That didn't mean it didn't hurt, though.

She took a deep breath and prepared to respond. She would have liked to simply walk away, but her position in camp prevented that. She had to maintain her authority, especially with the newcomers.

She opened her mouth, but another voice interrupted before she got out more than a single word.

"Marie! There you are!" Rafe appeared and placed one arm possessively around her shoulders. He smiled at the other girls. "Marla, Serena, Katherine, I hope you're enjoying the dance."

Marie wanted to roll her eyes. Of course he knew their names.

Katherine smiled back at him, but the other two were too busy looking between him and Marie in surprise.

"I'm glad to see you've met my dear friend, here," he said, giving Marie a small squeeze. "And I hope you'll excuse me if I steal her away."

He turned and gave Marie his most enchanting smile. "I won't be put off anymore, you've kept me waiting for my dance long enough."

"I didn't realize you two were friends." Marla sounded uneasy.

"Oh, really?" Rafe winked. "But you should know by now that I'm always friends with the most gorgeous girl in the room."

Katherine giggled, and Rafe grinned at her.

"But, jokes aside, yes. Marie and I are old friends. From before this whole rebellion business."

"Oh, I see, well…that's nice." Marla clearly didn't know what to say.

"Isn't it? It's nice to be surrounded by friends." Rafe smiled again, as if he had no idea what had been going on before his interruption, and then pulled Marie into the dance.

She waited until they had moved far enough away from the others, and then smiled up at him. She had been prepared to defend herself, but it turned out it was much nicer to be defended by someone else.

"Thank you," she said.

"For what?" Rafe's eyes laughed down at her.

"You know perfectly well for what!" She wanted to ask him if he really thought she was gorgeous but didn't quite dare.

"I spoke nothing but the truth," said Rafe.

"Really?" Marie raised both her eyebrows. "Old friends from before the rebellion, hey?"

Rafe laughed. "Well, all right, that one might have been stretching the truth, just a little. But I seem to remember it was you who first claimed old friend status!"

Marie shook her head. "And I suppose you've really been waiting impatiently all evening to dance with me, too."

Rafe's arm around her waist tightened, and the playfulness dropped out of his eyes. "Of course I have." His voice dropped so low she could barely hear it. "I shouldn't have been, but I was."

Marie's heartbeat quickened.

"In my defense," he said. "You look like the perfect forester in that dress."

Marie's heart sank. What was that supposed to mean?

"So, it's easy to forget who you really are, and that your brother would probably gut me if he saw me holding you this close." His arm around her didn't loosen.

Marie laughed, light-hearted with relief. "My brother has never decided who I dance with. I make my own choices there."

"I'm doubly flattered, then." Rafe looked down at her, his expression so intense that his eyes seemed to glow. "And as for before, I've already told you, Marie. I'll always do my best to protect you."

Marie looked away, unable to meet the intensity of his gaze.

"Not that you've needed much protecting yet," said Rafe, his voice returning to its usual light tones. "And you've seemed different the last few days—more sure of yourself or something. This dance was a great idea, by the way."

"Yes." Marie nodded. "I haven't seen a sword in two days."

"Plus, it gives me an excuse to do this." If possible, Rafe's arm around her waist tightened.

Marie looked up and saw that his usual charming grin hadn't erased the new intensity in his eyes. She blushed.

"You've tormented me all evening, making me admire you from afar," he said. "And I'm assuming it was with this purpose in mind?"

Marie looked around and realized he had maneuvered them to the entrance of the cave. She nodded, and together they slipped out into the rest of the cave system.

Rafe led them quickly down several stone passageways until they found themselves in a small, dim cave lit only by faint moonlight.

Marie drew a deep breath. Her pulse was racing, and her emotions were in turmoil. She needed to use this opportunity to tell Rafe the whole truth, but she suddenly didn't know where to start.

Before she could begin, Rafe's arms swept around her, and she found her back pressed against one wall of the cave, her whole vision filled with Rafe.

"I don't think I can do this anymore, Marie," he said.

"Do what?" His unexpected nearness completely disrupted

Marie's thought processes. She tried to tear her mind away from the feeling of being held in his arms so she could focus on his words.

He gave a small groan. "Keep my distance from you. Play at rebellion with you. I don't know. All of it?"

"I don't..." Marie cleared her throat and tried to make her voice stronger. "I don't understand. I thought things were going well. R's grip on the foresters seems to be weakening. And I have some things I need to tell you—about his plans."

Rafe's grip on her tightened in response to her words.

"Yes, R," he said, his voice suddenly grim. "He's the worst of it. Every time you disappear with him, it's all I can do not to go storming after you. I'm terrified of what he might do—that one day you won't come back."

Marie bit her lip, wondering how best to tell him that she, of all people, was in no immediate danger from R. Rafe's eyes staring down at her, pinning her against the wall more firmly than his arms, made it hard to form the right sentence.

He leaned in so close that she could feel his warm breath against her face. "I've tried to keep my distance. I'm the only one who knows who you really are and the last thing I want to do is take advantage of the situation. Living this sort of double life—I know it can create a false closeness."

Marie shook her head. "Nothing about this," she placed her hand on his chest, marveling at her own boldness, "is false."

He groaned again, lower this time, and stepped back. "I wish that were true," he said. "I wish there weren't secrets between us."

Marie bit her lip. So, she had been right, he did know she was keeping things from him.

"Back at home I'm known for being a light-hearted sort of fellow," he said, and Marie had to bite back a slightly hysterical giggle. "I try not to take things too seriously. But I don't think I can cope with having you here anymore. Every day it gets harder, knowing that you're in danger. R seems unbalanced to me. I keep waiting for him to flip. And when it finally happens, everything here will change. I just need to know you're far away from that."

He stepped close to her again but kept his arms at his side.

"Please, Marie, let me take you back to Northgate. Let me keep you safe."

Marie shook her head, her eyes remaining locked on his. "We're so close," she whispered. "We can't leave now. There's," she stopped to take a breath. "There are some things I need to tell you…"

Her voice trailed off as Rafe's head slowly lowered toward hers. He stopped with his lips a breath away from hers.

"But don't you see?" he whispered back to her. "None of that matters to me anymore, not compared to you."

And then his arms were around her again, and his lips were pressed against hers, and she couldn't think about anything but this one perfect moment.

CHAPTER 24

*M*arie had never imagined that anything could feel as perfect as Rafe's kiss. Held tightly against him, her face tilted up to meet his, she realized that being beautiful to everyone didn't matter. She just wanted to be beautiful to the right person.

And it made no difference that she was a princess. In this moment, she felt just like any other girl in the arms of the man she loved—amazed that this charming, handsome man had chosen her. It felt like a dream.

He began to pull back, and she pushed up onto her tiptoes, not wanting the moment to end. He responded, pressing his lips down on hers again, before abruptly breaking away. He let her go and stepped back, running his hand through his hair.

"Oh, Marie," he said. "What am I going to do with you?"

"Kiss me again?" she asked, hoping he could see the cheeky sparkle in her eyes despite the low light.

He chuckled. "Don't tempt me."

She grinned at him, and he grinned back at her. Neither seemed to want to break the moment. At last, however, he shook his head and spoke.

"You had something you wanted to tell me?"

His words brought reality crashing back in. Marie gave a half sob and covered her face with both hands. What was she thinking? She was about to tell Rafe that she had been lying to him the entire time—that she had even considered double crossing him and allying herself with the man he clearly considered evil. A man whose blood she shared.

And it didn't matter that she had eventually seen the truth. Even if her deceit didn't drive him away, her decision to return to her family made any future between them impossible. It would be William who would rule one day in Northgate, so it would be William who was permitted to make a marriage of love. Marie's own duty was clear. She must marry to benefit her kingdom.

Not that her parents would attempt to force her into a distasteful alliance. They loved her too much for that. But they would expect more than a wandering adventure-seeker. If she wished to remain with her family and continue to be a princess, she couldn't pick and choose which parts of that life she accepted. She slid down to sit, back pressed against the wall.

"Marie? What is it?" Rafe's concerned voice felt almost as painful as his kiss had felt wonderful.

He crouched down beside her and attempted to pry her hands away from her face.

"Come on, talk to me."

"Sit down," said Marie, her voice quiet. She couldn't bring herself to meet his eyes. "This might take a while."

It did take a while. Rafe's confused questions quickly subsided as he sank down onto the stone floor beside her and listened to her story without interruption. When she finished, the silence in the small cave seemed to deafen her with its echoes.

"I…" Rafe paused before trying again. "I'm going to need some time to think about all of that."

Marie nodded, her face miserable.

"But I'm going to want to talk to you again and soon." He looked at her with a ghost of his usual smile. "And I'm not waiting until you organize another dance. Tomorrow morning, I'll go hunting, early, while everyone is sleeping off their dancing-induced exhaustion. As soon as you can reasonably get away, come after me. I'll be waiting for you in the clearing where Peter attacked me. Do you remember how to get there?"

He waited until she nodded. "Don't forget! Tomorrow morning."

And with that, he was gone.

Marie returned to the dance but answered everyone who addressed her with absent-minded distraction. The last hour had been filled with too many emotions to properly process, and all she wanted was her bed.

Except, when she managed to escape to it, she found she couldn't sleep and had to stop herself from getting up and pacing. She didn't want to wake Lisa who had fallen straight into an exhausted slumber.

Marie envied her friend her light-hearted happiness. The other girl had confided to her before falling asleep that she had danced half the night with a particularly good looking young man from one of the other villages.

The next morning breakfast was delayed and most of the foresters slept late. Once they were up, Marie oversaw the beginnings of the clean-up before slipping away.

Her heart pounded as she raced through the forest. How had Rafe passed the night? Had he been able to sleep? What was he thinking now? What was he thinking of her?

She would have barreled straight into the clearing if a strong arm hadn't caught her around the waist, a hand coming down over her mouth.

She swung her leg, ready to kick back at her captor, but a familiar voice whispered in her ear. "Don't! It's me."

She stilled instantly.

Rafe let her go, and she spun around to see his finger on his lips, a warning in his eyes. He met her confused gaze and pointed into the clearing.

A voice suddenly sounded over the noises of the forest. The clearing was already occupied.

"Tracking you down was never part of our arrangement. What's more, I've had to leave my new recruits just as they were arriving at camp." R sighed and gave a small shake of his head. "This isn't the first time you've veered off course, either. You were a little, ah, let us say, *enthusiastic* in leading the assault on Greenwood. As it happened, it all turned out for the best, but it wasn't what I had in mind when I asked you to gather supplies." Marie moved quietly to one side, trying to get a view of who R was talking to.

She almost gasped aloud when she saw his companion.

"In spite of all this, you show great promise," R continued. Despite his words, Marie recognized the dangerous light that had come into his eyes. "I would hate to see such promise wasted, but I will not have you make a move against Marie."

"I don't know why you give her so much authority." Peter sounded sulky.

"She is my daughter and any disrespect to her is disrespect to me."

As much as Marie disliked Peter, she hoped he could read the warning in R's face. She hated to think how he would respond if Peter kept pushing him.

"Your daughter?" Even from a distance, Marie could see the forester's amazement.

"Yes indeed, and she's Princess Marie of Northhelm as well. Is she not *marvelous*?" The glitter in R's eyes issued a challenge.

Rafe shifted beside Marie, and she could almost feel his discomfort about her connection with R. She placed a calming hand on his arm.

"Yes," Peter mumbled, his confusion clear on his face, "marvelous."

"One day soon, she will take the throne and all my plans will be complete."

Marie could hear the gloat in R's voice. He sounded very sure of himself. She only hoped he was getting overconfident enough to make a mistake.

"The throne?" Peter shifted his weight. "But surely you will be the one to rule."

"Of course I shall." R giggled. "But look at me, boy. Surely you can't imagine that anyone in Northhelm would let me take the throne."

Peter bristled at the implied insult to R. "Of course they would!"

Peter's defense made sense given his thrall to R, but Marie knew better. R was right, he couldn't bewitch the entire kingdom.

R giggled again. "Take my word for it, there would be problems. My lovely daughter, on the other hand, will be accepted. Don't worry, I have plenty of experience working from the shadows. I shall rule by proxy."

"And if she doesn't comply?"

"Oh, she will. And if she tries to be difficult..." He shrugged. "I have four centuries of experience with turning situations and people to my advantage. Do you have any idea how many bargains it took to set up this moment? Every piece had to be perfectly orchestrated, the royal family manipulated, the supplies and weapons gathered, the camp prepared. I won't be outwitted by a teenager, I assure you. Not even my own flesh and blood. Everyone has a price. There is always a bargain to be made."

"But what of the king?" Peter seemed to be struggling to keep up with R, which Marie thought was fair enough given he only had half the story. "Even if you eliminate him, aren't you worried people will rally around the crown prince?"

"Ah, dear William." R's false affection made Marie grit her teeth. "I'm still deciding what is best to be done with him. The king and queen will have to go, of course, but it's possible the prince may still prove useful. It is unfortunate that he's resistant to the effects of my charm, but there may still be ways to use him. It's why I've kept him alive."

Marie sucked in her breath.

"That's the crown prince you have in that cave?" Peter shook his head. "I wondered who your prisoner was, but it never occurred to me…Hopefully you found someone else to take him food and water since I left camp."

"Yes, your disappearance was most inconvenient, I trust it won't happen again." The subtle warning was back in R's voice.

"It was that Rafe." Peter's indignation oozed off him. "I didn't want to leave, but he forced me away. I feared for my life! I've been trying to tell you, there's something strange about him. No one is that good a fighter." His voice sank to a sullen murmur. "But I suppose he's under your special protection as well."

"Not at all," said R. "In fact, I agree with you, there is something odd about him…" Marie stiffened as R's voice trailed off, and he stroked his hand across his chest where she knew the enchanted jewel lay under his clothes. "I think we may indeed have to do something about young Rafe."

Marie's hand, which was still on Rafe's arm, tightened. She glanced across at him, but his gaze was fixed on the pair in the clearing. His expression gave nothing away. She looked back at R.

His eyes had turned intense as he stared Peter down. "But

don't try anything on your own; you must wait for my guidance. The matter requires some consideration."

Peter looked reluctant, but he nodded his agreement.

"For now, I must get back to camp, my new recruits will be needing my guidance."

"And me?"

"You must return as well, of course. You can hardly take your place at the head of my army if you're cowering in the forest."

Peter muttered something that might have been a protest at the word 'cowering', but it was too quiet for Marie to hear.

"Now that we have gathered so many youths from the capital, we can begin to make our move. A good portion of the royal guard will stand down rather than attack their own children. And as for the rest..." The sound of his giggle was starting to make Marie feel sick. "Once enough of the youths have been killed, there will be an outcry from the kingdom. The king will be forced to step aside or risk civil war. And how much easier the decision will be when he is making way for his own daughter." R actually rubbed his hands together in his glee.

Marie shivered. His lies never ended. Once again, she felt ashamed to think she had ever been taken in by him, even a little.

She looked across at Rafe, and this time he was looking at her. He gestured with his head for her to follow him, and they carefully began to ease back from the clearing. As they moved away, R and Peter also left, heading toward the camp.

"We can't go back now," said Rafe, his expression grimmer than Marie had ever seen it. "We need to warn the king, and we need to get you out of R's reach. His plan needs you to succeed. Once he realizes you aren't going to support him, he'll have to resort to force. Or threats."

"No threat would make me give him the slightest bit of help!" Her outrage made her pause her flight through the forest.

Rafe stopped also, looking back at her with raised brows.

"Really? Don't forget, he apparently has William locked up somewhere."

"William!" Marie paled. She should have seen it herself. That was the sort of usefulness R envisioned for him. "We can't flee now. We have to rescue him!"

"We will," said Rafe, "or at least, the guard will. But not unless we have a chance to warn them about what's going on. If we go back to camp now and something happens to us, no one will ever know where he is. Everything could be lost."

Reluctantly, Marie acknowledged the wisdom of his words and began moving again. "We should go back via Greenwood," she said. "My father might have left a message for us. And we can leave a report there. Just in case…" She didn't think anything would happen to prevent them reaching the capital, but neither did she want to take any chances.

Rafe nodded without looking back and led them on through the forest.

CHAPTER 25

When they entered Greenwood, Rafe looked around and let out a low growl. "That cur!"

Marie couldn't help but agree with him. She had already disliked Peter, but knowing he was responsible for the destruction in Greenwood only strengthened her repugnance. And he had been helping to imprison William.

She kicked out at a broken chair, sending it flying into the wall of the closest house.

"Feel better?"

Marie looked at Rafe and actually managed to return his smile. "A bit," she said.

She didn't want to admit that seeing his familiar grin did more to ease her tension than the physical outburst had done. "I hope you know that I meant what I said last night. I had already decided not to help R, even before finding out his true plans."

Rafe looked at her, and the warmth in his eyes made her blush, her mind racing back to their kiss in the cave.

"I know," he said. "You can't help who your father is. And it's natural enough that you would have felt confused when you found out the truth so suddenly. I'm only sorry that you didn't trust me with the whole story from the beginning."

Marie looked down. "I know. I should have. In fact, I was going to, but then…" She bit her lip. "It's not that I didn't trust you!" She looked back up at him quickly. "The truth is that I've trusted you from our first conversation in the palace. It's that I didn't want to lose what we had, back there in the camp." Her voice dropped to almost a whisper, her eyes dipping down again. "I didn't want you to look at me differently."

"Hey." Rafe had approached while she was talking and now put a gentle hand under her chin, pulling her gaze back up to meet his. "I can hardly blame you for that. I've been guilty enough of the same thing myself."

Marie's breath quickened, and her eyes dropped to his lips.

Rafe gave a ragged laugh and stepped back. "I think I told you once before not to tempt me," he said. He took her hand and pulled her toward Lisa and Danny's old cottage. "Come on, we need to keep moving."

Standing in the doorway of the abandoned home felt surreal. Marie found it hard to believe she was the same person who had stood there mere weeks ago. She scanned the small space, trying to determine if the floor looked more or less trampled than she had left it.

Before she could decide, Rafe called her name. He held a sealed piece of parchment. She hurried over to his side and looked on as he broke it open.

Together they read the contents, and then stared at each other in horrified silence. Matters had progressed further than they had anticipated.

Marie read it again, struggling to wrap her mind around the full import of the words.

R's last trip had been to the capital, and word of his presence had reached the palace. Her father had sent a squad of young guards to capture him. Instead of returning with R, they had joined the rebels.

Concerned that the longer they waited, the bigger R's army became, the king had decided it was time to march against the rebel camp.

Apparently the Rangmeran delegation was still in Northgate and had advised the king that a quick attack, in force, was the only answer. The attack needed to be swift and decisive since the longer the soldiers were exposed to R, the more likely they would fall under his enchantment.

"This is all my fault!" Marie began to chew on her tongue as she read the missive for a third time, wishing the words would reform into a different message. "If I'd just found a way to leave camp and tell my father about the jewel's limitations, he could have sent older veterans to seize R in the city."

"Of course it's not your fault! You had no way of knowing what was happening in Northgate. There's only one person at fault in this situation." Rafe also looked back down at the parchment. "My concern is this Rangmeran contingent."

Marie sat down hard on the floor as the full ramifications burst through her mind. She had been too focused on the timeline to consider the additional news about the Rangmeran soldiers.

Queen Ava, upon hearing about the situation, had decided to show her support by sending a large contingent of her guard to stand with the Northhelmian forces against the rebels. Apparently, she felt some responsibility for allowing the jewel to escape into Northhelm.

"The Rangmerans have no connection to any of the rebels." Marie worked it through out loud. "So they won't have any reason to stand down or to go easy on them. They may not even answer to my father—it doesn't say what the chain of command is. They may have their own commander and be under orders to see this jewel destroyed no matter what the cost.

"And the rebels won't surrender while they're under R's enchantment. Which means this attack isn't going to end until they've all been killed!"

"Lisa and Danny and Robbie and all the rest will be slaughtered unless we can prevent it." Rafe's grim tone didn't suggest he felt a lot of optimism about their chances. "And who knows what the consequences will be? R suggested civil war, but if it's the Rangmerans who do the killing, the grieving families may demand a war with them."

"We need to get to my father at once! Tell him to stop the attack!"

Rafe shook his head. "Look at the date on this report," he said. "The attack force will have already left Northgate. We don't know what path they'll take or how far they might have gotten. The attack could start at any moment."

"Well, we can't do nothing." Marie leaped back up to her feet.

"No, of course not." Rafe ran his hand through his hair and paced the short length of the cottage. "Even if we could find the armed forces, we would have to convince them to listen to us. Your father may not be with them personally. No, I think we need to return to camp. If we hurry back immediately, hopefully we can arrive before the attack."

"And what will we do when we get there?"

"Somehow or other, we'll have to break the enchantment, convince the foresters to disperse before the attack begins."

"And how will we do that?" Marie's desperation wasn't producing any bright ideas.

"I don't know yet, but we don't have time to stop now and work it out. We'll have to think while we move. Come on, we need to hurry."

∼

The trip back through the forest felt like a nightmare. Marie pushed herself as fast as she could, aware that despite her newly increased fitness levels, she was slowing Rafe down. She suggested at one point that he go on without her, but he refused to leave her behind.

By the time they neared the camp, she was close to exhaustion, and her mind felt as empty of ideas as it had when they started. Despite keeping a close eye out, they had seen no sign of anyone else in the forest.

Marie had almost suggested hopefully that maybe the attackers were further away than they feared, but one look at Rafe's dark expression convinced her to remain silent. He clearly didn't share her optimism.

When they reached the edge of the clearing around the cave entrance, they paused. Marie's breath was coming in short bursts, and Rafe looked at her with concern.

"I'm fine," she said.

He turned to survey the clearing. There was no sign of any movement. Marie tried to calculate where the rebels would be in their schedule. Her stomach growled, telling her it was well past lunchtime. It reminded her of her first arrival at the camp, and she felt a small swell of pride to think that she had made it all the way to Greenwood and back again in less time than it had taken her to go one way the first time.

"The training session can't be over yet," she said. "It's not that late in the day. Perhaps they're all spending the free time after the meal resting."

"Maybe." Rafe didn't sound convinced. "Given the king's reaction, R must have brought back a large group from the capital. I would have expected to see someone outside."

"Well, I guess we go in and look for them then," said Marie.

Rafe watched her with concern. "R must be wondering where you are. He would have been expecting to see you when he got back. He might be angry at the state of the camp."

Marie shrugged. "That's a risk we have to take. You heard him talking to Peter. He's confident he can control me. I refuse to believe that's true, but as long as he continues to believe it, that gives us an advantage. He seems determined to see me as his perfect child—a carefully-prepared cog in his brilliant plan. We just have to hope his overconfidence blinds him to the truth."

Rafe reluctantly nodded.

"It's you I'm worried about," added Marie. "I think he suspects that you're immune to his enchantment. Who knows what he'll decide to do about it?"

Rafe shrugged. "I can take care of myself."

It was Marie's turn to reluctantly agree.

They looked at each other for a long moment, neither moving.

"So…do we actually have a plan?" Marie asked.

Rafe frowned back out at the empty clearing. She took that as a no.

"I don't like this," he said. "Something's changed. We don't know what we're walking into."

Marie sighed. "But we don't have a choice. One of us at least has to go in. I can go on my own, though. Of the two of us, it's safest for me."

"No!" Rafe spoke quickly. "Absolutely not."

Marie hadn't really expected him to agree, but she didn't want him going near R after what they'd overheard in the clearing.

She knew that she and Rafe had no future together; she also knew she would have to tell him the truth about that as soon as this crisis was past. But she still couldn't bear the idea of him coming to any harm. As long as he was safe and happy, she would simply have to learn to bear her own disappointment and loss.

She looked over at his handsome face and felt like crying. She had been happy enough for most of her life without him, and yet it seemed impossible to imagine now.

He raised his eyebrows at her, and she shook her head, pushing the thoughts away. They had a battle to stop and people to save. She couldn't afford to give in to her own emotions now.

"We go in together, then," she said. "Find out what's happening and decide how to proceed from there."

It was the flimsiest plan possible, and she could hardly believe she was suggesting it. But they were out of ideas and out of time, and the only other option was to stay outside and do nothing.

Rafe sighed and agreed, clearly as unhappy as she was about their lack of strategy.

Together they stepped forward into the clearing and proceeded without interruption into the cave system. No one was in sight.

Marie looked in the direction of the dining cavern, but she couldn't hear any sounds coming from it.

"Listen," said Rafe, "voices."

As soon as he said it, Marie heard them. The indistinct chatter of many people talking at once echoed confusingly around the cave. It took her a moment to identify the direction of the sound.

"The meeting cavern," she said. "R must have called a meeting."

She and Rafe shared a significant look. "He must have wanted them all together," said Rafe, "to reinforce the enchantment. After his being away for so long."

Marie sighed. All her efforts to detach the rebels from R's influence would be wiped out, just like that.

Before they could move, the sound of feet reverberated through the cave entryway, followed almost immediately by the first of the rebels. The trickle of young people quickly became a stream. They took no notice of Rafe or Marie, and most of the faces were unfamiliar.

"The group from Northgate," Rafe murmured to Marie, and she nodded her agreement.

The new rebels seemed cheerful enough, but Marie noticed they were mostly going in the same direction. Her eyes widened.

"The armory."

Rafe followed the direction of her gaze and let out a quiet curse. "Training session?"

"Maybe..." Marie had a bad feeling. "Come on," she said, "we need to keep moving."

The flow of people kept growing, and she started to recognize some of the faces. "I think we should split up. You go find Lisa and Danny and any of the others from Greenwood that you can. If we have any chance of convincing anyone, it's them. I'm going to find R. See if I can convince him to stand down."

Rafe looked alarmed. "I'm coming with you, then."

Marie shook her head. "I'll have a much better chance on my own." She didn't add that she wanted to keep Rafe as far away from R as she could.

Before he could protest any further, she took off into the caves, moving against the tide of rebels. Several of them called out greetings to her. She waved to each one but didn't stop. By the time she reached the meeting cavern, it was almost empty. She looked around for R but could see no sign of him.

Instead, her eyes fell on Peter. She stiffened.

He lingered up at the front of the cavern. Perhaps he had helped R lead the meeting. She tried to remind herself that he was under R's enchantment, but she couldn't help contrasting his behavior and attitude with Danny or Lisa's. And R himself had said he didn't order Peter to lay waste to Greenwood. No, clearly his natural temperament and inclinations aligned with those of R.

Peter caught sight of her, and his eyes narrowed, but he didn't approach her.

Marie forced herself to cross the large space and address him. "Where's R?"

"Gone."

"Gone where?"

Peter smirked, and Marie felt sure he knew where R was.

"He left straight after the meeting." Peter's grin got bigger. "He didn't say where he was going. When he couldn't find you, he told me to take charge until he returned."

"Fine, did he say when he would be back?" She didn't have time to quibble with Peter.

"No."

Marie turned around and walked away without another word. What was R up to? Why had he disappeared? Did he know the attack was coming? Was he planning to leave the rebels to face the soldiers alone? She was terribly afraid the answer was yes.

Hurrying back through the caves, she looked for Rafe, hoping he might have made some progress with Danny and Lisa. They had seemed so disconnected from R last time she had seen them, but she hardly dared to hope they would be the same way now.

There were faces everywhere, but she could see no sign of him in the ocean of rebels. She noted with foreboding that most of them now seemed to be armed. They milled around the caves, full of energy but little organization. She pushed through them, still searching.

When she finally caught sight of Rafe, his face had the first trace of hope she'd seen in it since they found the message in Greenwood. Her spirits lifted; he must have had success with Danny and Lisa. She looked around for them, but they were nowhere to be seen.

"Where are Danny and Lisa?" she asked.

Rafe shook his head. "I couldn't find them. I spoke to some of the others from Greenwood, but the conversation went nowhere. The enchantment is back in full force, and R has ordered them to prepare for an attack. They laughed off any suggestion of danger and got offended at the slightest criticism of R. We're not going to talk anyone around."

Marie's hopes deflated. "I couldn't even find R," she said. "Which means we're no closer to stopping this madness. I can't imagine why you're smiling."

Rafe's smile grew broader. "Because none of that matters anymore. I know how to defeat R."

PART III
REBELLION

CHAPTER 26

"*A*godmother!?!" Marie looked around the small cave Rafe had pulled her into, but there was no sign of wings anywhere.

"She already left. I was searching through the caves looking for Danny and Lisa, and I found her instead."

"My godmother?" Marie asked, still trying to wrap her head around it.

Rafe shrugged. "I don't know. I've never met your godmother. I suppose it could be the same one."

"You mean *you* have a godmother?"

He smiled his usual, charming grin. "I *am* a third son off seeking adventure, remember," he said. "Is it so surprising?"

"No, I guess not, when you put it like that." Marie spoke slowly. "And, you know, that might explain the source of our protection from R's jewel. Perhaps in its damaged state it can't affect young people under a godmother's direct blessing?"

Rafe nodded, his brow furrowed. "I didn't think of that, but you might be right."

"But why did she appear now?"

"She said she was sent because things had reached a crisis

point." The words seemed to echo those of Marie's godmother. "She said that in order to break R's enchantment, we need to discover his name. Apparently, it's part of the bargain he made to extend his life. All of his power is bound up in his name. All we have to do is speak it aloud in the vicinity of the enchantment, and all of the power will be gone."

"In the vicinity of the enchantment? So you mean if we walk up to Lisa and Danny and say R's true name, they'll simply wake up from his bewitchment?"

"Exactly."

"All right, then. How do we find his name?"

"That, she didn't say."

Marie stared at him incredulously. "She didn't say? My mother has spent years and years searching for his name without success! And she has all the resources of a queen available to her. The attack could come at any moment! How in the world are we supposed to find his name in the next few minutes?"

Rafe bit his lip and looked worried. "I asked her if she could tell me the name, or at least how to find it, but she said we have to work that out for ourselves. Apparently, that's part of the enchantment, too. It won't work if she just gives us the answer." He thought for a minute. "We do have an advantage over your mother, though."

"Oh, really? What's that?"

"We're here, where R lives. There must be a clue here somewhere."

Marie wished she could share his optimism. After a moment of consideration, however, she couldn't come up with any better idea.

"All right, then," she said. "Let's go to R's cave."

She led them back out into the main caves. A few rebels still milled about, but most of them must have trickled outside while Rafe and Marie talked. Ignoring them, Marie headed for R's personal cave.

"Don't expect much," she warned Rafe as they hurried through the stone corridors, "it's very impersonal."

She slid to a stop as they reached the right cave. Rafe caught her before she could lose her balance, and they both rushed straight in.

Marie's eyes raced around the space, not sure if she dreaded or hoped that she would see R. Only silence and stillness greeted them.

It looked just like she remembered from her previous visit—the same stools, the same pallet, and the same chest.

"The chest!" She pointed at it. "It's the only place anything could be concealed."

Rafe nodded and knelt in front of it. He reached out toward the clasp.

"Wait!" Marie's voice rang through the space between them.

Rafe paused, his hand suspended in the air.

"If there is anything in there, you need to be careful. We know R uses enchanted objects. He may have left something to guard his possessions." Marie moved forward, intending to join him, but Rafe waved for her to stay back.

"I'll be careful," he said. "But it's better if you stay back, just in case."

Marie opened her mouth to protest, but he gave her a stern look. She sighed and silently acknowledged that he was right. If there was an enchantment, it would do no good for them both to be caught in it.

She held her breath as Rafe reached out again, more tentatively this time, and opened the chest. He looked inside and then carefully stretched his arm down to feel the contents.

After the briefest examination, he sat back with a snort of disgust. "No need to guard this chest."

Marie sighed. It would have been too good to be true, anyway. Too easy. "Are you sure?" She didn't want to leave any stone unturned. "There aren't any hidden compartments or anything?"

Rafe reached back into the chest and pulled out two blankets, several sets of clothes and a pair of boots that he threw onto the floor of the cave. Once the chest was empty, he examined the inside and then rocked back to examine the outside.

He shook his head. "Not that I can see. The inside dimensions seem to match the outside."

Marie chewed on her tongue as she looked wildly around the cave. R had told her that she was always welcome there, but she had avoided the place. And she had been highly distracted during her single visit. Perhaps she had missed something.

Nothing leaped out at her.

While Rafe dismantled the pallet, she moved around the room, idly examining the stone walls.

"Rafe!"

He looked up, surrounded by the destruction of R's sleeping space.

"Come over here!"

He leaped to his feet and was beside her in seconds. Together, they stared at the opening in the far corner of the room. A natural passageway extended out from the opposite side of the cave to the main entrance.

"I don't understand how I didn't see it before…" Marie shook her head at her poor observation.

"No, it's understandable enough," said Rafe. "The shape of the walls, and the way the light falls, masks it almost completely. Take a couple of steps backward and it's almost invisible."

Marie did as he suggested and shook her head in amazement at how well camouflaged the opening was.

"It's dark in there," she said, and then wished she hadn't. She sounded afraid.

Rafe took several steps into the passageway and then turned back to her with a shrug. "There's enough light to see. Just."

She took a deep breath and followed him.

The rock walls of this hidden path seemed much rougher

than the stone that lined the rest of the cave system. As if whoever had constructed the whole thing had added this extra space as a hasty after thought.

They hadn't gone far before the path curved abruptly, and they lost all sight of the entrance back into R's cave. A minute later, it turned again and then widened to become a small cave. Unlike the passageway, this cavern had the same ventilation holes as the rest of the cave system. Marie felt secretly glad for the increase in light and the fresher air. The stale darkness of the passageway had unnerved her.

Once again, the first thing Marie did was scan for any sign of R. This time, she felt nothing but relief at his absence. She couldn't imagine he would welcome finding them in his secret retreat.

At first glance, the contents of the space seemed unexciting. A table and a single chair stood in the center of the room. Marie crossed over to look at the papers resting on top of it. A large map that showed the capital and a large region of the forest, including their current location, took up most of the space.

Villages had been marked with notations next to them. Recruit numbers, she assumed. Troop movements were also noted, and she called out to Rafe, pointing at how close the royal guard had come to the cave system. R must have been here updating the map recently.

Rafe joined her and leaned over the table, examining the map. He quickly picked up and leafed through the rest of the papers on the table before letting them drop to the floor. He shook his head, muttering to himself too quietly for Marie to hear.

Moving away from the table, he strode to the far edge of the room and knelt before another chest, identical to the one in R's sleeping cavern. Marie turned to watch him.

He moved more quickly this time, throwing back the lid of the chest without pausing. He reached inside and then froze.

"Marie." His voice sounded strangled.

"What is it?" She rushed toward him.

"Stop, don't come any closer."

She also froze, and they stared at each other across the short distance.

"What is it?" she asked again.

"I don't know, but I can't move." Rafe's flat expression and emotionless tone were so different from his normal liveliness that they conveyed his terror more effectively than fear would have done.

For a long moment they remained in their respective positions.

Finally, Marie snorted and continued toward Rafe. "Whatever it is, I can't do any good all the way over there."

"Well, don't touch me—or the chest!"

She shook her head. "I'm not stupid."

"Sorry." The strain sounded in his voice. "I know you're not."

She knelt beside him, careful not to let even her clothes brush against anything, and peered into the chest. It contained a large stack of empty parchment, several stacks of books and a couple of pouches that looked like they might contain gold.

It all looked harmless.

Marie stared helplessly up at Rafe, who watched her with concern in his eyes, and then glanced down his arm to where his hand rested inside the chest.

She gave a small shriek.

CHAPTER 27

"What?" Rafe followed the direction of her gaze. "Oh."

"Does...does it hurt?" Marie was almost afraid to ask.

"No, I can't feel it at all." The curious interest in Rafe's voice gave Marie a small measure of reassurance.

She could only just see that his hand rested against a small bottle of ink. She glanced over at the bottle on the table. It looked similar but not identical.

The ink from the chest had begun to creep out of the bottle and onto Rafe. It had already nearly covered his hand and had started up his arm. It looked thick and black and unlike any ink she had ever seen.

It looked like darkness in physical form. It looked like magic.

"Well, I guess we found his guarding enchantment," said Rafe. "Which means we must have found something of value."

"What will happen when it reaches your head?" Marie kept her voice steady, forcing herself to consider the issue dispassionately.

"I don't know about you," said Rafe, with something of his normal charm, "but personally, I'd rather not find out."

"You can't pull your hand out?" The answer seemed obvious, but Marie couldn't help asking the question.

"I can't move anything but my head. The rest of me is completely frozen."

"Hmmm. Then I guess we'd better find out R's name so we can break the enchantment."

Marie reached into the chest.

"Don't!"

She shook her head at Rafe without stopping. "I'm not going to touch you or that bottle, but I'm also not going to sit back and let you be swallowed up by that...*ink*." She shuddered as she said the word. "There's nothing else in the room. If there are any clues, they have to be in here."

She ignored the stack of parchment but pulled everything else out of the chest. Stacking it on the floor a safe distance away from Rafe, she quickly looked through the pouches. She had been right. They contained gold and several jewels. They looked ordinary enough, but she carefully avoided touching any of the gems, just in case.

The books presented a more difficult challenge. It would take her hours and hours to read through them all.

She glanced back at Rafe and saw that the ink now covered most of his arm. Apparently, the bottle held a limitless supply. He was still frozen in a kneeling position before the chest, but his head was strained as far away from his ink-covered arm as possible.

"Don't look at it," he said, his voice quiet.

She tore her eyes away from the slowly creeping ink and looked at his face.

"Just focus on your task."

His words steadied her. She swallowed and nodded, turning back to the books. She would never be able to read them all. If one of them contained R's true name, then she needed a clue to direct her where to look.

"Hello? Hello? Is there someone out there?" The voice sounded rough and faint.

Marie's head jerked up. She looked first at Rafe and then toward the source of the sound. The words had definitely come from the passageway, which didn't end in the cave but continued on from the opposite wall. It must curve again, though, because she could only make out a short stretch of stone.

She stood up and stepped toward the opening.

"Marie."

She stopped and looked down at Rafe. He didn't need to say anything; she could read his emotions on his face.

"Don't worry," she said. "I'll be careful."

"Draw one of your knives, just in case."

She nodded. Rafe had insisted that she start carrying two concealed knives, and for the first time she felt glad of their presence. The hilt was reassuringly solid in her hand.

Carefully, she crept down the passageway. Sure enough, it turned after only a handful of steps. Once again, the light levels dropped, and the air quickly turned stale. Even so, she could see a long corridor before her, stretching into distant darkness.

"Hello?"

The voice sounded much clearer this time, and she gasped.

"William?" She almost screamed his name. "William, where are you?"

There was an excruciatingly long pause.

"Marie?" He sounded incredulous. "Is this some sort of trick?"

She ran down the passageway toward his voice.

An arm suddenly appeared before her, and she swung around to face it. Sure enough, despite the gloom, she could just make out her brother's familiar features. His arm stretched out between two bars of a cell door that had somehow been secured in the stone opening of a small cave. He looked terrible, pale with large circles under his eyes. But he also looked unharmed.

She gripped his arm and cried tears of relief. "William, you're here! You're alive! Are you all right?"

He laughed a little shakily. "Come on, Mare, no tears. That's not like you. I'm fine. The real question is what in the kingdoms are you doing here?"

She dried her cheeks and shook her head. "That's much too long a story. How do I get you out?"

She looked around, hoping a key would miraculously appear. It didn't.

"Is that a knife you've got there?" William held out his hand. "Here, give it to me."

She did, and he twisted both arms through the bars, gripping the large lock.

"Hopefully this should only take a minute...almost there..." A loud grating sound echoed against the stone. "Got it!" He sounded triumphant. "That has got to be the worst lock I've ever seen. I could have saved myself some very boring days if only they hadn't taken my knives away before they put me in here."

Marie stepped back, and he swung the door open, stepping out and putting both arms around her.

"Thanks, little sis," he said. "Looks like I owe you one."

His endearment reminded her of just how much he didn't know. But it hardly seemed like the right moment to tell him everything. It would take too long.

She gasped at the thought of all the time that had already passed. "Rafe! Quick."

William kept pace with her as she hurried back down the corridor. "What? Is he here, too? You're really going to have to tell me what's going on."

Marie shook her head. "There's no time! You'll see." She raised her voice. "Rafe, Rafe, it's William! I've found William."

They raced into the cave, and William almost collided with her, his attention caught by Rafe's kneeling figure.

"What in the...?" he trailed off, his eyes huge as he stared at the darkness that now coated Rafe's shoulder and the top of his chest. It seemed to be flowing downward rather than up his neck. Still, it was clearly only a matter of time.

"William, good to see you." Rafe managed to sound remarkably like his usual self. "I'd explain the whole matter in detail, but I'm afraid I'm a little short on time at the moment."

"Yes, yes, no time for explanations," said Marie, plonking herself back down in front of the books. "For now, all you need to know is that we're looking for a name. The name of a prince who was born over four centuries ago. He was the eldest son of the king of Northhelm at the time, but he lost the kingdom to his younger brother."

"Um, as fascinating as that bit of history sounds," said William, his horrified face still focused on the ink dripping down Rafe's body, "you might have noticed that our friend here seems to be in a spot of bother. Do you think we should maybe save the reading for later?"

"Of course I've noticed!" Marie sighed in exasperation. "I've told you, there's no time to explain. We need the name to free Rafe from that trap. Oh, and also to stop a battle and save the kingdom."

"Well, all right, then," said William, tearing his eyes away from Rafe. "That makes perfect sense. How can I help?"

She ignored his witticism and picked up the first book from the stack. Reading the title, she discarded it and picked up the next one. "I have no idea, that's the problem." She dropped the second one as well and picked up a third. "I don't even really know what I'm looking for."

She had almost reached the bottom of the pile when she paused, her eyes caught by the slim volume of fairy tales in her hand.

What was it her godmother had said to her? About finding answers? *I suggest that you start by thinking back on all the old tales.*

She rocked back onto her heels as she thought it through. She and Rafe actually had a second advantage over her mother. R, in his eagerness to win her to his cause, had told Marie something of his history. Her mother had known nothing about him beyond his appearance and his bargain-making. Marie, as she had just told her brother, knew that he had been born, centuries ago, as the crown prince of Northhelm. She also knew that, when he lost the kingdom to his younger brother, a godmother had been involved.

"I don't like to hurry you," said Rafe, "but is there a reason that you've stopped?"

She looked up at him and saw that the ink now covered most of his chest.

"The old tales," she said, holding up the book. "Perhaps there's one that tells R's original story. Perhaps it recorded his name."

Rafe looked thoughtful. "It's worth a try. Look for a tale you're not familiar with."

Marie nodded and opened the volume, scanning its contents. Most of the tales listed inside were old ones she remembered hearing as a child. Several were new to her, however. She opened to the first of these.

After only a few paragraphs, it became obvious the story centered around a peasant boy and some magic beans. She turned to the next one and read the name aloud.

"Puss in Boots."

"Oh, I've heard of that one," said William. "No princes in it, though, it's about a cat."

Marie looked at Rafe. Half of his body appeared black. She turned to the next tale. Quickly skimming it, she shook her head.

"I like this one," she said. "It's about a girl who becomes a soldier and saves her entire empire. No sign of R, though."

She flipped forward to the next one.

"Bluebeard," read William, over her shoulder. "I haven't heard of that one. R doesn't have a beard though, blue or otherwise."

"I know that one," said Rafe. "It was always my least favorite as a child. I can easily imagine R as Bluebeard, he has the right level of creepiness." He shivered. "But Bluebeard isn't a prince, plus he dies at the end."

Marie nodded and turned to the last unfamiliar story in the book. She held her breath as she read it.

"I think...I think this might be it," she said, looking up at William for confirmation.

He nodded slowly, reaching the end of the story himself. "I think you might be right. It fits. Three princes set out to retrieve the water of life from the High King in order to save their dying father. The older two are tested by the godmothers and found unworthy. Only the youngest succeeds, and he is named heir in consequence."

"The water of life sounds like one of those enchanted objects," said Marie. "It might have been what started R on his obsession with them."

"Well, don't keep me in suspense," said Rafe. "What's his name?"

Marie looked over at him and hesitated. What if it wasn't the right story? She had reached the end of the book, and the ink had covered all of Rafe's body except for his left shoulder. If the name was wrong, they were out of time. As long as she didn't actually say the name, there was still hope.

William obviously didn't share her reluctance.

"Rumpelstiltskin," he said.

A sound almost like a sigh filled the cave, and the darkness sloughed off Rafe, dripping onto the floor, where it pooled in a small depression in the ground.

Marie stared down at it. It looked like ordinary ink. She looked up at Rafe. No sign of black remained anywhere on his skin or clothes.

Slowly he pushed himself up to his feet, his usual broad grin returned to his face.

"Well done, Marie," he said.

She leaped to her own feet, but her leg had gone to sleep from resting on the hard ground. She stumbled, tripping into his arms. He caught her and held her close.

Meeting his eyes, she felt as if her face might break apart under the pressure of her own smile.

"Ahem." A pointed throat clearing made them fall apart.

William watched them with raised brows. "It seems I missed a lot while I was keeping that cell back there entertained."

Marie blushed, and Rafe looked uncomfortable.

William looked between them. "Never mind," he said, shaking his head. "Now is hardly the time. Didn't someone say something about having a battle to stop?"

CHAPTER 28

"At least we know the name works," said Rafe. "I guess now we just run around, yelling it at all the rebels." He led the way back toward R's sleeping cavern.

"You know, you're going to have to explain things to me at some point," said William, following behind them. "Because you're really not making any sense."

Marie laughed, almost light-headed in her relief.

"Maybe you can start by telling me who this Rumpelstiltskin fellow is?" He hadn't finished speaking when a loud rumbling shook the passageway.

Rafe, who was still in the lead, shouted a warning and pushed them both back. The stone began to shake, and Marie fell to the ground.

Rafe threw himself protectively over her, and for a long minute her whole world was consumed by shaking and the grumbling of breaking rock.

Finally, the ground settled and only dust continued to fall around them. Slowly, Rafe pushed himself up and helped her to her feet.

"That is going to be a problem," he said.

She followed his gaze in the now-darkened corridor. The entryway back into R's cave had disappeared. Facing them was a solid wall of rocks.

"Strange timing for a cave-in," said William grimly.

"I don't think it was a coincidence," said Rafe.

"Me neither," said Marie. "I thought from the beginning that these caves couldn't be entirely natural. Looks like you said R's name at just the wrong moment, William. We must have been passing some crucial part of the enchantment he used to make them."

"Did I mention already that you're *really* going to have to tell me what's going on?"

"First, we decide what to do next," said Rafe. "I don't see us digging through that stone anytime soon."

"We'll have to go the other way then," said Marie. "And hope there's another way out." Her happiness from only minutes before now seemed impossibly far away. "The passage continued after William's cell. Hopefully it leads somewhere."

"All right then," agreed Rafe. "We can talk as we go."

Making their way carefully back through the darkened corridor, they passed through the cave, giving the chest and the puddle of ink a wide berth, and continued on down the passageway. The further they went, the darker it became and the more slowly they had to go. Every now and then, the walls around them would shake slightly and a new rain of dust sprinkled over them.

Marie shuddered each time it happened, but there were no more cave-ins.

As they walked, she filled William in on what had happened in his absence, keeping it as brief as possible. Her voice trembled slightly when she told him the truth about her birth, and Rafe reached out and took her hand. She squeezed it, grateful for his presence and acceptance.

"Well, I guess that makes a strange sort of sense," said William.

"Sense?" Definitely not the reaction Marie had been expecting.

"You always used to complain when you were younger that you didn't look like a princess. Now you know why." He shrugged.

"Really? That's your only response to discovering I'm not really your sister?" Marie couldn't believe it.

William shook his head at her. "It's not an accident of birth that made you my sister. You're my sister because you took the blame for that pie we stole from the cook when you were three." Even in the dim light, Marie could see his cheeky grin.

"So you do remember! You really are shameless, you know." After a brief pause, she added, "But I knew there was a reason you're my favorite brother."

He laughed. "And your least favorite, don't forget." They shared a smile as they both recalled the frequent joke from their childhood.

"What happened to you?" asked Marie. "How did you get captured?"

William grimaced. "I decided to follow Rafe so I could have a look at the rebel camp for myself." He gave Rafe an apologetic look. "I was pretty sure you could be trusted, but I figured it would be better to be sure."

Rafe shrugged. "No offense taken. In fact, that was my guess as to what had happened. But why didn't you return to Northgate?"

"Because as soon as I got near the camp, someone, or something, hit me on the back of the head. I woke up in that cave back there." He gestured back toward the cell, which they had already passed. "I don't know how they found me, but somehow this R fellow knew I was there. He seemed disappointed that I wasn't ready to drop everything and join his little rebellion. Unfortunately, in my initial disorientation and anger, I made my position quite clear. It was only later that I thought of the much better plan of playing along. And by then, he wouldn't believe me.

"I'd pretty much given up hope when I heard Marie here shriek. That rebel, Peter, is contemptible and that R is an odd one, but I can't see either of them shrieking. I wasn't sure whether to respond at first. I thought it might be a trap. But eventually I figured since I was already locked away in a cell, I didn't have much to lose. That's when I called out to you."

"I can't believe you were locked up so close to me all those weeks!" said Marie. "I should have come looking for you."

"I don't see how you could possibly have known," said William. "But...wait. What do you mean you've been here for weeks? What exactly happened after Mother told you the truth?"

"I'm afraid I didn't take it very well," said Marie and proceeded to tell him the rest of the story.

She admitted, shamefacedly, that she had been tempted by R but left out the part about falling for Rafe. Although given their embrace in the cave earlier, and that she hadn't let go of his hand, it probably didn't need much explanation on her part.

There was a long moment of silence when she finished that was filled by another ominous bout of shaking.

"So, assuming the roof doesn't collapse on our heads, and we actually find our way out of here, all we have to do is break the enchantment with R's name and the rebels should all wake up and surrender," said William. "Then we can sort things out with the guard. Seems simple enough."

"Yes, simple enough," agreed Marie, "assuming they haven't all been killed while we're bumbling around in here."

"And even if they haven't," added Rafe, "we'll almost certainly be walking out into the middle of a battle, so we should probably try to avoid being accidentally killed ourselves."

Another grim silence reigned.

"Well, you lot are a bunch of laughs," said William.

For a moment, Marie felt annoyed, but then she recognized the expression on his face. It wasn't that he didn't understand the seriousness of the situation—he was just trying to keep up her spirits. He'd done it often enough back at the palace.

She gave him a grateful smile. And then the whole world exploded.

~

She shook her head groggily and took stock of her body. She was lying on the stone floor of the corridor, but she couldn't feel any injuries. All of her limbs still seemed to be working. She looked around.

The path behind her was once again blocked by stone and, far worse, this time she could see no sign of either of the other two. She pushed herself quickly to her feet, almost losing her balance from the fear that flooded her senses.

"Rafe? William?" She listened intently but heard nothing. "RAFE? WILLIAM?"

"Marie? Are you all right?" Rafe's voice was faint but just discernible, coming from behind the wall of rock. Marie almost sank back down to the ground in her relief.

"Is William with you?" she called.

"Yes, I'm here."

A second rush of relief quickly faded. They were both trapped.

She examined the broken stone closely but, if anything, it looked thicker than the first cave-in. She suspected it would take days for the three of them to move enough of the rocks to create an opening.

Reluctantly, she concluded that she had no other option but to abandon them.

"I'm going to have to leave you both there," she called. Silence greeted her statement, so she kept talking. "But don't worry.

Once I've freed the rebels and sorted things out with the guard, I'll bring a bunch of them back to dig you out."

"Marie, no! You can't go alone, it's too dangerous. You'll be walking into the middle of a battle." All trace of joviality had disappeared from her brother's voice.

She appreciated his concern, but she didn't see what choice any of them had.

"Be careful, Marie." That was Rafe. "Don't get yourself killed."

"Rafe!" William sounded angry. "How can you agree to this crazy plan?"

"You've been locked up for weeks," said Rafe. "You haven't seen how far she's come. Your sister was always brave and resourceful. Now she has some skill with weapons to go with it. She can take care of herself."

Marie felt herself grow taller in response to Rafe's faith in her.

"Well, then. I guess you don't need us at all." Marie could tell that William still wasn't happy about the situation, but she appreciated his acceptance.

"We'll try to dig our way out and join you, if we can." He tried for a lighter tone. "And, don't worry, if we do get out, I'll keep your man here safe."

Marie laughed. "You haven't seen him fight," she said. "I'll be trusting him to keep *you* safe."

"Hey!"

She could hear indistinct bickering and shook her head, a smile on her face.

"See you soon!" she called and set off alone.

CHAPTER 29

The dim stone passageway seemed much creepier without companions. Marie steeled herself and kept moving, looking around for any opening or even an increase in the light.

For what felt like a long time, the passage seemed to get only darker and danker. Marie had nearly given up hope when she thought she perceived a slight lightening of the darkness. She hurried forward with renewed energy, and after another minute the increased light was undeniable.

As the light continuously increased, her pace also picked up until she was almost running. *Please don't just be another lot of ventilation shafts*, she thought.

Even as she thought it, the passageway opened into a large cavernous space. The stone of this cave was rough, and the ground was covered in jagged bumps and ridges. Marie searched the space, trying to find the origin of the light. She eventually spied a small opening on the far side of the cavern. Carefully maneuvering across the uneven floor, she made her way over to it.

The hole was small, but she could see a tree through it. She stared at it, wondering what would happen to them all if she got halfway through and got stuck. Taking a deep breath, she knelt down and squeezed her head and shoulders into the gap.

The rough stone scraped her shoulders through her clothes. Scrabbling with her feet, she pushed harder. Her shoulders popped through and her arms came free. She stopped to take another breath.

Now able to use both her feet and her arms, Marie managed to squeeze the rest of her body through the narrow space. Tumbling forward onto the forest floor, she took a moment to gather herself. Looking back at the size of the opening, she hoped that Rafe and William had returned to the original cave-in site to begin their digging. Neither of them would fit through this exit.

Her mind flashed back to the many ominous rumblings they had felt before the second cave-in. Would attempts to dig through the collapsed stone prompt yet another cave-in?

She jumped up and looked around. She needed to hurry.

She didn't recognize her surroundings, so she'd clearly come out some distance from the entrance to the cave system. *What would Rafe do?* she asked herself. She thought about how he moved through the forest and closed her eyes, focusing on her other senses.

It took her a few moments to filter through all the sounds, but she managed to identify a noise that didn't match the others. People.

She hurried toward it.

The closer she got, the clearer the noise became. She knew she should go cautiously, but the sound of shouting, the clomp of boots and the clang of weapons filled her with fear. She pictured Lisa, lying on the forest floor, bleeding, and her feet flew even faster.

She had been following the edge of the hill that housed the cave system. Trees covered it, but she could feel the gentle start of the slope beneath her feet. It led her straight to the cave entrance.

She burst out into the clearing at full speed, sliding to a frantic stop. It took only half a second to absorb the scene before her. Rows of rebels filled the clearing, barring passage between the forest and the beginning of the caves. Swords glittered in their hands and Peter stood at their head, no longer looking quite so sure of himself.

Marie recognized Lisa and many of the Greenwood foresters in the front row. She couldn't help but suspect Peter had placed them there purposefully. There was no sign of Danny, however.

Facing the rebels was what looked like a far larger force of royal guards. Some of them wore Northhelmian colors, while others flew the Rangmeran flag. It was difficult to determine their exact numbers since they were spread throughout the trees. Many of them shifted uncomfortably, but they held their ground. Marie noticed that most of the front ranks were filled with Rangmerans.

But where was Danny? He would never have left Lisa, of that she was sure. A slight movement drew her eyes upward. The trees that ringed the clearing were filled with rebels, bows drawn and arrows nocked. Danny clearly led them, perched high in the biggest tree, closest to the guard.

The noise she had been hearing had died away but, even with her inexperience of battle, she recognized it as the lull before hostilities began. Into the stillness, a familiar voice rang out.

"Ready..." It was Danny, calling to his archers.

Marie sucked in the biggest breath she could. If the archers started shooting, there would be no stopping the battle in the chaos that would surely ensue.

"Stop!" she screamed as loudly as she could.

Danny looked around, clearly recognizing her and confused by her sudden appearance. She drew another full breath.

"RUMPELSTILTSKIN!" she yelled, putting everything she had into making the name ring through the clearing.

Her efforts were followed by a deafening silence.

She looked across the clearing at Danny. He was shaking his head, the confused look on his face deepening. After a moment, he looked around, his eyes landing on Lisa. The confusion changed to fear.

Marie wanted to cheer. It looked like the sound of the name had worked. The enchantment had been broken.

"Princess Marie?" The tentative call came from the guard, and Marie looked over to see Ferdinand stepping forward through the other guards. Her brother's friend looked as confused as Danny.

All across the clearing, rebels shook their heads, looking from the swords in their hands to their friends beside them. A number of them focused on the guard in front of them. Everywhere, confusion reigned as they tried to remember what they were doing there.

Only one person seemed unaffected by Rumpelstiltskin's name. Peter glared across at Marie and then turned his angry face on the swordsmen behind him. His expression transformed into one of cunning.

"We're under attack!" he called. "Defend yourself!" He raised his sword above his head.

Marie stared aghast as many of the rebels responded, raising their own swords. Peter was taking advantage of their confusion, directing their focus toward the threatening guard and away from working out what was really going on.

She heard the guard shift, preparing a counterattack of their own.

Panic gripped her. She had only seconds to defuse the situation.

Glancing around wildly, her eyes fell on Danny. His gaze was still locked on Lisa, who was attempting to push her way through the other rebels toward his tree. Marie could only hope his natural determination and focus would be enough to pull him out of his confusion more quickly than the others.

"Danny!" she screamed.

He spun to face her. She pointed at Peter, and he followed her finger, his brow creased.

"Please, please, please," she whispered.

He raised his bow, and for a horrifying moment she thought he had mistaken her. That he was preparing to re-join Peter in the fight.

And then his arrow flew across the clearing and pierced Peter's upraised arm.

Peter yelled and dropped his sword. The other rebels lowered their own blades, looking in renewed confusion between Peter and Danny.

Marie raced across the clearing toward the guard. Ferdinand had reached the front line now, and she came to a stop in front of him.

"Ferdy, you have to get the guard to stand down," she said, her words coming out between pants. "The rebels have been under an enchantment, and it's just been broken. If they have a minute to understand what's happening, they'll all surrender. But if the guard attacks now, it will be a slaughter."

Understanding filled his face, and he turned without a word to rush back through the rows of guards. She saw him reach a huddle of men dressed as officers and could see his mouth moving quickly. After another minute, they all dispersed, and a ripple spread through the ranks of the guard as they slowly stood down, drawing back from the clearing.

She closed her eyes and took a moment to just breathe. She had done it.

Opening her eyes, she spotted a familiar figure moving toward her. The captain of the Northhelmian guard was accompanied by an equally senior-looking guard wearing the colors of

Rangmere. She composed herself, ready to answer their questions.

"You!" The growled word pulled her attention back toward the clearing.

Peter stood behind her, his face twisted in anger, framed by a scene of pandemonium. The rebels had mostly dropped their weapons and were either surging back toward the safety of the caves, or sitting on the ground, their hands on their heads in surrender.

"I don't care what R says." The light in Peter's eyes looked crazed. "This is all your fault." He had pulled the arrow from his arm and held the limb cradled against his side, the blood dripping down.

The sight of his injury had distracted Marie from his other hand. Almost too late, she saw that it held a long knife.

She leaped backward as the blade flashed toward her. Jumping back a second time, she drew one of her own blades, bringing it up in a defensive stance. She only just got it up in time.

CHAPTER 30

*P*eter lunged forward again, his movements clumsy since he used his left hand. She deflected the blow and then lunged forward herself, slashing her blade along his exposed left arm.

He screamed and fell to the ground, both arms now covered in blood.

Marie stared down at her knife, shaking with the leftover energy from the sudden attack.

"Well done, Your Highness," said the captain of the guard. He put a steadying hand on her arm. "I could have sworn you didn't know how to do that last time I saw you."

She smiled up at him, grateful for his solid presence. "I've learned a trick or two in the last few weeks."

The Rangmeran with him was barking orders at several guards who had rushed forward in response to the attack. Within moments, they had Peter back on his feet and were escorting him away into the forest.

Marie watched him go with mixed feelings.

"Don't worry," said the captain of the guard, seeming to read her mind. "We have doctors with us. They'll have him patched up and ready to stand trial in no time."

She smiled at him again. As much as she disliked Peter, she didn't want to be responsible for anyone's death. Untangling how many of his actions had been done of his own free will would be difficult but, thankfully, it was a problem for another day.

Looking around, she spotted Danny and Lisa. All of the archers had come down from the trees, but the siblings had broken off from the rest of the rebels to approach Marie.

Several of the guards stepped forward, weapons raised ready to defend her.

"No, no," she said, waving them off. "They aren't a threat, I promise."

"Are you sure, Your Highness? I'd really prefer you stepped back behind the lines until we have this whole situation sorted out..." The captain didn't have a chance to finish speaking before his words were cut off by Lisa.

"Marie!" She threw both her arms around her friend and began to cry into her neck.

Marie met the captain's eyes and shrugged awkwardly through her friend's embrace. "With all due respect, Captain, I think I might be of some help in getting things straightened out."

He raised one brow and spread his arms wide to signal defeat.

Now that the guards had seen that tears, rather than weapons, were on the agenda, most of them stepped back. Marie wanted to laugh at their reluctance to get involved in the situation. She would have bet they, at least, were glad to have her stick around and help deal with the now-subdued rebels.

"Come on, Lise." Danny stepped forward and tried to detach his sister from Marie. "Everyone's all right." He paused. "Well, except for Peter, I suppose, but that's hardly something to cry over."

Lisa gave a weak chuckle and stepped back from Marie.

"Sorry, Marie," she said, wiping at her cheeks. "I don't know what came over me." She frowned. "To be honest, I don't know what's come over me at all lately."

"You've been under an enchantment."

"An enchantment?" Danny's sharp tone matched his expression. "R, I suppose."

Marie nodded.

"Well that explains a lot. But how?"

"It's complicated," said Marie, unwilling to go into the whole story. "The important thing is that the key to breaking the enchantment is his true name. Rumpelstiltskin." She turned to the captain. "Make sure every member of the guard knows it, and we won't have any trouble from him again."

"His name? That's it?" The older man sounded skeptical.

She shrugged. "It's an enchantment, it doesn't follow the usual rules. And you saw me use it earlier. You saw them all respond when I yelled out his name."

"That's true enough," said the Rangmeran. "It sounded like gibberish to me, but it was certainly effective." He gave a gruff laugh. "I mistook you for some madwoman at first."

The captain of the guard glared at him, and the man grimaced.

"My mistake, of course, no offense intended."

"None taken," said Marie. She gave them both her most royal stare. "And I hope there is no thought of punishing any of the rebels. Everyone here is witness to the fact that every one of them, except for Peter, stood down as soon as the enchantment was lifted."

The Rangmeran shrugged. "That's a matter for Northhelm to decide. We are here merely to show Her Majesty's support for her valued allies."

Marie hid a smile. The man, whoever he was, had remembered his coaching and returned to the official diplomatic line.

"Aye," the captain of the guard nodded. "I can't see His

MELANIE CELLIER

Majesty wanting to charge any of them. The sooner this whole
business can be put behind us, the better."

"I'm glad to hear it," said Marie. "This is Danny and Lisa of
Greenwood." She gestured at her friends. "They're smart, have
good sense, and they know the former rebels. Now that they're
free from Rumpelstiltskin's influence, I would trust them with
my life. You couldn't find anyone better positioned to help you
sort things out here."

Lisa blushed at Marie's praise, and even Danny looked
pleased.

"And what of you, Your Highness?" The captain's eyes
narrowed, and Marie remembered that he'd always been an
astute man.

"I need Ferdy and his squad, and any engineers and diggers
you brought with you."

"Engineers, Your Highness?" The captain raised both his
eyebrows.

"I don't have time to explain right now," said Marie, "as it's a
matter of some urgency. But I promise to give a full account on
my return."

The captain hesitated, and she drew herself up to her full
height, glad for once of her unusual stature. She met his eyes and
raised her own brows.

He grimaced. "As you say, Your Highness." He turned toward
the trees and signaled to one of the guard hovering nearby.
"Fetch the major and the other men requested by the princess.
And make it quick."

The man dashed off and soon returned with at least twenty
men. Marie gestured for them to follow her and led the way
toward the cave entrance at a half-jog. Ferdinand kept pace
beside her.

"What's all this then, Your Highness?" he asked.

"It's William." She met his eyes. "He might be in danger."

230

"So, he's alive, then?" He looked relieved, and Marie realized how worried he must have been all this time.

"He was when I left, but he was also trapped behind a cave-in. An unstable one."

Understanding filled Ferdinand's eyes, and he picked up his speed, calling to his men to hurry. "Now I understand the engineers and diggers," he said. "But is it safe for you to accompany us?"

"You need me to show you the way." Marie narrowed her eyes at him. "And don't even think about trying to send me away once we get there. I outrank you, remember?"

Ferdinand chuckled. "Duly noted, Your Highness."

They passed through the caves, dodging ex-rebels who quickly made way for them. Only Robbie came forward.

"Where are Danny and Lisa?" he asked Marie. "I can't find them."

Ferdinand turned astonished eyes on him, presumably surprised at the informal way he addressed Marie, and the forester boy shifted uncomfortably. He held his ground, however.

Marie replied without thinking, struck by a sudden thought. "They're outside, with the captain of the guard."

Robbie drew in a quick breath, and Marie realized how her words had sounded.

"No, no," she rushed to assure him, "they're helping the captain. You've all been under an enchantment and the guard knows it. They're going to sort everything out and help you all get home."

"Home." Robbie's eyes dropped to the floor, and she suspected he was remembering what they had done in Greenwood.

"It will be all right, Robbie, I promise you," she said. "But at least some of these caves are affected by the enchantment. And now that it's failing, they're not safe. There have already been some cave-ins."

Robbie looked up quickly, fear in his face.

"I need you to spread the word," she continued. "Tell everyone to get out of the caves as quickly as they can. Let them know that they have a promise of immunity from the royal family themselves. They'll be much safer out there than in here."

"All right." Robbie nodded. "You can count on me, Marie. I'll get them all out. I haven't seen Rafe, though. Not since before this all started."

"I know." Marie fought to keep her voice steady. "He's caught in one of the cave-ins. We're on our way to rescue him now." She gestured at the accompanying guard.

Robbie's eyes widened.

Marie spoke again before he could say anything. "If anyone can get him out, these guards can. The rest of the people here need you."

Reluctantly Robbie nodded, and Marie started moving again. Every delay felt painful, but she couldn't have left the ex-rebels in danger without at least warning them. Neither Rafe nor William would want that.

It didn't take long to reach R's cavern. Its previous ordered calm had been disrupted by the small stones and dust that had dispersed throughout the room. The entryway to the hidden passage now drew the eye, filled as it was with a mound of rubble that sloped into the rest of the cave.

"They're behind that," she said, pointing.

Ferdinand instantly fell back to consult with two men Marie didn't recognize. She stepped aside, aware she would only be in the way, and collapsed onto one of the stools. She stared at the pile of stones, wishing she could clear them with the power of her mind.

What we need is a godmother, she thought and looked around hopefully. No one appeared. Obviously, this was one problem they were going to have to solve with sweat. She sighed.

Ferdinand approached the wall of stone. "William! Can you hear me? Are you back there?"

A pause ensued as they all listened intently.

"Ferdy? Is that you?"

A broad grin stretched across Ferdinand's face. "It sure is, old friend, it sure is," he called back. "I've got a whole team here and we're going to get you out in no time."

"And what about Marie?" That was Rafe. "Is the princess with you? Is she all right?"

"She's here," said Ferdinand, shouting to be heard through the stone. "She's been a hero all the way through, and she's saved everyone. Now let's get you out so you can hear the whole story."

He looked over at Marie. "I suppose that's the Rafe you mentioned?" he asked at normal volume.

Marie nodded.

While they had been talking, the men from the guard had brought forward various pieces of equipment. At a nod from Ferdinand, they called for William and Rafe to step back and then got to work.

Marie watched them in exhausted silence, impressed with their efficiency. They worked at the top of the mountain of stone, and their headway was soon obvious.

They had just managed to clear a small hole, the size of a fist, when the whole room began to shake.

CHAPTER 31

*E*veryone froze, except for one man who lost his balance and slid painfully down the slope. Two others, who were working at the bottom to clear away the rocks being handed down, hurried forward to help him. The rest of them grimly returned to work.

The slight shake had refilled their hole, but they had it clear again within minutes and quickly expanded it. Marie, holding her breath, noticed that they worked even more quickly than they had before.

It seemed like no time at all before the gap had widened enough for a person to slip through. The guard at the top stuck his head through, and she could hear the indistinct sound of voices. He pulled back out again, and then extended his hand in to help her brother through the hole.

A cheer went up when the crown prince appeared, and he grinned down at them all.

"Thanks for the welcoming committee," he said. "Next time, perhaps you could drop round a few weeks earlier."

Marie rolled her eyes, but his squad mates chuckled, clearly used to his joking ways.

Rafe emerged, a sack over one shoulder, while the men greeted William, and soon both of them were safely on the ground. Marie stood up, intending to rush to them, but Ferdinand spoke before she could.

"I'd say it's well past time we all got out of here," he said.

"No complaints here," said William. "I haven't seen the sky in weeks. Lead the way."

Marie and her brother were ushered from the cave in front of the guards and she could do nothing but throw a quick glance at Rafe over her shoulder. His eyes were fixed on her, relief filling his face. She felt the same relief at seeing that he was unharmed.

"What's in the sack?" she asked William, pointing back toward Rafe.

"Huh?" He turned back to look. "Oh, that. We had plenty of time, so we figured it was worth gathering up R's things."

Marie looked at him in horror.

"Oh, not that weird inky stuff," he assured her. "Just the papers and the books and the pouches. You'd already touched them all anyway, so we knew they were safe, even without R's name."

William glanced back at Rafe again. "I like Rafe," he said, lowering his voice. "But you know our parents are never going to approve."

"I know," said Marie, sure that her misery must be evident in her face.

"All right then," said William, his own eyes filled with pity. "I am sorry, Mare. If there was anything I could do…"

She shook her head wordlessly.

While they had been talking, the group had nearly reached the entrance of the caves. William looked down at her again and then suddenly picked up his pace.

"Come on, you lot, stop your dilly-dallying," he called, and led the men out into the open air. Marie found herself alone in the deserted entrance cave with Rafe.

He looked after the men, then back at Marie. She moved toward him, and he quickly dropped the sack, opening his arms to receive her.

She melted into his embrace with a sigh.

"Thank goodness you're safe," he said. "I've been sick with worry."

She smiled up at him. "I thought you had full confidence in me."

"I did." He smiled back down at her. "It was everyone else I wasn't so sure about."

"Well, you would be right where Peter was concerned," said Marie, her eyes narrowing. "He was the only one who didn't change his mind about the rebellion as soon as he heard R's name. He even attacked me!"

"What? Again?" Rafe's arms tightened around her. "When I get my hands on that…"

"Well, you won't," said Marie, suddenly proud of herself. "Danny took out one of his arms with an arrow, and I got the other one with one of my knives. And then he was arrested. Despite his crimes, you can hardly attack an incarcerated man without the use of either arm!"

Rafe sank his face into Marie's hair. "That's my girl," he said softly.

A single tear leaked down Marie's face, and she silently thanked her brother for this final opportunity.

Rafe raised his head, and she looked up at him, her heart in her eyes. The hopeless situation made her bold.

"I love you, Rafe," she said.

He stared down at her, his face filled with wonder.

"I want you to know that," she continued. "But it doesn't change anything. By choosing to be a princess, I'm also choosing duty to my kingdom."

He ran a thumb along her jaw. "One of the many things I love about you, Princess Marie," he said. "And in case there was any doubt, I love you, too." He moved his thumb to one of her eyebrows. "I think I have since the moment you first raised this eyebrow at me and asked what it was, exactly, that people said about the Northhelmian princess."

Marie smiled through the misted tears in her eyes. "Such a long time ago," she murmured. "Or it feels like it."

He lowered his head toward hers, but stopped, interrupted by a fresh rumble. Gripping her hand instead, he pulled her out of the cave and into the clearing. Behind them, the stone collapsed and the echoes of it crashed through the forest.

The noise went on for a long time.

"Goodness," said Ferdinand mildly. "I think half the hill must have collapsed that time."

Rafe let Marie's hand drop and nodded his agreement with the other man.

Marie wanted to reach after him, but she knew it was no use.

He turned away to greet the foresters who still lingered in the clearing, and she let him go.

"Marie." Yet another familiar voice greeted her. Only this one she hadn't been expecting.

Spinning around slowly she faced her adoptive father.

"Father," she said, "I didn't realize you were here."

"My advisors recommended against it," he said, carefully examining her with his eyes. "But I was hardly going to stay away when both of my children were missing. I'm relieved to see you both looking so well." He glanced over at William. "Although your brother looks like he needs a decent night's sleep and a few days in the sun."

"*Both* of your children?" Marie couldn't help the small hitch in her voice.

"Of course," said the king, his voice measured as always. "Every father fears for his children's safety. And I have never preferred one of my children over the other."

"Oh Father," she said. "I'm so sorry I ran away. But why didn't you tell me the truth?"

"For this very reason," he replied, gesturing around them. "We didn't want to lose you. Or to have you doubt our love. Nothing could be fiercer than the love of a parent for their child. It never mattered to us that we chose you instead of birthing you."

Tears slipped down Marie's cheeks.

"I choose you, too, Father," she said. "All of you. I understand that now, I think. We can choose where we belong. And I choose to receive the love you've been giving me all these years. You and Mother and William. I hope you'll be willing to accept me back."

King Richard smiled down at her. "You were never gone from our hearts."

She laughed aloud at the sentimental words delivered in his usual matter-of-fact tone. Reaching forward, she pulled him into a tight hug.

"Thank you, Father," she said. She felt clean and fresh, the guilt gone in the wave of love, forgiveness and acceptance.

Well, most of it. "How's Mother?" She pulled back and grimaced. "She must be beside herself with worry."

"She has been concerned, yes," said the king, and Marie almost laughed again at what she could only assume was a massive understatement.

"It would probably be wise if we all hurried back to her," he added.

Marie nodded her agreement. "As soon as I'm sure that everyone here is safe."

"Spoken like a true princess." The pride in her father's voice filled Marie with joy. Gone were her days of questioning herself. She was a princess because she chose to act like one and because her family chose to make her one. Her looks and birth had never mattered.

William strolled up to them and slung an arm over her shoulders.

"Hello, Father," he said cheerfully. "Good to see some old family bonding going on. I hate to interrupt, but I've just been chatting with Rafe, and we have a quick question."

"Yes?" Their father was as used to his son's light-hearted ways as William's squad.

"Has anyone seen this Rumpelstiltskin fellow?"

All of the warmth filling Marie turned to ice.

"No," she said, drawing out the word. "Have you checked with Danny and Lisa?"

"Rafe's been asking around. No one's seen him since some meeting or other, apparently."

Marie frowned. Despite the ability to reverse his enchantments, R was a loose end she wasn't willing to leave hanging. "We should talk to Peter. He might know where R went."

"I'd love to have a chat with him," said William, his fisted hands contrasting with his light tone.

"Men." Marie rolled her eyes. "He's been arrested, William. And he's wounded. Neither you, nor Rafe, can have it out with him."

William's hands relaxed. "Well, that's too bad." He grinned at her. "I'll just have to hope for his full recovery."

Marie shook her head and led him toward the forest. "They took him off this way. If we can find the captain of the guard, I'm sure he knows where he is."

Marie assumed their father was following them. Until she reached the edge of the trees, and a loud scream rose above the chatter in the clearing.

Turning, she saw that he remained where they had left him, standing in the middle of a large empty space.

Empty except for Rumpelstiltskin, who held a dagger to the king's throat.

CHAPTER 32

*M*arie wasn't the only one to turn around in response to the forester's scream. A ripple spread out from the clearing as more and more people turned to see the threat to the king.

William took two strides toward their father but halted when Rumpelstiltskin shook his head and pressed the blade harder against the king's throat.

"Tut, tut, tut," he said, grinning at them. "Keep your distance, if you please."

Marie could actually feel the surge of restrained energy from the guards who still ringed the clearing. She hoped no overeager guard would rush forward despite the warning and seal her father's fate.

She stepped forward to stand beside her brother. "What are you doing?" She stared across the space, hoping desperately that she still held some sway with her birth father.

Rumpelstiltskin's face grew hard as he gazed back at her. All the subtle threats she had ever witnessed in his eyes seemed to solidify in his face. "Don't speak to me," he said. "You are the biggest disappointment of all. I had hoped for so much more from you."

Marie stared back at him, putting all of her emotions into her expression. "And I had hoped for so much more from you. You have done nothing but lie and kill and steal. I want no part of you or any kingdom you would rule."

"Four centuries I have planned my return. I will not be defeated now." The grin on Rumpelstiltskin's face grew, and he looked truly insane. "If I can't have the kingdom, I can at least have revenge."

He drew his knife along the king's throat, and several drops of blood dripped down his neck. King Richard didn't move, and his face remained as calm and unafraid as it had since Marie had turned around. A shudder moved through the watching troops, however. Marie held her breath, but none of them broke rank to attempt to save the king.

"Killing me will achieve nothing," said the king. "You have lost your hold over my daughter and over our people, and that is the only thing that matters to me. I live, as always, to serve my kingdom."

"Disgusting!" Rumpelstiltskin turned his head and spat on the ground. "You sound like my brother." His twisted face with its strange skin looked barely human.

Marie felt paralyzed. She wished she had her bow and enough confidence to shoot Rumpelstiltskin without injuring her father.

Just as the thought raced through her mind, she heard the whoosh of an arrow followed by a high-pitched scream. A flurry of movement in the center of the clearing followed the sound, and it took a moment for Marie to understand what she was seeing.

Rumpelstiltskin, now cursing instead of screaming, was ripping an arrow from his hand. His knife lay at his feet, and the king, released from his hold, had also dropped to the ground, out of his reach.

William, quicker to grasp the implications of the scene before them, was already racing toward them both. But he wasn't the only one moving into the open space.

Rafe, also running toward the conflict, threw down his bow and drew his sword. Marie realized that he must have been the archer who had shot Rumpelstiltskin with such precision.

"Get him out of here!" yelled Rafe to William, gesturing toward the king.

For the briefest moment, William looked torn, his own sword halfway out of its sheath. Then he pushed it back in and leaned down to pull his father to his feet. Together they hurried back across the clearing toward Marie. She ran forward to meet them halfway, grabbing her father's other arm and hauling him toward the trees.

As she ran, she glanced back over her shoulder, concern for Rafe almost causing her to stumble. Rumpelstiltskin had produced a sword from somewhere and now faced the younger man, his face even more twisted with hate and pain.

"You've been a thorn in my side from the beginning," he snarled. "There's something strange about you. I sensed it as soon as I saw you. I would have worked it out eventually, but I'll happily kill you instead."

They'd reached the trees without Marie even realizing and were swarmed with soldiers. The captain was directing his men to take the royals further into the forest, away from any possible danger, but Marie pulled back against the arms that grabbed at her. Blindly she fought them, her eyes still focused on the men in the clearing.

Rafe seemed entirely unperturbed by Rumpelstiltskin's words. "I think you'll find I'm not so easy to kill."

The older man lunged forward, and Rafe deftly parried him, dancing backward out of reach.

Rumpelstiltskin cursed again and reached into his jacket. His hand closed over something that was hidden from Marie's sight. A moment later, she gasped.

Rumpelstiltskin had disappeared

She looked around wildly. Where had he gone? He couldn't possibly have left the clearing without her noticing.

Rafe, his sword held defensively in front of him, narrowed his eyes.

"Rumpelstiltskin," he said, his confident voice echoing across the clearing.

For a moment, Marie's eyesight seemed to waver, and then Rumpelstiltskin appeared in front of Rafe. Of course, she thought. Another enchantment.

Rumpelstiltskin was halfway through another attack, his blade pointed directly at Rafe's heart. The younger man leaped backward, only just avoiding the tip of the sword, and parried again. Only this time, he followed the maneuver with a counter-attack. He lunged forward, his arm extended, and his blade pierced Rumpelstiltskin's chest.

This time, Rumpelstiltskin didn't scream. He merely stared down at the sword in surprise. Dropping his own weapon, he sank to his knees. Rafe had let his sword go and Rumpelstiltskin gripped the hilt, but he didn't attempt to pull it out.

Instead, he looked up and met Marie's eyes. Something strange flashed across his face. *Fear?* she wondered. *Or regret?*

Whatever the emotion was, it was quickly gone, replaced by an empty look. Slowly he tipped to one side and lay motionless on the ground.

Rafe stood over his body, panting. His expression held sadness instead of triumph. Marie was already running across the clearing toward him, so she was close enough to hear his quiet words.

"You will never hurt her, or this kingdom, or anyone, ever again."

In another second he had turned away and opened his arms to receive Marie, who tumbled into them.

CHAPTER 33

*M*arie's heart raced, and she struggled to calm it, her breath coming more raggedly than the short run warranted.

"Shhh," said Rafe, stroking her hair, "it's all right now."

"I know," said Marie. "But you, my father..." She shook her head, not even sure which father she referred to.

After another moment, she took a deep breath and drew back. "I'm sorry," she said. "I shouldn't be doing this."

He smiled down at her, and she wondered how he could smile so easily when her own heart was breaking.

"Thank you, young man," said the king. He seemed to have shaken off the guards who had been attempting to carry him to safety. "I owe you my life, and my kingdom owes you a debt for ridding us of such a dangerous threat."

Rafe instantly released Marie and bowed to the king. "I am pleased to have been of service to Northhelm and, even more, to you." He glanced at William, who stood beside his father, and then down at Marie. "You see, I have a request to make of you. And if you would grant it, I would be far more in your debt than you could ever be in mine."

"Rafe, no," said Marie quietly. "You know I can't." She knew what he wanted to ask and couldn't bear to hear her father reject him.

Rafe ignored her.

"I have never met a woman I admire more than your daughter. In fact, I love her. She is brave and strong and true. And beautiful, of course." He grinned down at Marie. "That goes without saying."

He looked back up at the king. "And if you would be willing to grant me her hand in marriage, I would treasure her every day for as long as we live."

Marie's heart melted, and for a single beautiful moment, the whole clearing stood frozen, the silence absolute. Then the king opened his mouth to reply, and she prepared her heart to be shattered.

But she never got to hear what he had to say. Before he could speak, Rafe continued.

"Before you give me an answer, however, I have a confession to make."

Marie spun around and stared at him.

"I haven't been completely truthful with any of you."

Marie sucked in a breath. She felt as if someone had punched her in the gut. *Would it ever end?* she wondered. *Could she ever trust anyone to be truthful with her again?*

Rafe saw her expression and reached over to grip her hand. "It's killed me, Marie, not to tell you everything. I wanted to so many times. But you told me once you were scared of changing things between us. And I felt the same way."

She could read the desperation and sincerity in his eyes. Slowly, she returned the grip of his hand. Who was she to judge him? Hadn't she done the exact same thing?

"But I swear to you," he continued. "Nothing I have said to you has been a lie. And this is the only truth I withheld. And, if you'll agree to marry me, I promise that I will never hide anything from you ever again."

His eyes pleaded with her for her understanding, and her heart responded without hesitation.

"A pretty speech," said the king, his voice as measured as if he was conducting another meeting in his council room. "But you have yet to enlighten us as to this great deception."

Rafe looked up, and something of his usual cheeky good-humor crept into his face.

"I told you my name is Rafe and that I'm a third son," he said, "which is true. What I didn't tell you is that my full name is Raphael Alexander Michael and I'm the third son of Their Majesties King Leonardo and Queen Viktoria of Lanover. I set out some time ago and had been traveling as simply Rafe before I ever entered Northhelm. When I met you, in the palace, I was afraid that if you knew my true identity, you would feel obligated to prevent my going undercover with the rebels."

He smiled down at Marie. "It hadn't occurred to me, then, that I might have a very important reason for wanting you to know who I was."

She smiled back at him, still trying to absorb the wonder of his news. Rafe—a prince!

"One of my sisters is under a curse, you see, and I have been wandering the kingdoms searching for a way to break it. I thought, perhaps, this Rumpelstiltskin might hold the answer."

"And do you think he is behind her curse?" the king asked.

Marie wanted to shake him. What did Rumpelstiltskin matter? He hadn't answered Rafe's question.

William snorted quietly, and she glared at him. He knew her too well and was too easily able to guess her thoughts.

Rafe didn't take his eyes from her father, but the silent chuckle that shook his body told her that he was aware of the wordless exchange between the siblings.

She glared at him, too.

"I don't know, Your Majesty," he said. "But now that we have the key to breaking his enchantments, I can only hope so. When I return to Lanover, I will attempt to free her."

"And I sincerely hope you're successful," said Marie, unable to restrain herself any longer. "But personally, I'm rather eager to know the answer to your earlier question." She raised both eyebrows at her father.

He stared back at her, his face expressionless. Then, slowly, a broad smile began to grow. When it had reached full size, he let out a chuckle that sounded remarkably like one of William's.

"How could I say no to a prince who has not only saved my life but who obviously loves my daughter as much as I do?" He chuckled again. "I can assure you Lanover's wealth and excellent standing among the Four Kingdoms doesn't weigh with me at all."

Rafe grinned back at him and executed another small bow. "I can see your reputation for excellent judgment and unwavering good sense is well-deserved."

Marie rolled her eyes and jabbed him in the side with her elbow.

He turned to her and the grin softened into an expression of such tender love that it took her breath away.

"As for you, dearest Marie," he said, "it will give me the greatest of pleasures to ensure that no one can ever question your status as princess again." He reached out and pulled her against him. His smiling eyes seemed to match her own joy and rebound it in even greater amounts. "And since I never want there to be even the slightest shade of untruth between us again, I have one last confession to make. I told you once that you would always be a princess to me, but the truth is, in my heart, you will always be queen."

Marie rolled her eyes again, reached up and pulled his face

down to meet hers. She would wait for a more private moment to tell him that being queen of his heart meant far more to her than any title of princess ever had.

NOTE FROM THE AUTHOR

The story continues in the Four Kingdoms novella, *A Midwinter's Wedding: A Retelling of The Frog Prince*. Discover the danger and romance awaiting Rafe's younger sister when she travels to Northhelm for his wedding. Turn the page now for a sneak peek.

Thank you for taking the time to read my book. If you enjoyed it, please spread the word! You could start by leaving a review on <u>Amazon</u> (or <u>Goodreads</u> or <u>Facebook</u> or any other social media site). Your review would be very much appreciated!

To be kept informed of my new releases and for free extra content, including an exclusive bonus chapter of Book One in the Four Kingdoms series, *The Princess Companion: A Retelling of The Princess and the Pea*, please sign up to my mailing list at www.melaniecellier.com. At my website, you'll also find an array of free extra content, including an epilogue to *The Princess Pact*.

A GIFT

"*I*t's a present."

Princess Cordelia looked down at the golden ball and then up into the stunningly beautiful face of her sister. "Umm, thanks?"

Ever since the curse, Cordelia was used to her sister doing senseless, empty-headed things, but the unexpected gift seemed odd even for her. It wasn't as if it was Cordelia's birthday or anything.

"It's not for you, silly!" Celeste laughed, and the golden, musical sound filled the small garden. Her laugh was almost as irresistible as her face.

If any courtiers had been there, they would have sighed and murmured to each other. Cordelia could easily imagine what they would say. *Such a beautiful girl. Such a pity about the curse.*

She almost sighed herself. Not because of the wasted beauty of her older sister, though. Life as a sixth child had enough challenges of its own. No one noticed you when you were constantly surrounded by the beauty and talents of your older siblings. And Cordelia wasn't even the baby of the family, a position that attracted at least some attention.

She reminded herself, for the thousandth time, that she should be grateful. After all, if she'd been the most beautiful of them all, then she would have been the one with the curse.

But despite the reminder, she couldn't help wishing that, just once, she could stand on her own. That she could meet someone who would see her as Cordelia, rather than as yet another one of that horde up at the palace. Even poor, cursed Celeste had gone on a visit of state to their northern neighbor Arcadia a year and a half ago, when she was Cordelia's age.

Celeste was still smiling, apparently oblivious to Cordelia's discontent. "It's for Princess Marie. As a wedding present. She's marrying our brother Rafe, remember?"

"Of course I remember!" snapped Cordelia and then instantly regretted it. It wasn't Celeste's fault that she was such a fool. She softened her tone. "But I don't know why you're giving it to me."

"Oh! Haven't you heard? The wedding is to be held on Midwinter's Day, which means any attendees will be snowed in for the whole season. Mother and Father have decided they can't be away for that long. But Rafe will be so sad if none of us attend." Her smile grew even brighter. "So they've decided to send you."

"Me?" Cordelia stared at her, hardly able to believe her good fortune. "Only me?"

"That's why I'm giving you the ball. For our new sister."

Cordelia tried to contain her glee. It seemed too good to be true. And Rafe was her favorite brother, too. She bit her lip. She would have to think of an amazing wedding gift for him. She glanced down at the golden ball that her sister had deposited in her hands.

"Is it real gold?" she asked, curiosity momentarily distracting her. "It's very light."

"Of course it's real! Only the best for our dear Rafe." Celeste leaned forward as if imparting a secret. "I think it might be magic. I got it from Godmother. It's supposed to help you find true love."

"Well it doesn't seem to have helped you," pointed out Cordelia.

She didn't mean it harshly. It was just the truth. The three youngest Lanoverian princesses often bemoaned the lack of romance in their lives.

Celeste leaned back and looked puzzled. "No, it hasn't, has it? Maybe it's not magic after all. That might have been a game I was playing... I can't quite remember now." Her words trailed off as she began to hum to herself happily.

Cordelia bit back an impatient retort. Celeste couldn't be held responsible for the foolish things she said. Still, the younger princess couldn't resist asking the obvious question. "Well, if it *is* magic, why would you give it to a bride? She's already found true love."

Celeste stopped humming and leaned forward again. "I've heard rumors of dangerous things afoot in Northhelm. I thought a godmother item might help, and it's the only one I have."

Cordelia considered reminding her sister that Rafe and Marie had already defeated the danger in Northhelm but decided against it. She had far more important things to do—like pack!

But first she would find her mother and make sure Celeste was telling the truth. She ran out of the garden with a light heart.

CHAPTER 1

$\mathcal{C}$ ordelia bounced once on the seat of the carriage and then subsided after a stern look from her personal maid. She would have made a face except she could hear Celeste's warnings in her mind. Celeste had told her many times that a princess should never make faces since it diminished her beauty. And beauty was the one topic where Celeste's judgment couldn't be questioned.

Cordelia settled for a small sigh instead.

She had been so excited when her mother had confirmed that she would be traveling to Northhelm to attend Rafe's wedding. The emotion had been somewhat dampened, however, when her mother insisted that Priscilla accompany her. As a personal maid, Priscilla left a lot to be desired. As a combination of nanny, governess, and parental substitute, Queen Viktoria thought she was perfect. And nothing Cordelia could say had convinced her mother that she was too old to need a baby-sitter.

She supposed she should be grateful she had been allowed to come at all. Her parents hadn't wanted any of the family to travel so far and be gone for so long. Instead they had dispatched the

Duchess of Sessily, along with a large retinue, to support Rafe in the various negotiations and treaties that would surround the wedding. The older woman was a diplomatic genius, and the kingdom had proven safe in her hands many times before.

When their children had questioned the decision, the king and queen had assured them that they would fund a royal tour for the newlyweds to visit Lanover after the wedding. They would all get the chance to meet their new sister.

Except when Rafe heard that the duchess was already on her way without any of his family, he had sent a letter pleading on behalf of his three younger sisters. King Leonardo and Queen Viktoria had decided that, while Celeste had already had her turn in Arcadia and Celine was far too young, Cordelia should be allowed to attend after all.

Celine had complained—that went without saying—but their mother had done nothing but repeat the same placid, unmoving reply. "You're too young." Of course none of the princesses were fooled by this. Celine wasn't too young. She was too wild and too tempestuous.

At least those were the words Priscilla used. Their two oldest brothers used even less complimentary words. And their mother simply sighed and reminded them all that she was still young yet.

Cordelia threw off thoughts of her sisters. The carriage had entered Northgate, the capital of Northhelm, several minutes before, and she wanted to stick her head out the window so she could get a good look at the city. She snuck a glance at Priscilla and then decided against it. The older woman watched her with a hawk-like stare.

She sighed again and contented herself with absorbing as much of the view as she could see from inside the vehicle. Priscilla had been nanny to the older Lanoverian princes and princesses but had handed over the role before Cordelia arrived. Cordelia wished the dour woman had retired instead of staying on in the palace. Even Celeste, who didn't normally worry about much apart from her looks, found Priscilla overly strict.

The city seemed smaller than the Lanoverian capital, and the differences didn't stop there. The warmer southern climate meant Cordelia had grown up in a sprawling, dusty city, composed mostly of single-story buildings made of reddish sandstone. Even her own home, the palace, consisted of only one story.

In contrast, Northgate had quaint cobbled streets lined by tall houses, each connected to the neighboring home to form long unbroken rows of buildings. Their window boxes were empty of flowers due to the season, but the streets were brightened by lanterns on black metal poles.

The sun hadn't set, but the lanterns already glowed, combating the overcast sky. The whole effect was already quaint and picturesque even without the added advantage of softly falling snow.

"Look, Priscilla!" Cordelia couldn't contain her glee. "It's snowing!"

"I have observed, Your Highness."

Cordelia tightened her lips and kept her eyes glued to the window. She refused to let the other woman ruin her enjoyment of the moment. The travelers had pushed themselves for weeks to make it to Northhelm before the winter weather made travel impossible. Cordelia was just glad they were there.

"Ohh…" The soft sound of enchantment slipped unconsciously from her mouth. The palace had come into view, and the tall building of white stone looked even more beautiful than she had imagined.

According to Celeste, the elegant Arcadian palace was even more impressive than this one. But Cordelia was in the mood to be impressed, and she found the Northhelmian palace more than lived up to her expectations.

She was still admiring it when her carriage passed through the gates and pulled to a stop in the front courtyard.

"Stay here," said Priscilla before climbing out and beginning to order about their various guards and grooms, as well as the Northhelmian servants who had come rushing out to help. With four carriages, a great many riders, and even more luggage, the traveling party took some time to disperse.

Cordelia restrained her impatience, occupying herself with her usual game. Staring at the seat in front of her, she formed a mental picture of what was happening outside. She could hear three Northhelmian grooms directing the Lanoverians where to send their horses. Several more servants unloaded the luggage under the direction of both Priscilla and a Northhelmian woman, presumably the housekeeper.

She was entertaining herself by imagining the faces that belonged to the voices when another voice caught her ear. The tone marked it as belonging to a noble, and it sounded distant from the melee around the carriage.

Cordelia doubted any of the other Lanoverians could hear it; even she had nearly missed it, and she not only had excellent hearing but was paying close attention. She let the other noises fade away and focused in the direction of the voice.

"So, the first of them arrives." That was a second voice, markedly less noble.

"No, no, that's a Lanoverian royal carriage. And, anyway, the southerners only sent one of the younger princesses." The noble voice sounded impatient.

"Oh." A pause. "Aren't we interested in Lanover then?"

"So far, Lanover appears to have escaped the general madness. Only their third prince has been infected, and he's defected to Northhelm from what we hear."

Cordelia frowned and bit her lip. The voices were speaking about her and Rafe, but the words didn't quite make sense. They did, however, make her feel uneasy. Madness? Defection? What did they mean? She decided to peek out the window and see if she could spy the owners of the voices.

As she began to move toward the far window, the door on the palace side opened.

"Your Highness."

Cordelia froze, half off the seat. She reminded herself that looking out the window wasn't a crime—even in Priscilla's strict rulebook. She had no reason to feel guilty.

Priscilla looked around the interior of the vehicle, as if searching for the source of Cordelia's guilt, and then settled for shaking her head. Stepping back, she gestured for the princess to alight.

Cordelia glanced once more toward the window and then hopped out of the carriage. From an unobstructed view, the palace looked even more impressive. All of its windows were ablaze, and the light shone on the softly falling snow. She forgot momentarily about the strange overheard conversation at the beautiful sight.

Her carriage was already being whisked away by several grooms, and the mountains of luggage they had brought with them had disappeared into the palace. Cordelia looked around, hoping that Rafe might have come to greet her.

As she surveyed the large courtyard, she admitted to herself that she would be happy enough to see anyone. Well, anyone more sympathetic than Priscilla, anyway.

Even as she thought it, a lone rider trotted through the palace gates. He wore a military uniform and rode a beautiful chestnut horse. Cordelia's love for horses gave her a soft spot for anyone who could ride well. And this man had one of the best seats she'd seen in a long time.

He pulled up, facing away from her, and began a conversation with a groom. Cordelia ignored Priscilla, who was motioning for her to proceed inside, and lingered in the courtyard, hoping the rider might dismount and move toward the palace doors.

Sure enough, the newcomer swung down from the saddle and handed his reins to the groom. A little thrill rushed through her body. In truth, she wanted an audience as much as she wanted sympathy.

After all, she was one of the Lanoverian princesses, famed throughout the Four Kingdoms for their great beauty. Every day her mirror told her how lovely she was to look at. Unfortunately, her eyes also told her that she was the least remarkable of her six siblings. What was the point being beautiful if you spent your life standing next to Celeste?

But now her chance had come. Only one of her siblings was in Northhelm with her, and he didn't count. She resisted the urge to pat her hair and straighten her dress, and instead put on a bright smile.

The rider turned and took two steps toward the palace before he looked up and noticed Priscilla and Cordelia. His gaze glanced over the older lady and then settled on the princess.

Cordelia smiled encouragingly.

His look of shocked surprise was familiar—she had seen it often enough on the faces of young men the first time they saw Celeste. How entirely different it felt, though, to have it directed at her.

Except his expression didn't progress to one of admiration. Instead it transformed into a look much more closely resembling distaste. After a frozen moment, he wheeled around and hurried past the side of the palace and out of sight.

Cordelia's smile dropped. She ducked her head and rushed up the palace steps, propelled forward by the heat in her cheeks. Her gut churned with embarrassment, and the warmth from her face seemed to wash over her whole body. Her one relief was that no one but Priscilla had been present to witness her foolishness.

What had she been thinking? A few weeks of travel hadn't made her experienced and sophisticated. She was as unimportant in Northhelm as she had always been in Lanover.

Read on in *A Midwinter's Wedding: A Retelling of the Frog Prince*

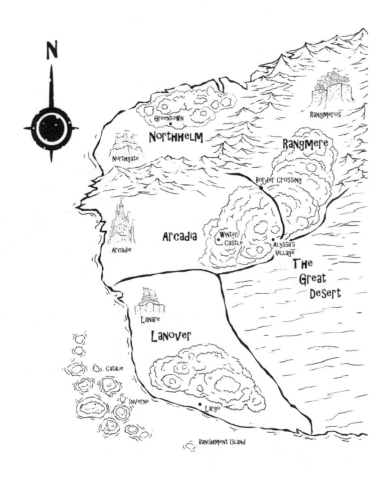

N

Greentown

Northhelm

Northgate

Rangmeros

Rangmere

Border Crossing

Arcadia

Winter
Castle

Alyssa's
Village

Arcadie

The
Great
Desert

Lanare

Lanover

Catalie

Inverne

Largo

Banishment Island

ACKNOWLEDGMENTS

This book was written during one of the hardest and darkest periods of my life. It was a time full of pain and deep loss. But in the midst of all the difficulty, there were also glimmers of joy and light, and this book was one of the positive things that came out of that season. Marie was a great character in The Princess Companion, and I had been looking forward to seeing her get her own happy ending in The Princess Pact. I can only hope others have enjoyed discovering Marie's story as much as I did.

So many friends and family supported me during the months I was writing this book that I couldn't possibly name them all. But I hope they all know how much they mean to me, and that I couldn't have made it through without them. A special thanks, however, goes to Robyn who was always there to step in whenever things were at their worst. You are a true friend and have been a lifeline to us.

For specific book assistance, I need to thank my beta readers and editors: Katie, Priya, Rachel, Debs, M.M. Chabot and J.D. Cunegan. And, as always, my parents and Marc, who are always willing to help in any way they can and who deserve the biggest thanks of all.

Once again, the beautiful cover is thanks to Karri. Somehow, I love each cover just as much as the last!

Bringing good from the worst of circumstances is the special province of God, so all thanks go to Him for sustaining and inspiring me through this last year.

ABOUT THE AUTHOR

 Melanie Cellier grew up on a staple diet of books, books and more books. And although she got older, she never stopped loving children's and young adult novels.

She always wanted to write one herself, but it took three careers and three different continents before she actually managed it.

She now feels incredibly fortunate to spend her time writing from her home in Adelaide, Australia where she keeps an eye out for koalas in her backyard. Her staple diet hasn't changed much, although she's added choc mint Rooibos tea and Chicken Crimpies to the list.

She writes young adult fantasy including her *Spoken Mage* series, and her *Four Kingdoms* and *Beyond the Four Kingdoms* series which are made up of linked stand-alone stories that retell classic fairy tales.

Printed in the USA
CPSIA information can be obtained
at www.ICGtesting.com
LVHW092257300924
792598LV00032B/149